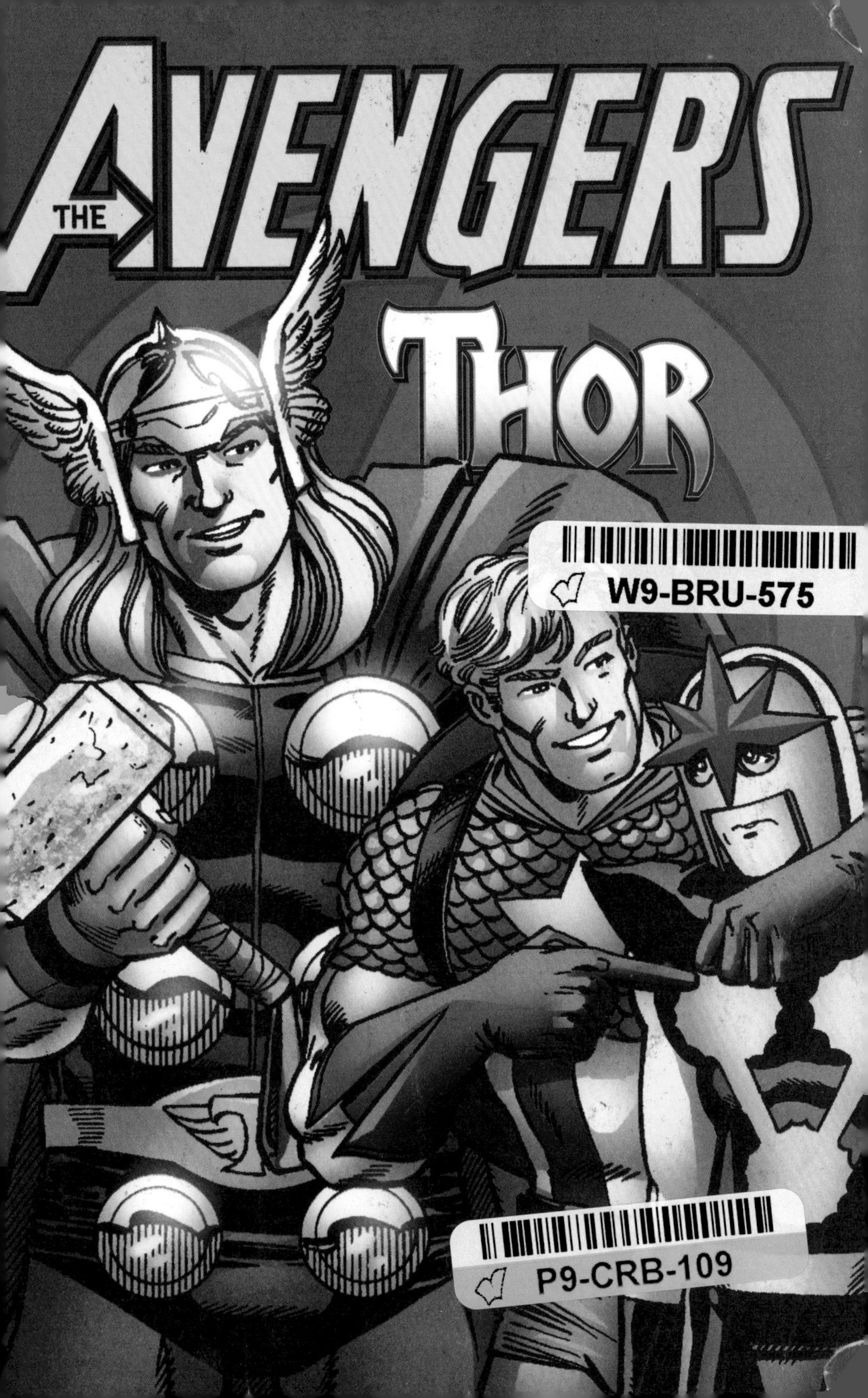
THE AVENGERS
THOR

THE AVENGERS

THOR

Writer: **Paul Tobin**
Pencilers: **Chriscross (Issue #5)**
Ronan Cliquet (Issue #6)
Scott Koblish (Issues #7 & 8)
Inkers: **Rick Ketcham (Issue #5)**
Amilton Santos (Issue #6)
Scott Koblish (Issues #7 & 8)

Colorist: **Sotocolor**
Letterer: **Dave Sharpe**
Cover Artist: **Clayton Henry**
with **Guru eFX & Sotocolor**
Assistant Editors: **Michael Horwitz & John Denning**
Editor: **Nathan Cosby**

Captain America created by Joe Simon & Jack Kirby

Collection Editor: Cory Levine
Editorial Assistants: James Emmett & Joe Hochstein
Assistant Editors: Matt Masdeu, Alex Starbuck & Nelson Ribeiro
Editors, Special Projects: Jennifer Grünwald & Mark D. Beazley
Senior Editor, Special Projects: Jeff Youngquist
Senior Vice President of Sales: David Gabriel

Editor in Chief: Joe Quesada
Publisher: Dan Buckley
Executive Producer: Alan Fine

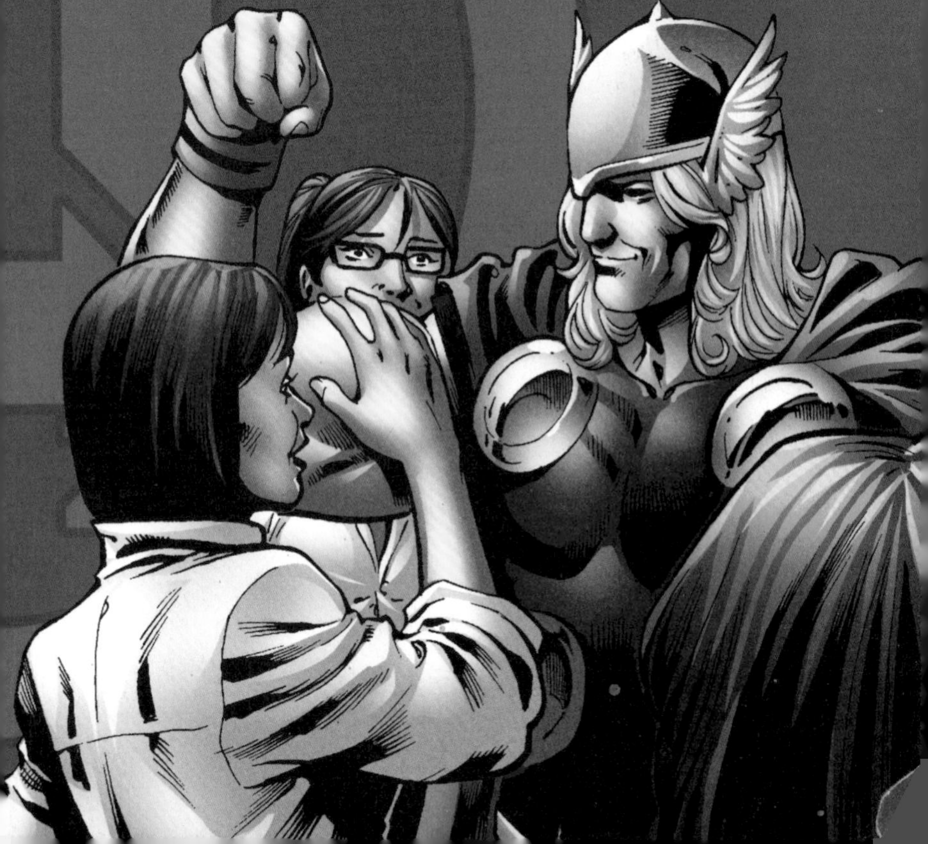

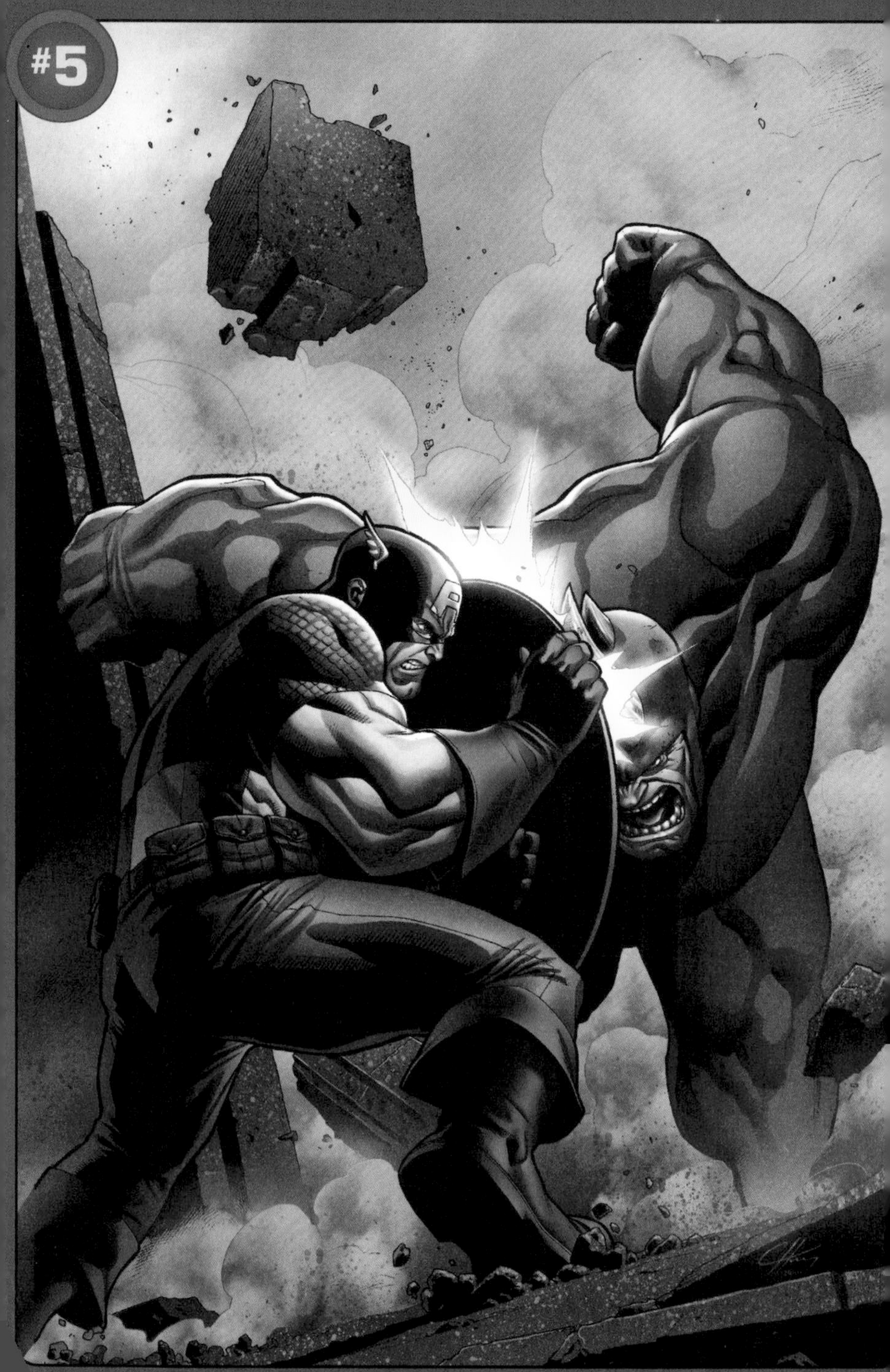
#5

CAPTAIN AMERICA

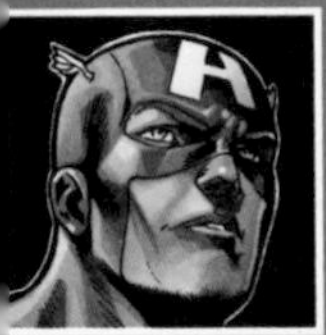

STEVE ROGERS
PEAK PHYSICAL SOLDIER, MASTER STRATEGIST

THE VISION

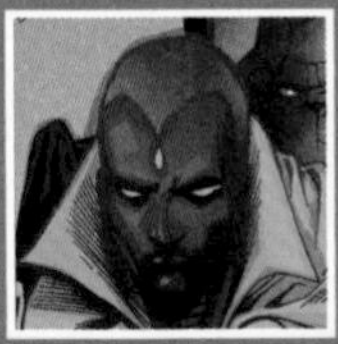

ANDROID, PHASES THROUGH MATTER, SUPER-STRENGTH

IRON MAN

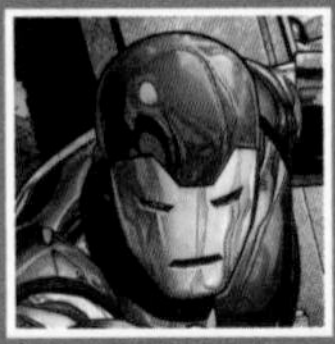

TONY STARK
BILLIONAIRE INVENTOR, ONE-MAN ARMORED TANK

INVISIBLE WOMAN

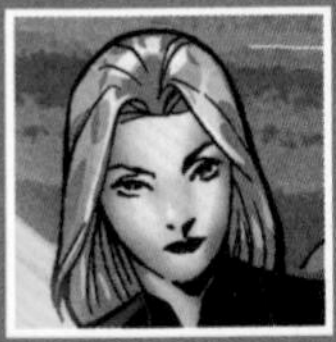

SUSAN STORM
TURNS INVISIBLE, CREATES FORCE BUBBLES

THOR

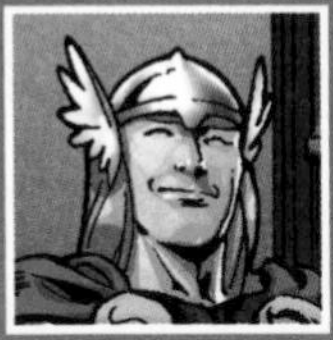

ASGARDIAN GOD, WIELDS MAGICAL HAMMER

BLACK WIDOW

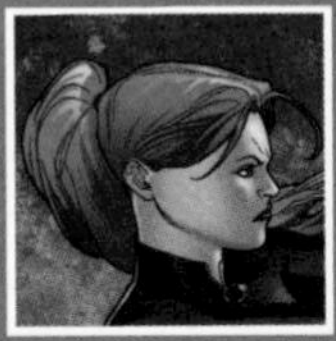

NATASHA ROMANOVA
SUPER-SPY, COVERT SPECIALIST

NOVA

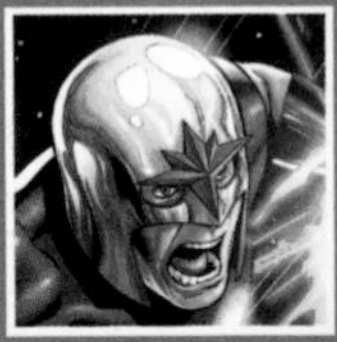

RICHARD RIDER
COSMIC-POWERED KID, STRONG & FAST FLIER

THERE ARE DANGERS THAT MANKIND CANNOT CONQUER. A MIGHTY FEW WOULD RISK THEIR LIVES TO DEFEND US ALL. THEY ARE

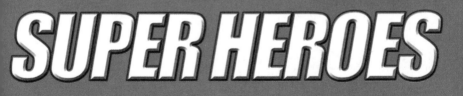

SUPER HEROES

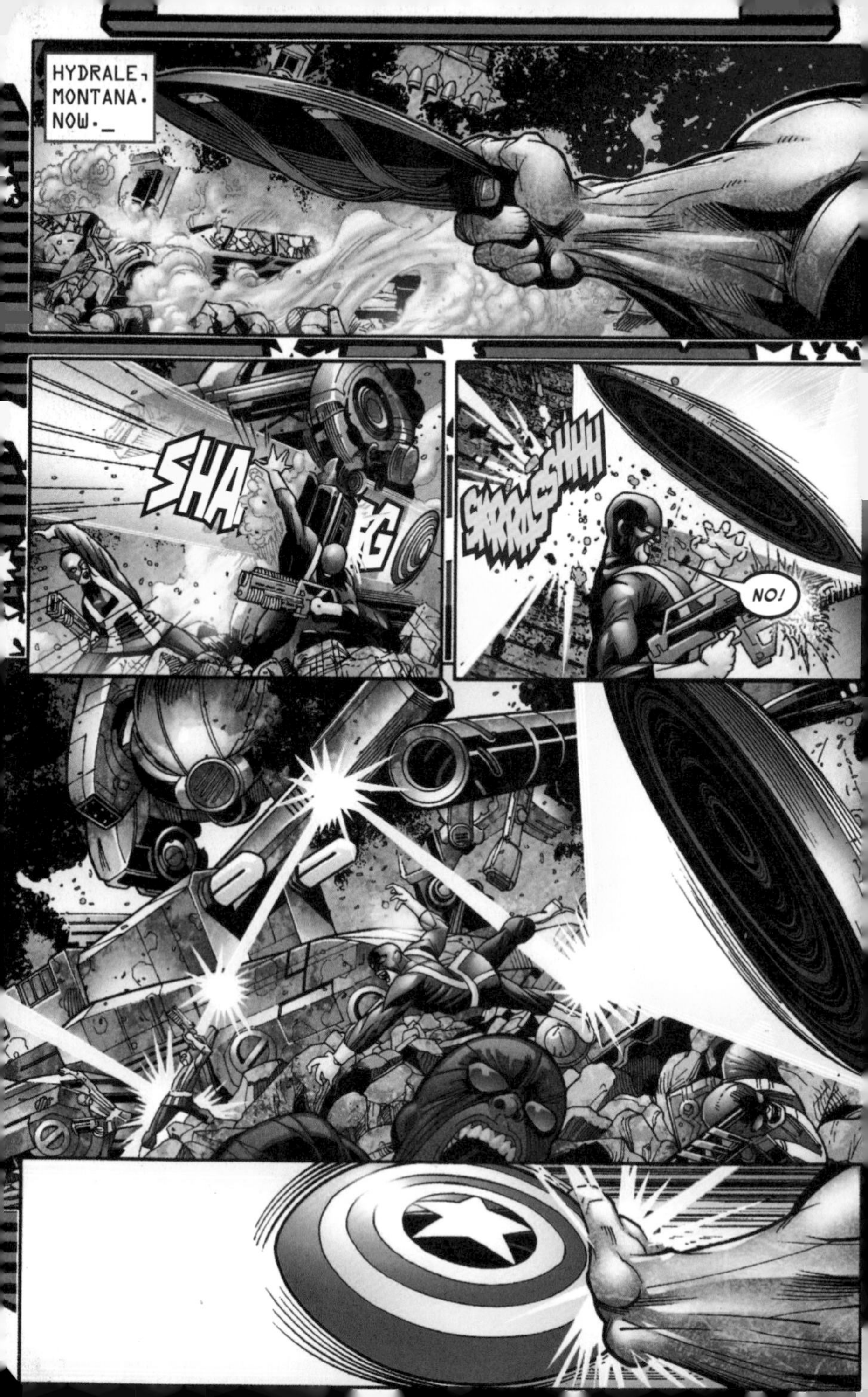
HYDRALE, MONTANA. NOW._
SHA
EG
SKRRASHHH
NO!

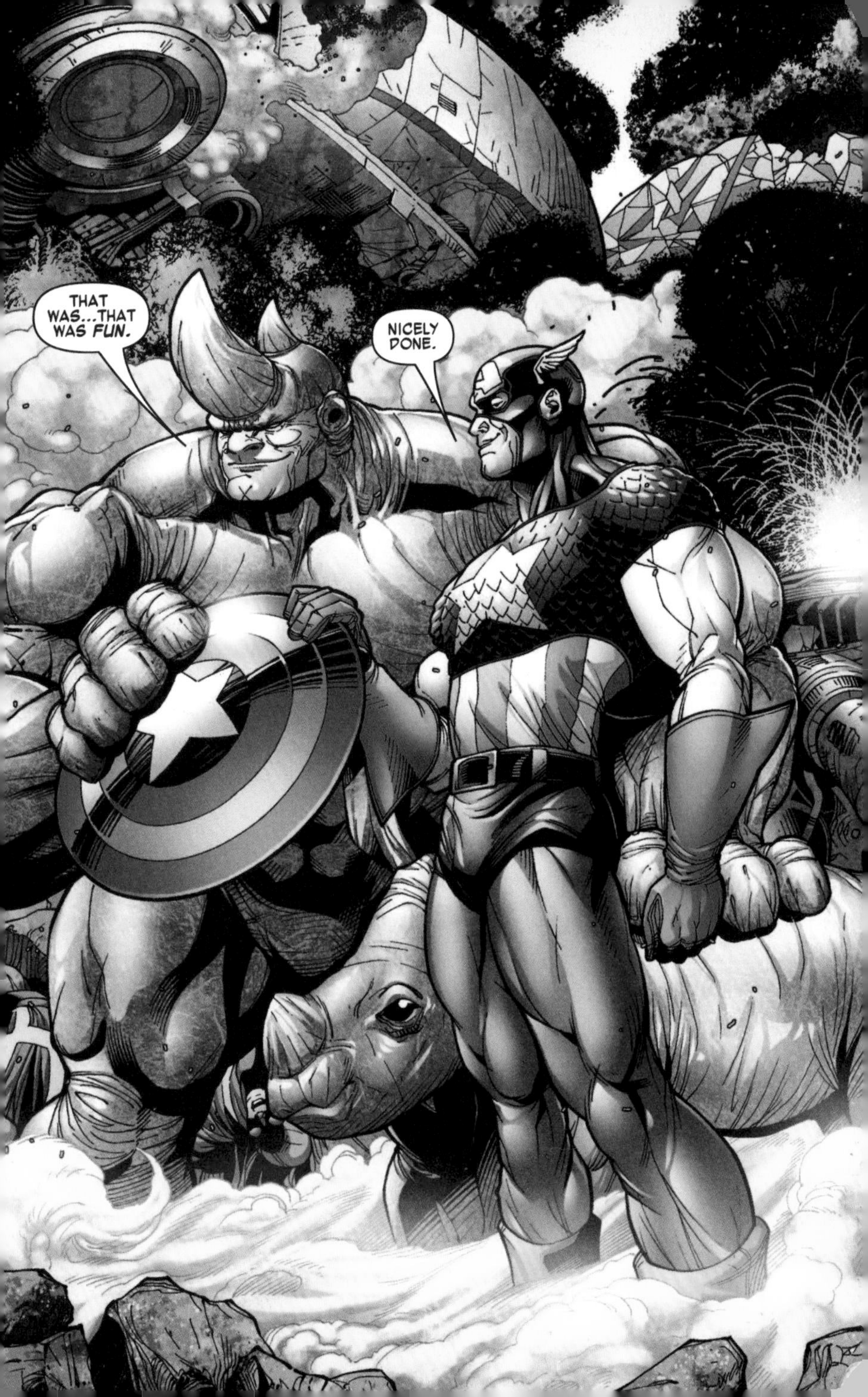
THAT WAS...THAT WAS FUN.
NICELY DONE.

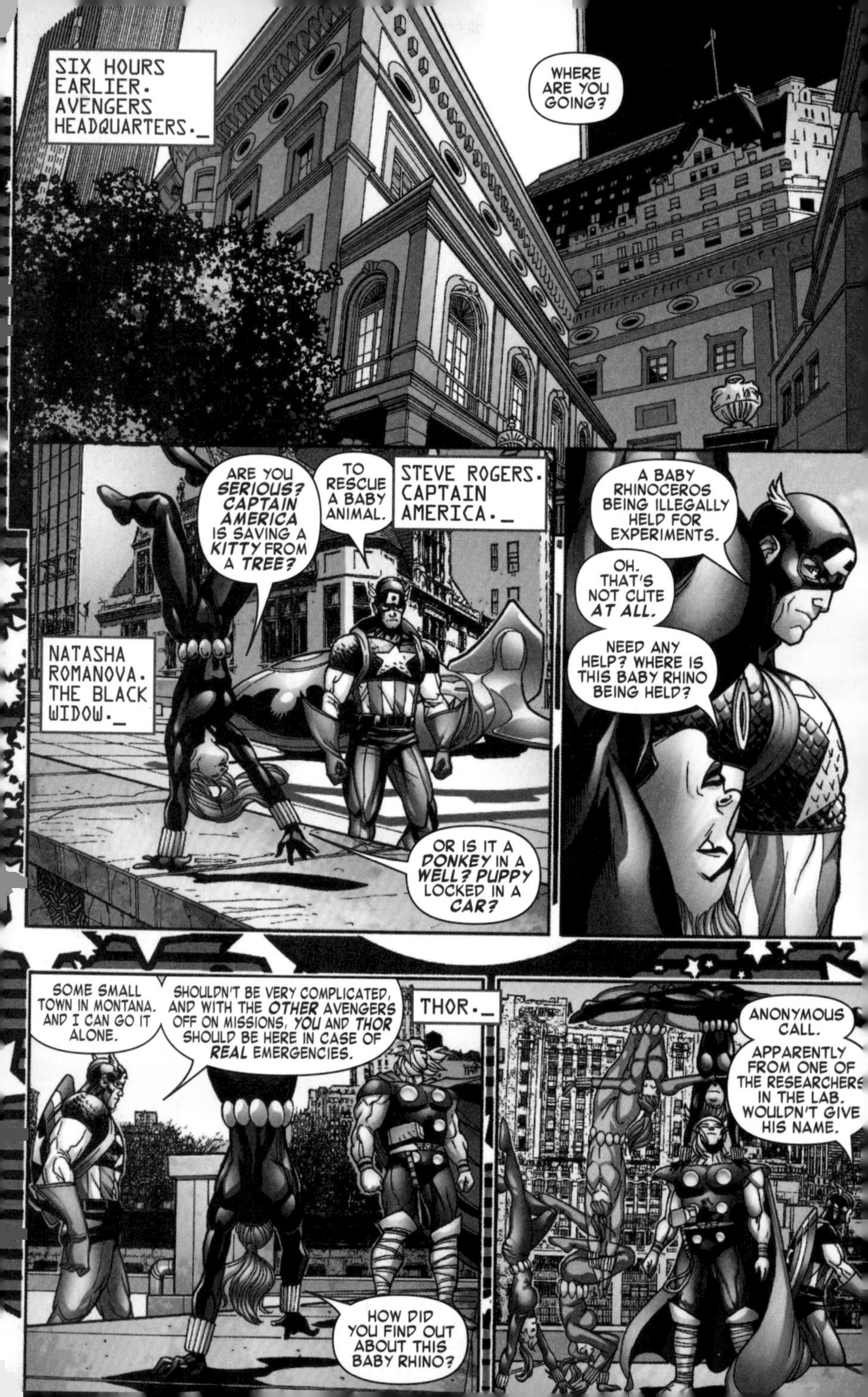

SIX HOURS EARLIER. AVENGERS HEADQUARTERS._
WHERE ARE YOU GOING?
STEVE ROGERS. CAPTAIN AMERICA._
TO RESCUE A BABY ANIMAL.
ARE YOU SERIOUS? CAPTAIN AMERICA IS SAVING A KITTY FROM A TREE?
NATASHA ROMANOVA. THE BLACK WIDOW._
OR IS IT A DONKEY IN A WELL? PUPPY LOCKED IN A CAR?
A BABY RHINOCEROS BEING ILLEGALLY HELD FOR EXPERIMENTS.
OH. THAT'S NOT CUTE AT ALL.
NEED ANY HELP? WHERE IS THIS BABY RHINO BEING HELD?
SOME SMALL TOWN IN MONTANA. AND I CAN GO IT ALONE.
SHOULDN'T BE VERY COMPLICATED, AND WITH THE OTHER AVENGERS OFF ON MISSIONS, YOU AND THOR SHOULD BE HERE IN CASE OF REAL EMERGENCIES.
THOR._
HOW DID YOU FIND OUT ABOUT THIS BABY RHINO?
ANONYMOUS CALL.
APPARENTLY FROM ONE OF THE RESEARCHERS IN THE LAB. WOULDN'T GIVE HIS NAME.

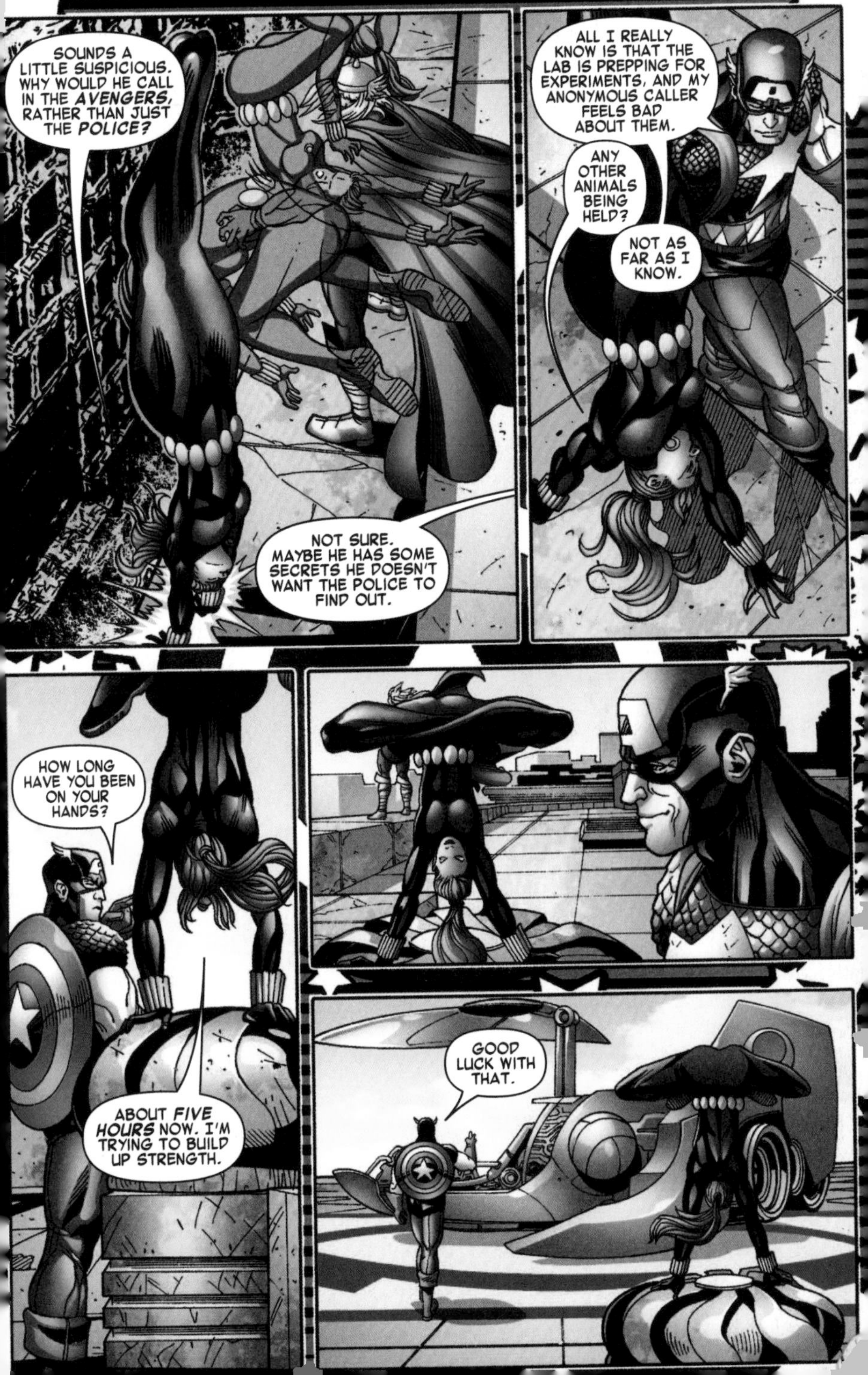
SOUNDS A LITTLE SUSPICIOUS. WHY WOULD HE CALL IN THE *AVENGERS,* RATHER THAN JUST THE *POLICE?*
NOT SURE. MAYBE HE HAS SOME SECRETS HE DOESN'T WANT THE POLICE TO FIND OUT.
ALL I REALLY KNOW IS THAT THE LAB IS PREPPING FOR EXPERIMENTS, AND MY ANONYMOUS CALLER FEELS BAD ABOUT THEM.
ANY OTHER ANIMALS BEING HELD?
NOT AS FAR AS I KNOW.
HOW LONG HAVE YOU BEEN ON YOUR HANDS?
ABOUT *FIVE HOURS* NOW. I'M TRYING TO BUILD UP STRENGTH.
GOOD LUCK WITH THAT.

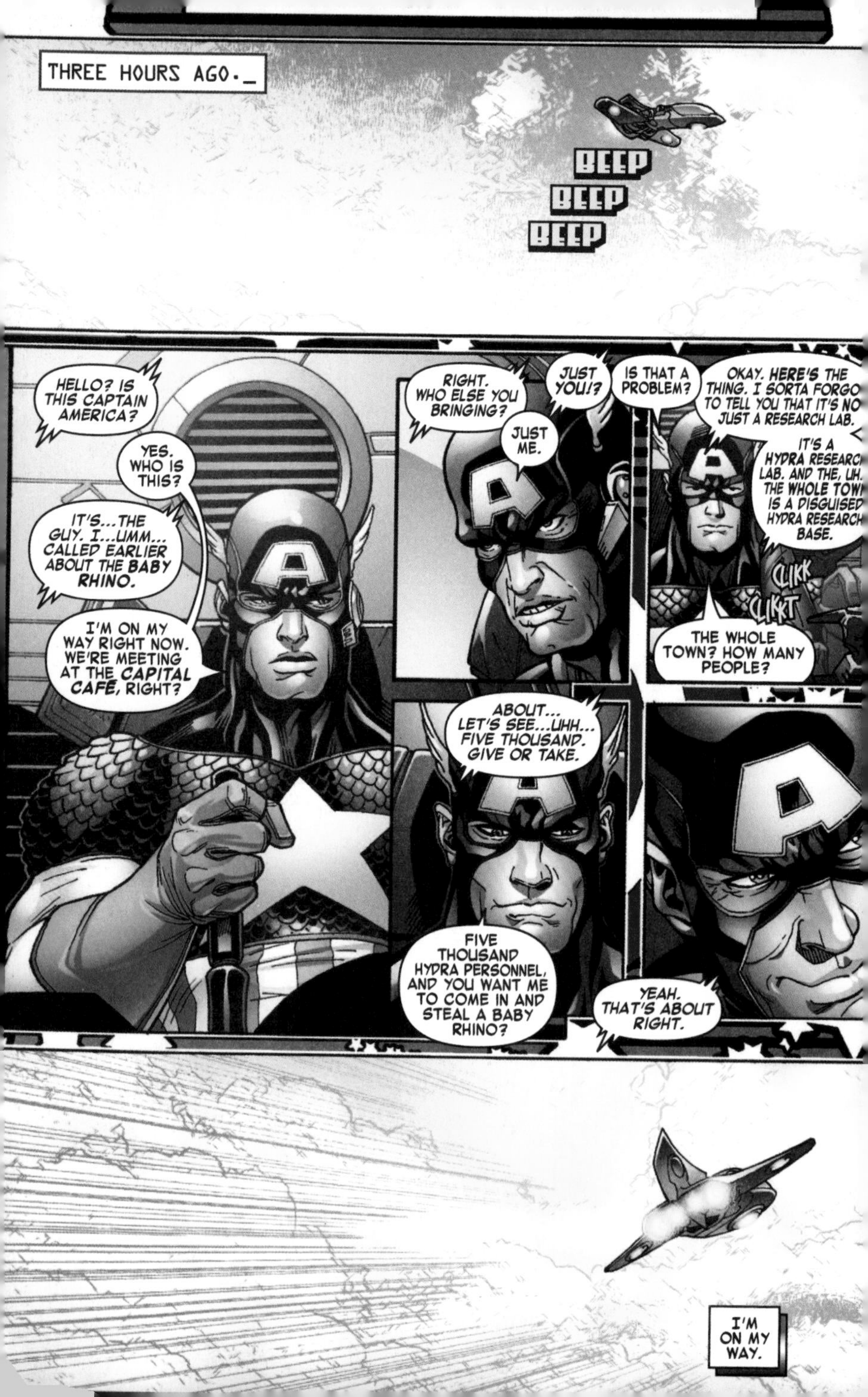
THREE HOURS AGO._
BEEP
BEEP
BEEP
HELLO? IS THIS CAPTAIN AMERICA?
YES. WHO IS THIS?
IT'S...THE GUY. I...UMM... CALLED EARLIER ABOUT THE BABY RHINO.
I'M ON MY WAY RIGHT NOW. WE'RE MEETING AT THE CAPITAL CAFÉ, RIGHT?
RIGHT. WHO ELSE YOU BRINGING?
JUST ME.
JUST YOU!?
IS THAT A PROBLEM?
OKAY. HERE'S THE THING. I SORTA FORGO TO TELL YOU THAT IT'S NO JUST A RESEARCH LAB.
IT'S A HYDRA RESEARC LAB. AND THE, UH. THE WHOLE TOW IS A DISGUISED HYDRA RESEARCH BASE.
CLIKK
CLIKKT
THE WHOLE TOWN? HOW MANY PEOPLE?
ABOUT... LET'S SEE...UHH... FIVE THOUSAND. GIVE OR TAKE.
FIVE THOUSAND HYDRA PERSONNEL, AND YOU WANT ME TO COME IN AND STEAL A BABY RHINO?
YEAH. THAT'S ABOUT RIGHT.
I'M ON MY WAY.

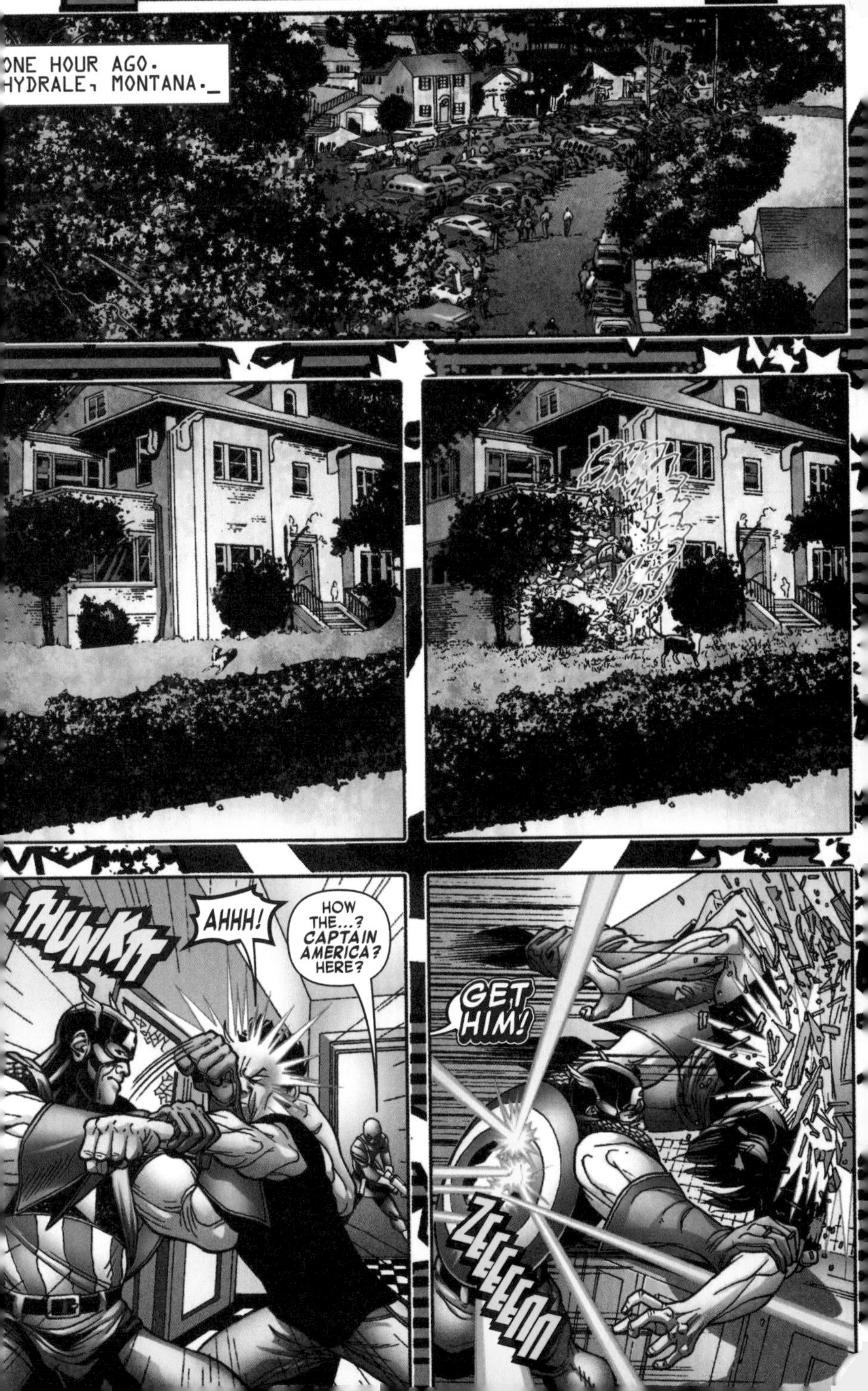

ONE HOUR AGO.
HYDRALE, MONTANA._
THUNKT
AHHH!
HOW THE...? CAPTAIN AMERICA? HERE?
GET HIM!
ZEEEEEOW

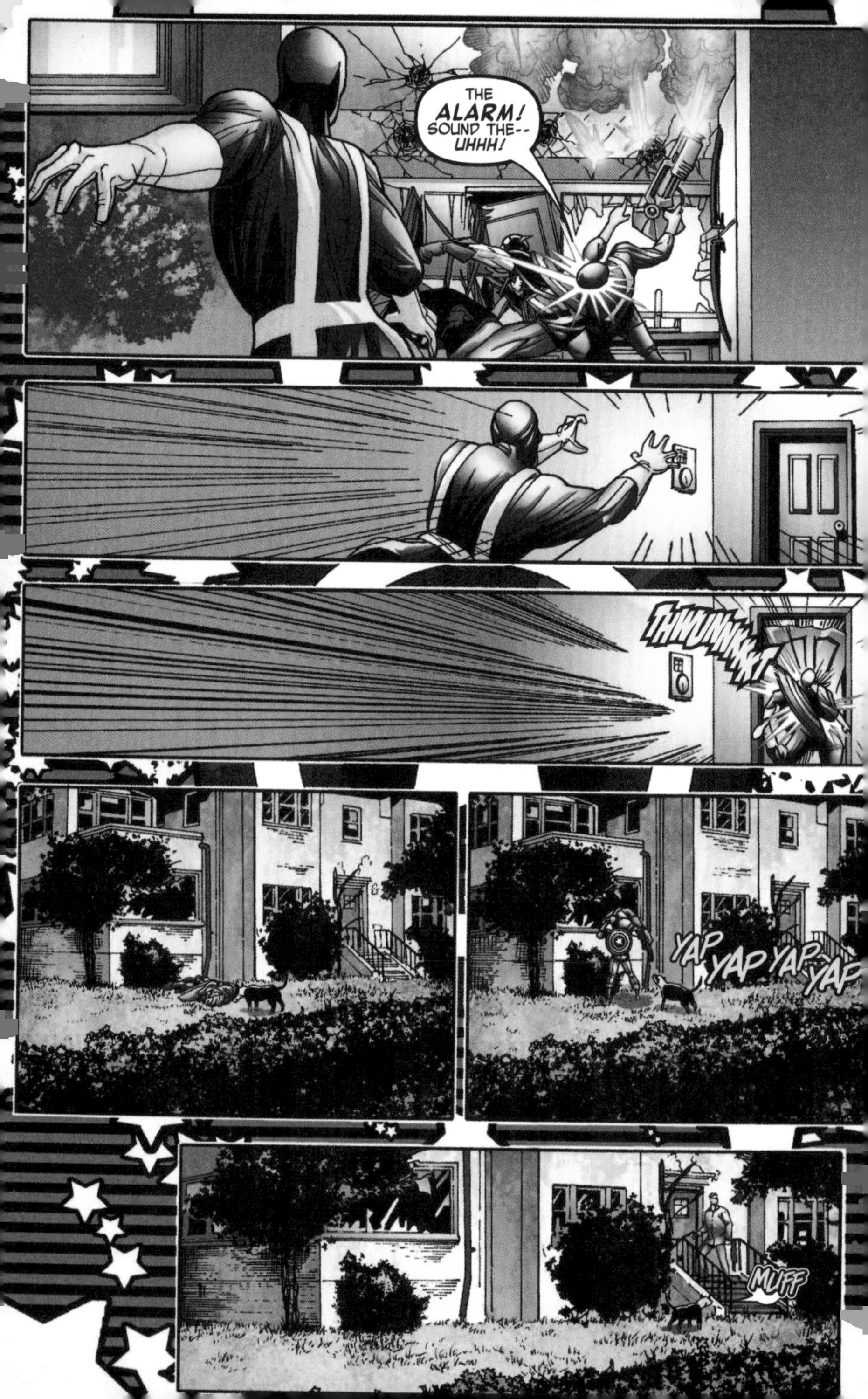
THE ALARM! SOUND THE-- UHHH!
THWUNNKKT
YAP YAP YAP YAP
MUFF

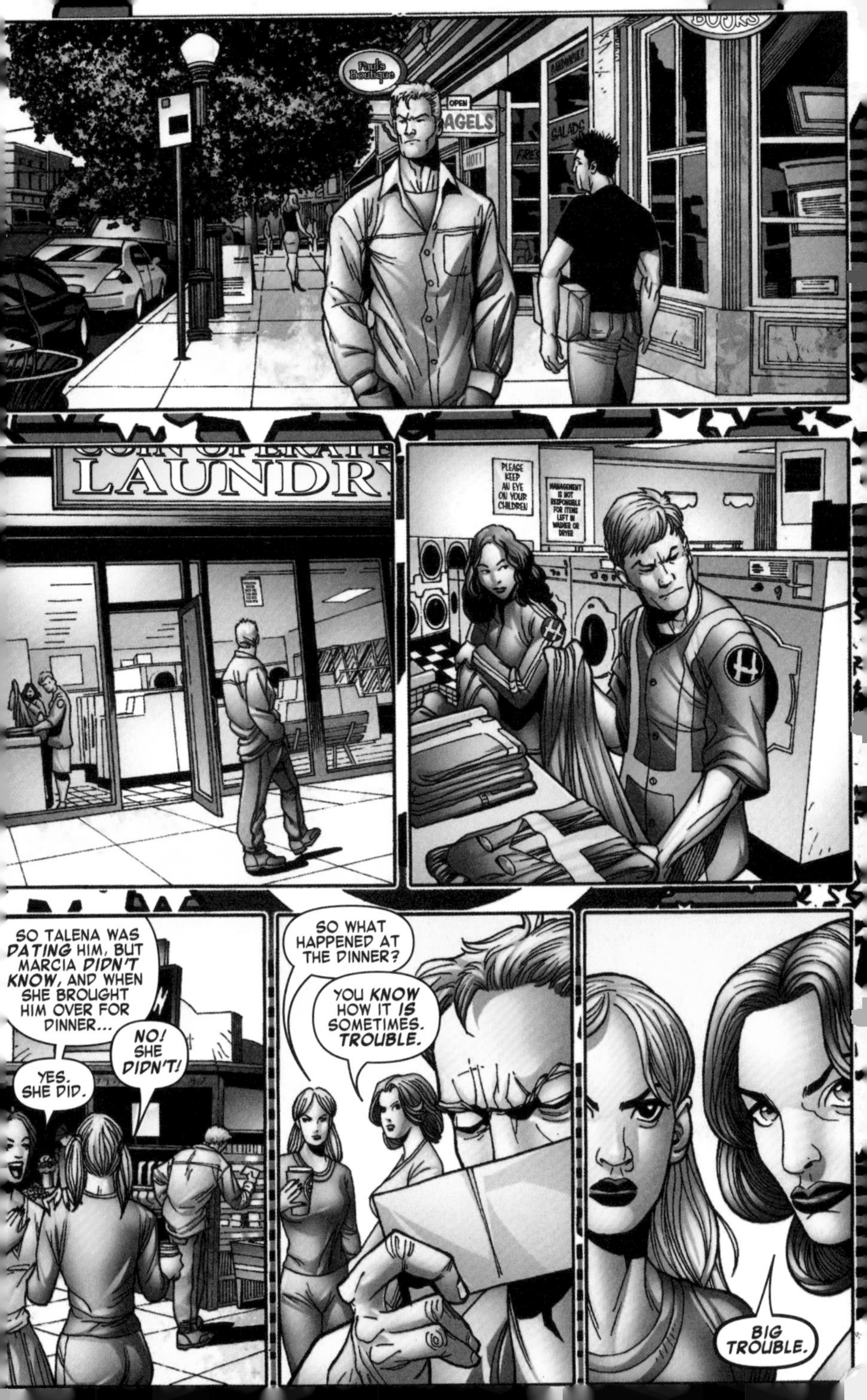
Paul's Boutique
OPEN
AGELS
SALADS
BOOKS
COIN OPERATED
LAUNDRY
PLEASE KEEP AN EYE ON YOUR CHILDREN
MANAGEMENT IS NOT RESPONSIBLE FOR ITEMS LEFT IN WASHER OR DRYER
SO TALENA WAS DATING HIM, BUT MARCIA DIDN'T KNOW, AND WHEN SHE BROUGHT HIM OVER FOR DINNER...
NO! SHE DIDN'T!
YES. SHE DID.
SO WHAT HAPPENED AT THE DINNER?
YOU KNOW HOW IT IS SOMETIMES. TROUBLE.
BIG TROUBLE.

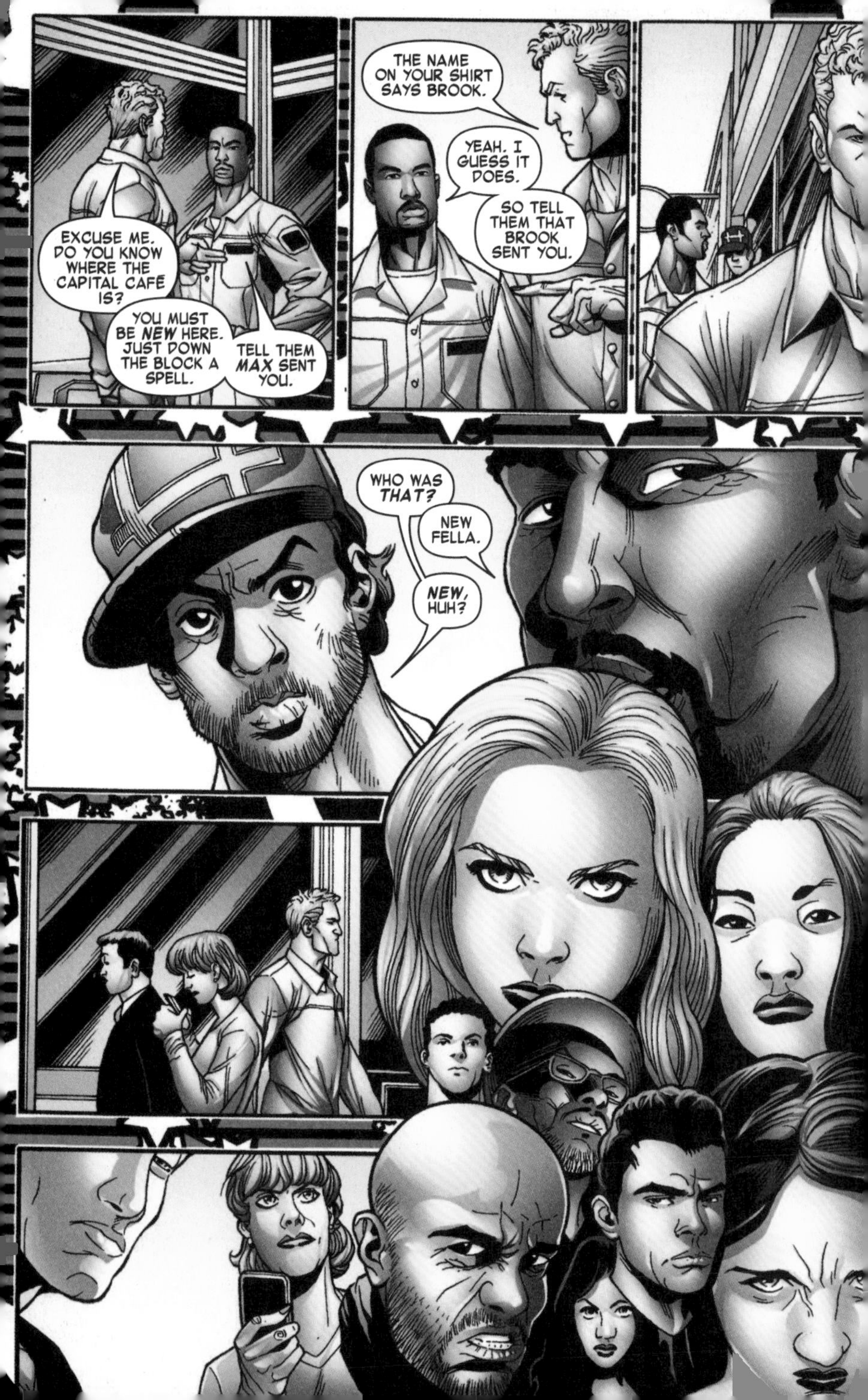
EXCUSE ME. DO YOU KNOW WHERE THE CAPITAL CAFÉ IS?
YOU MUST BE NEW HERE. JUST DOWN THE BLOCK A SPELL.
TELL THEM MAX SENT YOU.
THE NAME ON YOUR SHIRT SAYS BROOK.
YEAH. I GUESS IT DOES.
SO TELL THEM THAT BROOK SENT YOU.
WHO WAS THAT?
NEW FELLA.
NEW, HUH?

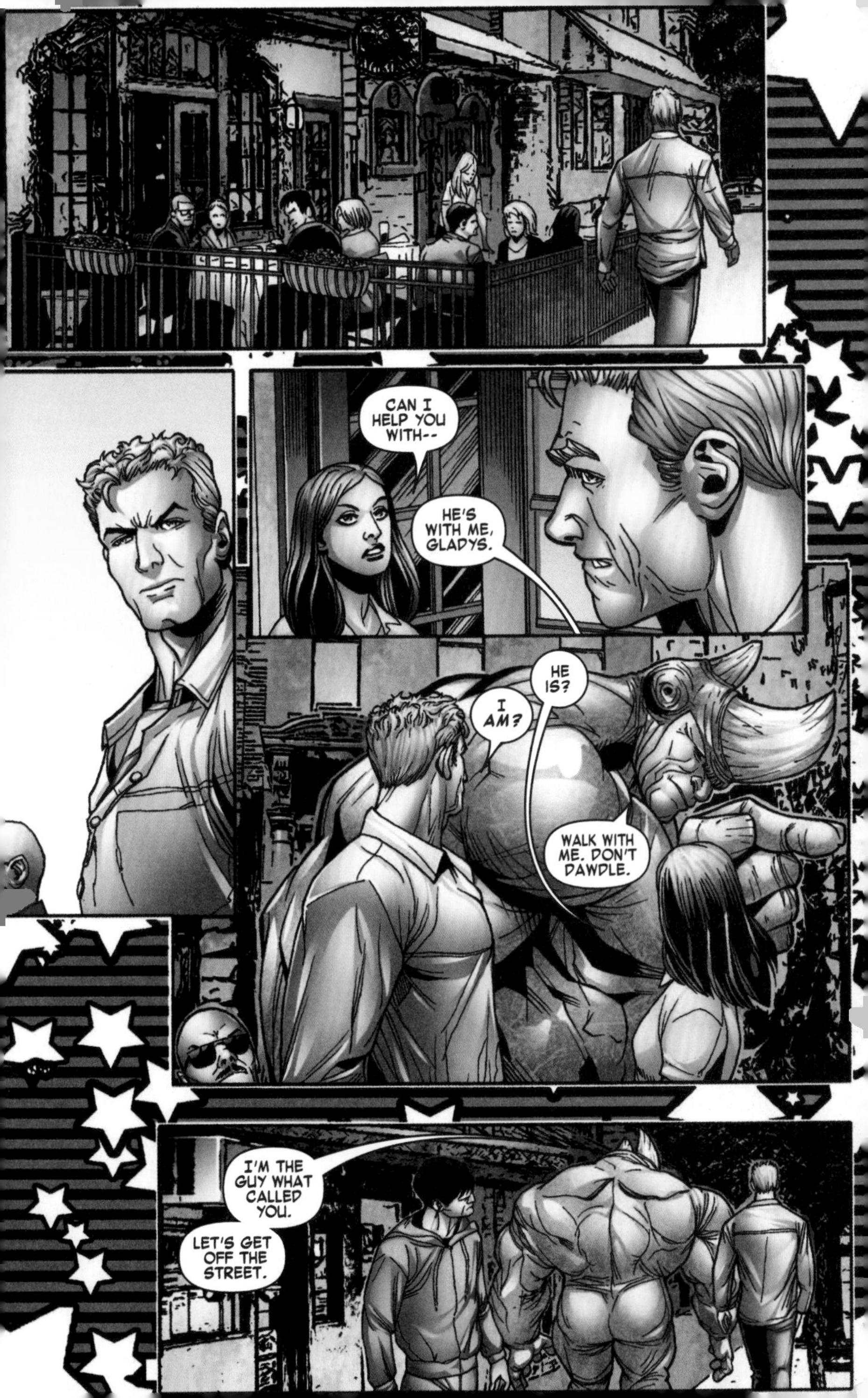
CAN I HELP YOU WITH--
HE'S WITH ME, GLADYS.
HE IS?
I AM?
WALK WITH ME. DON'T DAWDLE.
I'M THE GUY WHAT CALLED YOU.
LET'S GET OFF THE STREET.

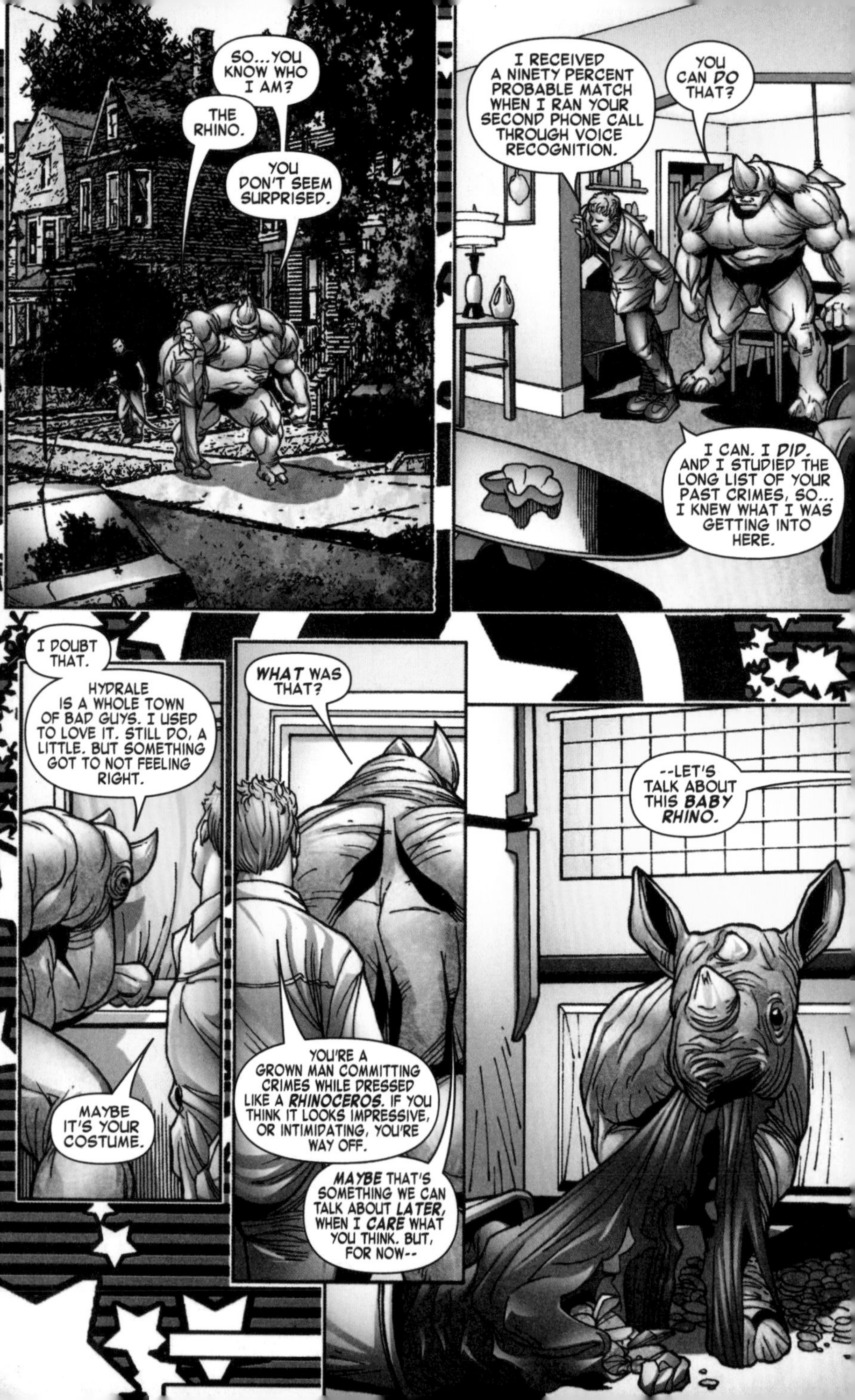
SO...YOU KNOW WHO I AM?
THE RHINO.
YOU DON'T SEEM SURPRISED.
I RECEIVED A NINETY PERCENT PROBABLE MATCH WHEN I RAN YOUR SECOND PHONE CALL THROUGH VOICE RECOGNITION.
YOU CAN DO THAT?
I CAN. I DID. AND I STUDIED THE LONG LIST OF YOUR PAST CRIMES, SO... I KNEW WHAT I WAS GETTING INTO HERE.
I DOUBT THAT.
HYDRALE IS A WHOLE TOWN OF BAD GUYS. I USED TO LOVE IT. STILL DO, A LITTLE. BUT SOMETHING GOT TO NOT FEELING RIGHT.
MAYBE IT'S YOUR COSTUME.
WHAT WAS THAT?
YOU'RE A GROWN MAN COMMITTING CRIMES WHILE DRESSED LIKE A RHINOCEROS. IF YOU THINK IT LOOKS IMPRESSIVE, OR INTIMIDATING, YOU'RE WAY OFF.
MAYBE THAT'S SOMETHING WE CAN TALK ABOUT LATER, WHEN I CARE WHAT YOU THINK. BUT, FOR NOW--
--LET'S TALK ABOUT THIS BABY RHINO.

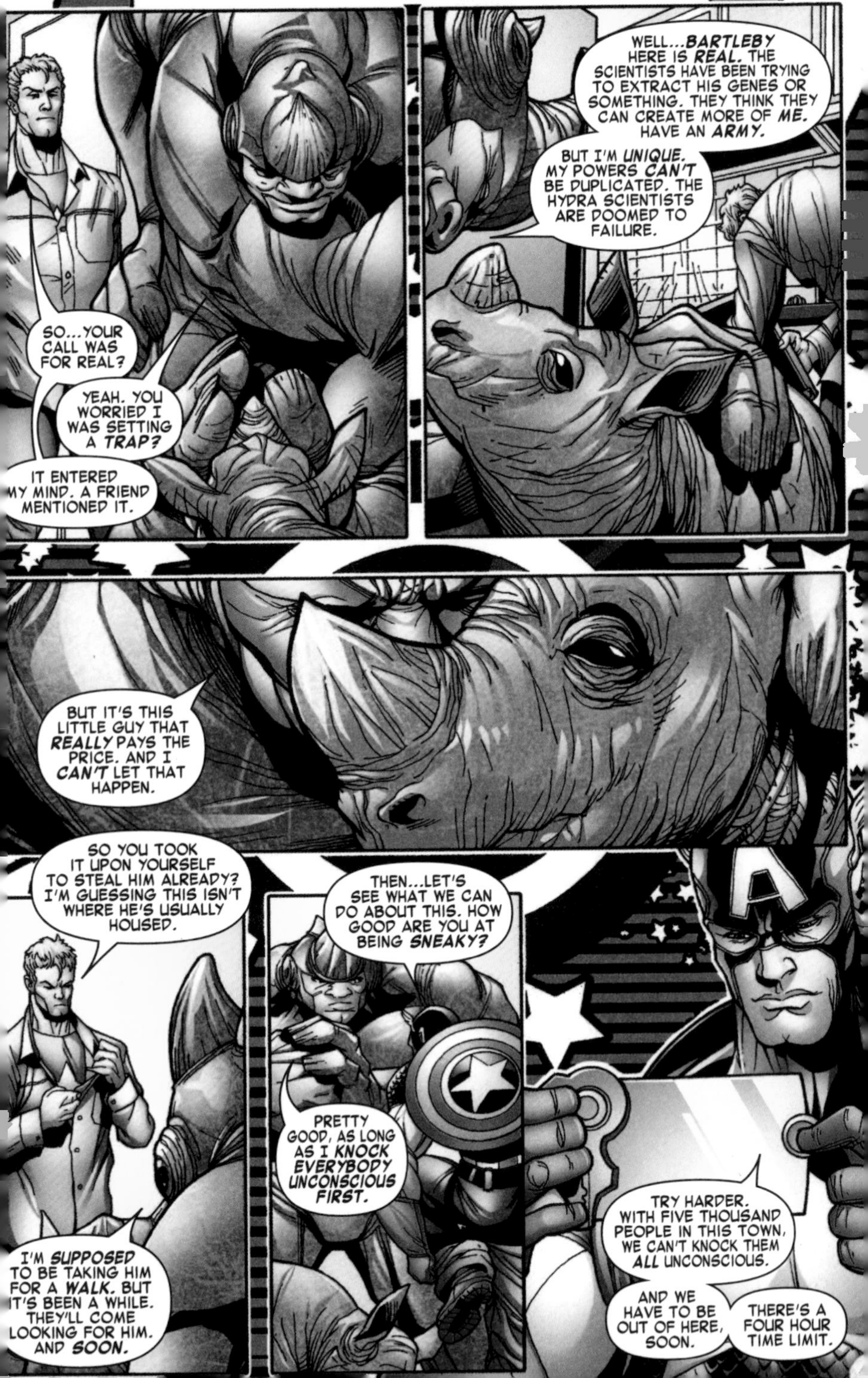

SO...YOUR CALL WAS FOR REAL?
YEAH. YOU WORRIED I WAS SETTING A TRAP?
IT ENTERED MY MIND. A FRIEND MENTIONED IT.
WELL...BARTLEBY HERE IS REAL. THE SCIENTISTS HAVE BEEN TRYING TO EXTRACT HIS GENES OR SOMETHING. THEY THINK THEY CAN CREATE MORE OF ME. HAVE AN ARMY.
BUT I'M UNIQUE. MY POWERS CAN'T BE DUPLICATED. THE HYDRA SCIENTISTS ARE DOOMED TO FAILURE.
BUT IT'S THIS LITTLE GUY THAT REALLY PAYS THE PRICE. AND I CAN'T LET THAT HAPPEN.
SO YOU TOOK IT UPON YOURSELF TO STEAL HIM ALREADY? I'M GUESSING THIS ISN'T WHERE HE'S USUALLY HOUSED.
I'M SUPPOSED TO BE TAKING HIM FOR A WALK. BUT IT'S BEEN A WHILE. THEY'LL COME LOOKING FOR HIM. AND SOON.
THEN...LET'S SEE WHAT WE CAN DO ABOUT THIS. HOW GOOD ARE YOU AT BEING SNEAKY?
PRETTY GOOD, AS LONG AS I KNOCK EVERYBODY UNCONSCIOUS FIRST.
TRY HARDER. WITH FIVE THOUSAND PEOPLE IN THIS TOWN, WE CAN'T KNOCK THEM ALL UNCONSCIOUS.
AND WE HAVE TO BE OUT OF HERE, SOON.
THERE'S A FOUR HOUR TIME LIMIT.

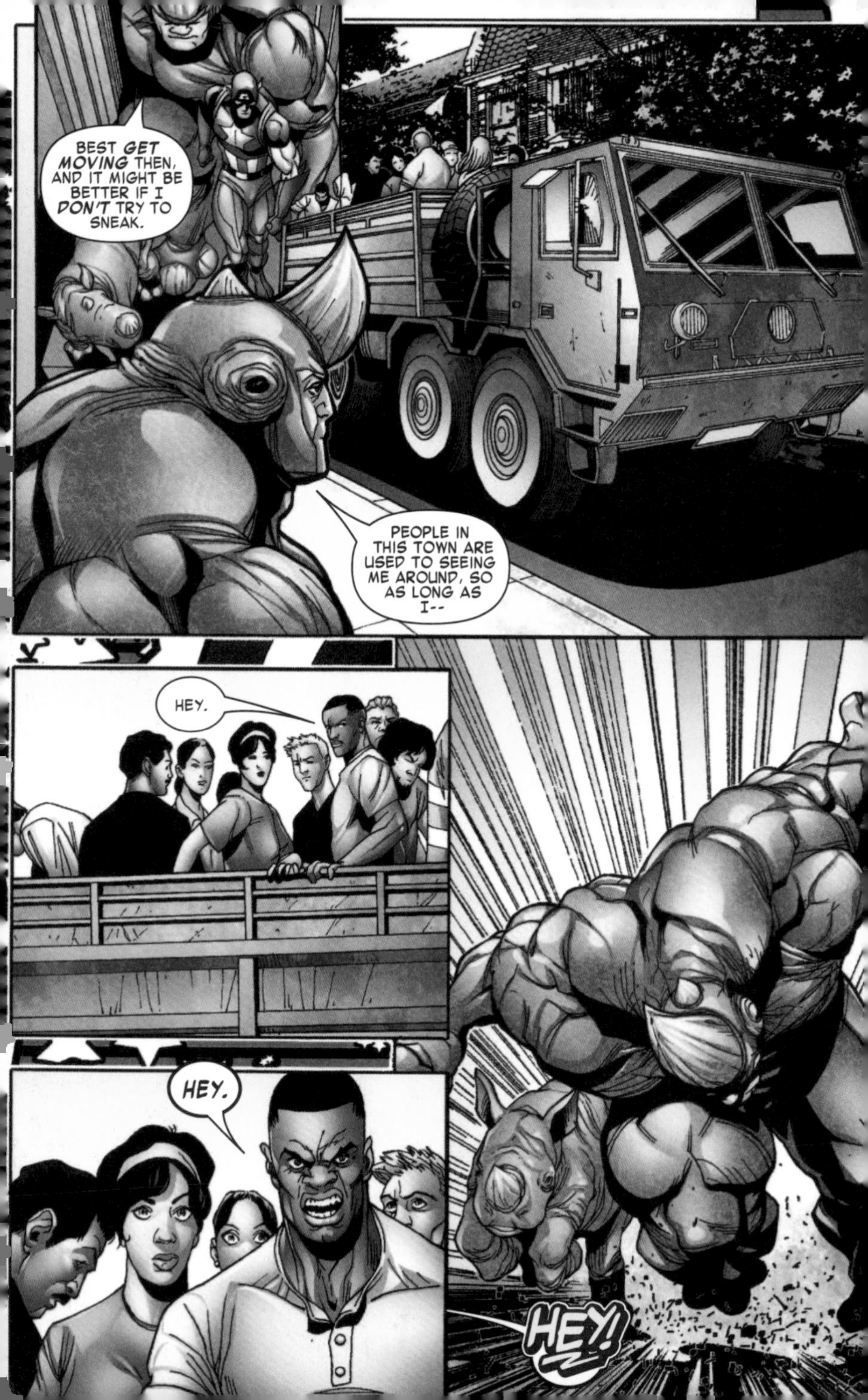

BEST GET MOVING THEN, AND IT MIGHT BE BETTER IF I DON'T TRY TO SNEAK.
PEOPLE IN THIS TOWN ARE USED TO SEEING ME AROUND, SO AS LONG AS I--
HEY.
HEY.
HEY!

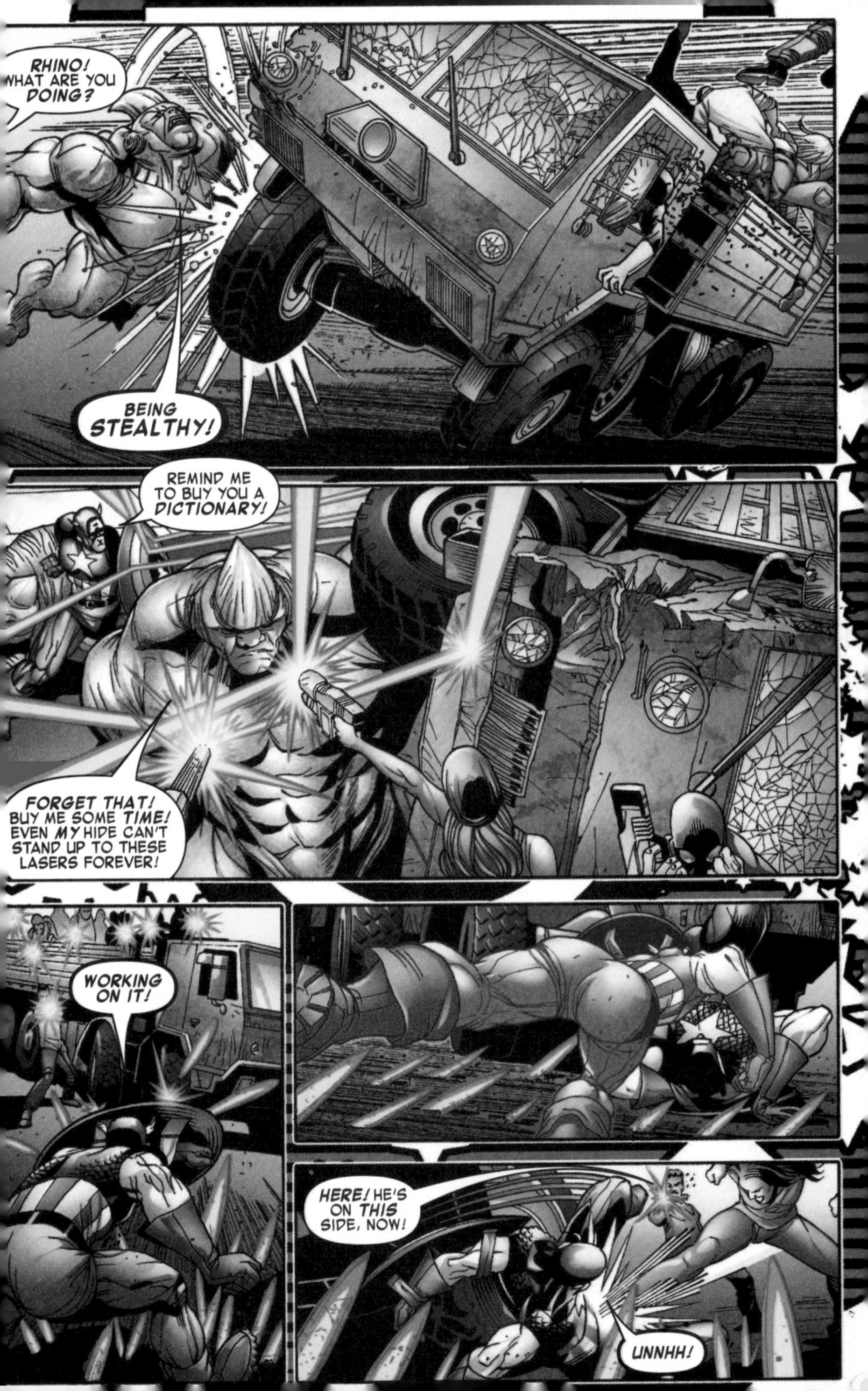
RHINO! WHAT ARE YOU DOING?
BEING STEALTHY!
REMIND ME TO BUY YOU A DICTIONARY!
FORGET THAT! BUY ME SOME TIME! EVEN MY HIDE CAN'T STAND UP TO THESE LASERS FOREVER!
WORKING ON IT!
HERE! HE'S ON THIS SIDE, NOW!
UNNHH!

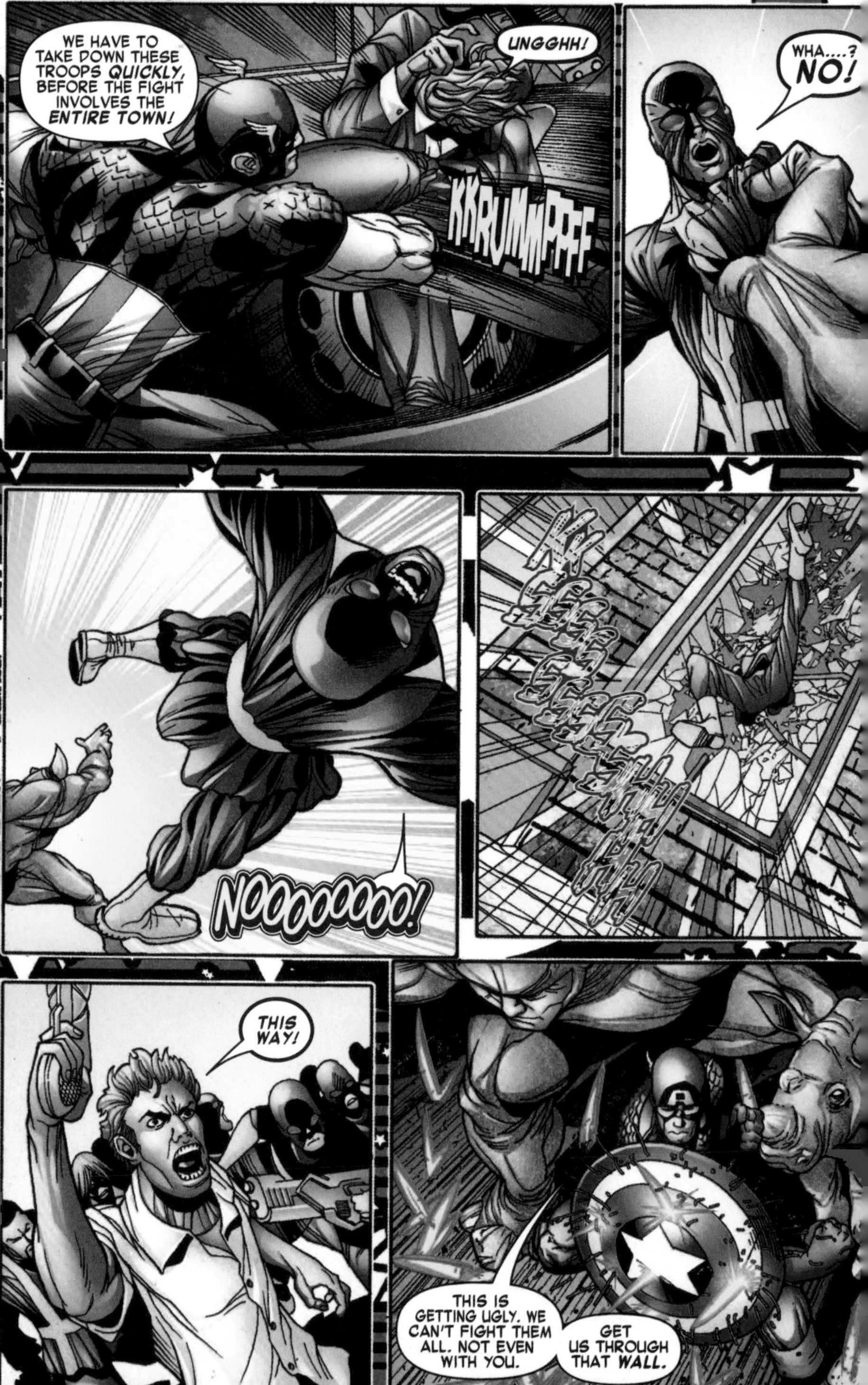
WE HAVE TO TAKE DOWN THESE TROOPS QUICKLY, BEFORE THE FIGHT INVOLVES THE ENTIRE TOWN!
UNGGHH!
KKRUMMPFF
WHA....? NO!
NOOOOOOOOO!
THIS WAY!
THIS IS GETTING UGLY. WE CAN'T FIGHT THEM ALL. NOT EVEN WITH YOU.
GET US THROUGH THAT WALL.

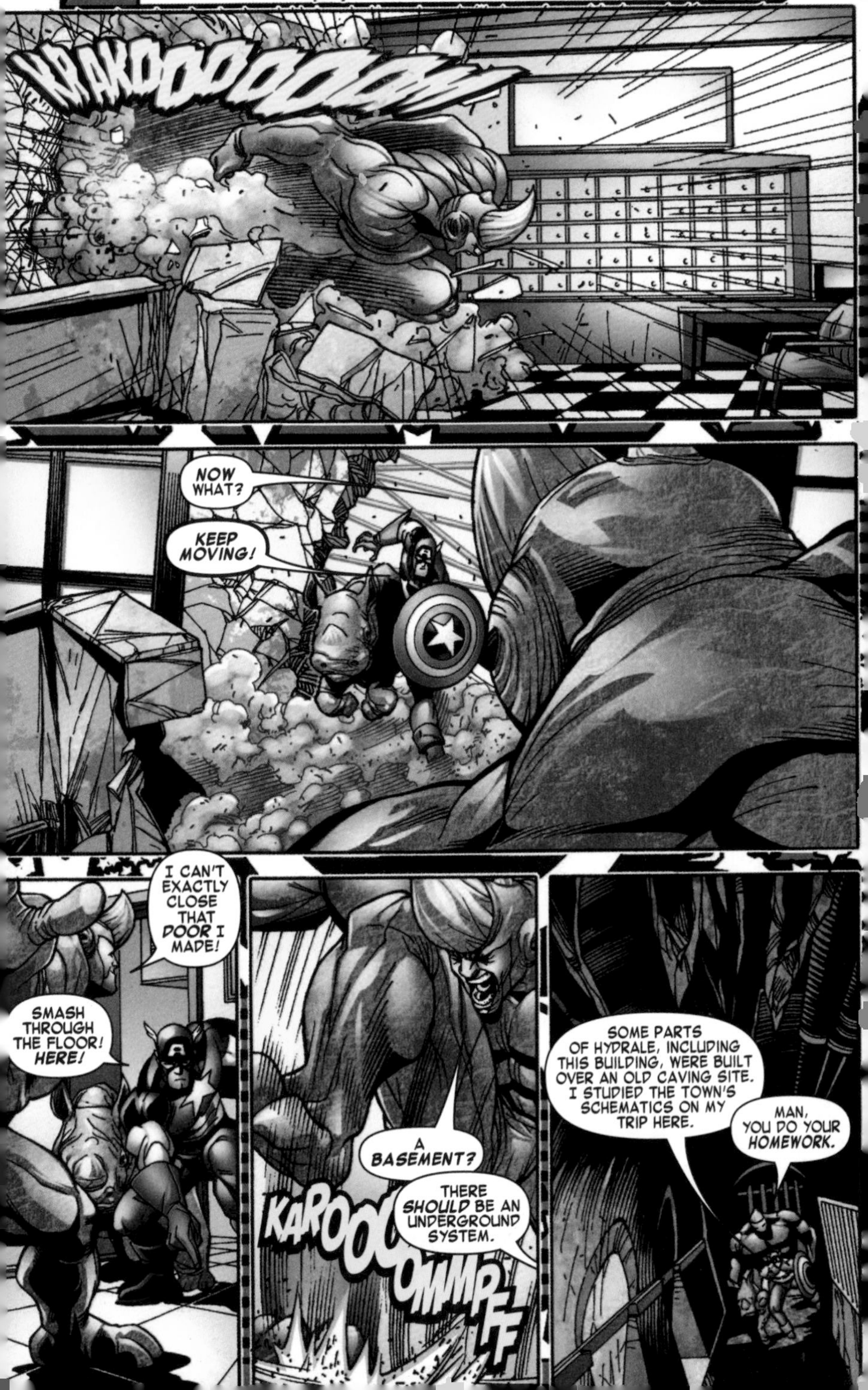
KRAKOOOOOOM
NOW WHAT?
KEEP MOVING!
I CAN'T EXACTLY CLOSE THAT DOOR I MADE!
SMASH THROUGH THE FLOOR! HERE!
A BASEMENT?
THERE SHOULD BE AN UNDERGROUND SYSTEM.
KAROOOOOMMMPFF
SOME PARTS OF HYDRALE, INCLUDING THIS BUILDING, WERE BUILT OVER AN OLD CAVING SITE. I STUDIED THE TOWN'S SCHEMATICS ON MY TRIP HERE.
MAN, YOU DO YOUR HOMEWORK.

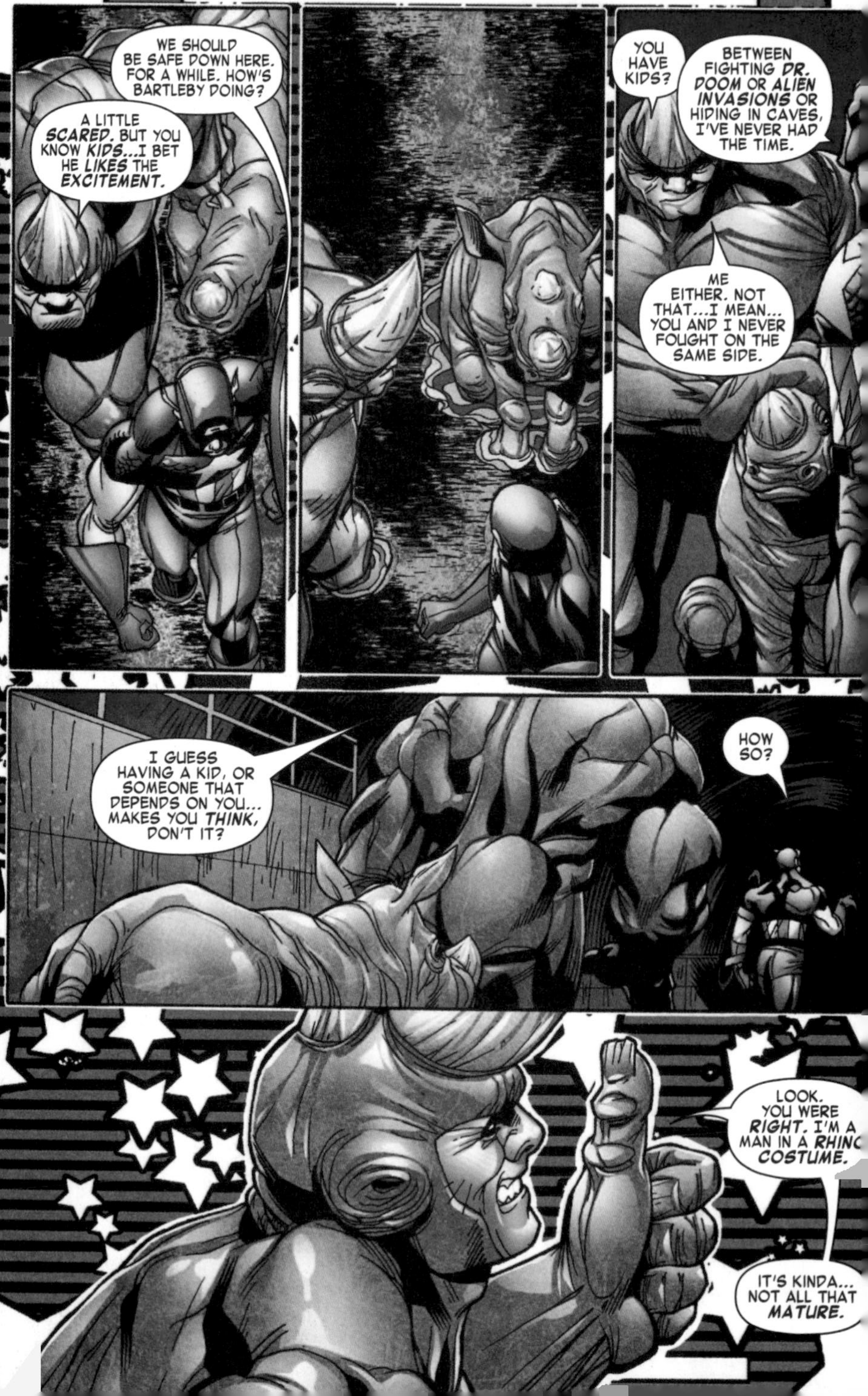
WE SHOULD BE SAFE DOWN HERE. FOR A WHILE. HOW'S BARTLEBY DOING?
A LITTLE SCARED. BUT YOU KNOW KIDS...I BET HE LIKES THE EXCITEMENT.
YOU HAVE KIDS?
BETWEEN FIGHTING DR. DOOM OR ALIEN INVASIONS OR HIDING IN CAVES, I'VE NEVER HAD THE TIME.
ME EITHER. NOT THAT...I MEAN... YOU AND I NEVER FOUGHT ON THE SAME SIDE.
I GUESS HAVING A KID, OR SOMEONE THAT DEPENDS ON YOU... MAKES YOU THINK, DON'T IT?
HOW SO?
LOOK. YOU WERE RIGHT. I'M A MAN IN A RHINO COSTUME.
IT'S KINDA... NOT ALL THAT MATURE.

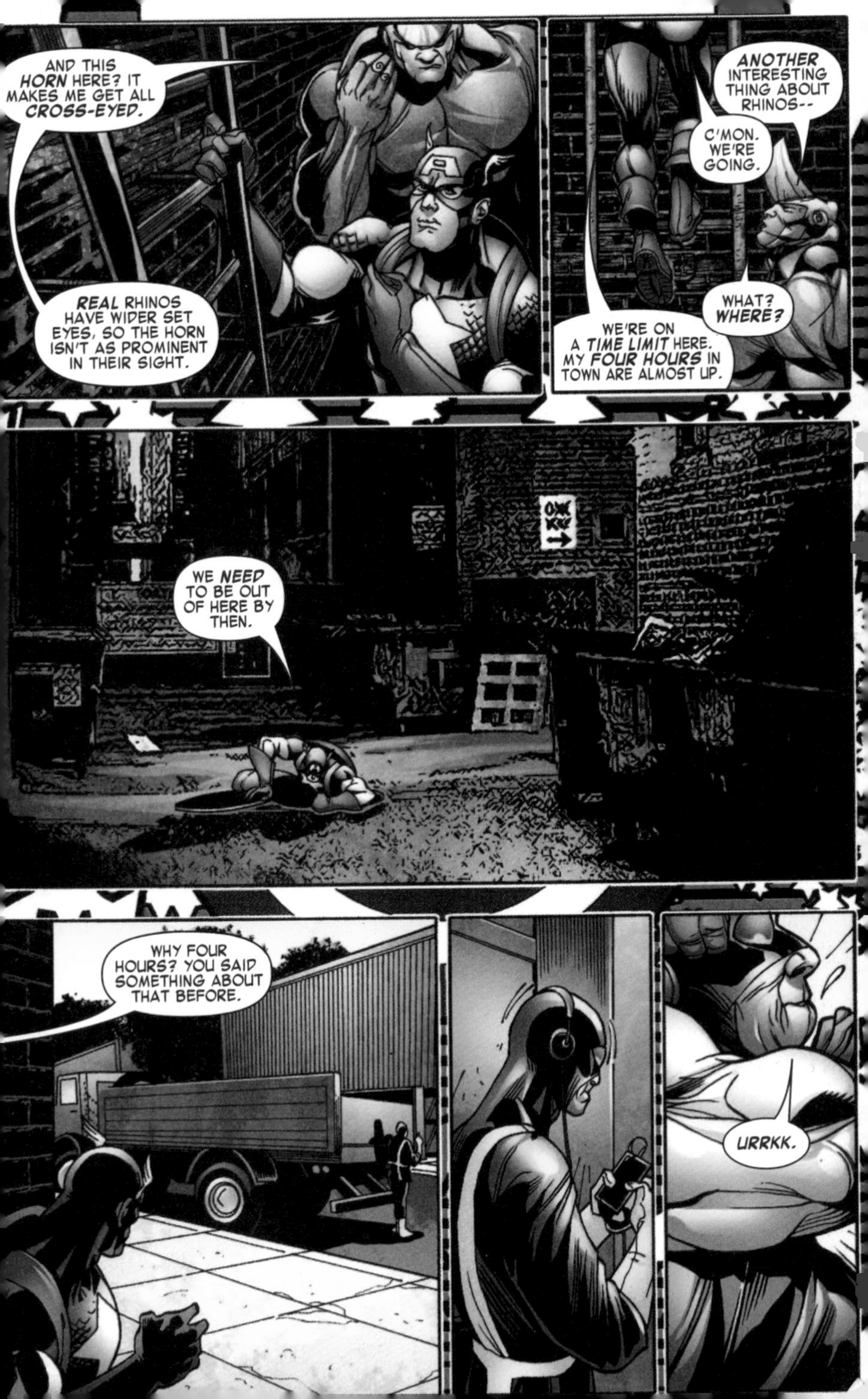
AND THIS HORN HERE? IT MAKES ME GET ALL CROSS-EYED.
REAL RHINOS HAVE WIDER SET EYES, SO THE HORN ISN'T AS PROMINENT IN THEIR SIGHT.
ANOTHER INTERESTING THING ABOUT RHINOS--
C'MON. WE'RE GOING.
WHAT? WHERE?
WE'RE ON A TIME LIMIT HERE. MY FOUR HOURS IN TOWN ARE ALMOST UP.
WE NEED TO BE OUT OF HERE BY THEN.
WHY FOUR HOURS? YOU SAID SOMETHING ABOUT THAT BEFORE.
URRKK.

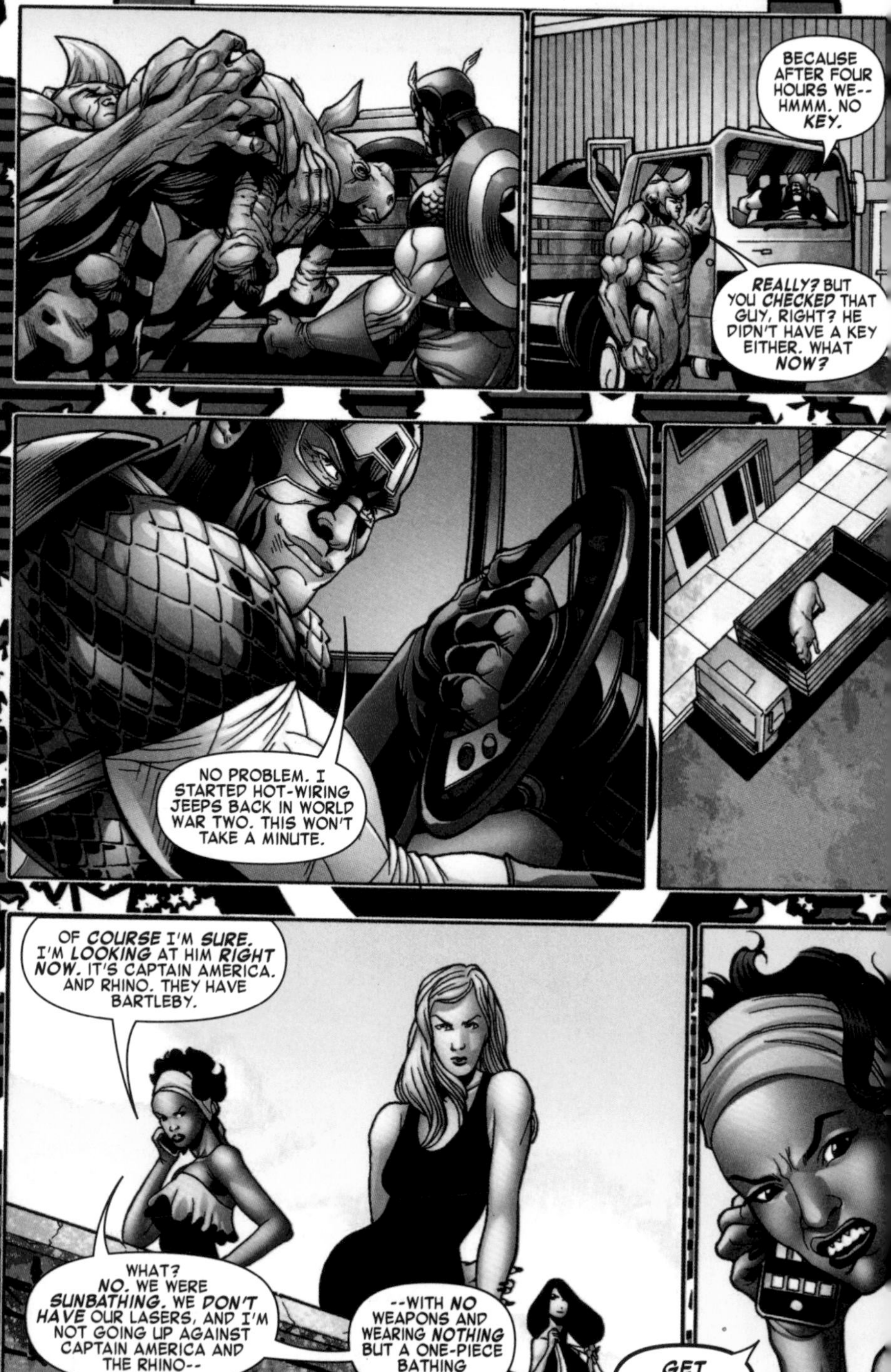
BECAUSE AFTER FOUR HOURS WE-- HMMM. NO KEY.
REALLY? BUT YOU CHECKED THAT GUY, RIGHT? HE DIDN'T HAVE A KEY EITHER. WHAT NOW?
NO PROBLEM. I STARTED HOT-WIRING JEEPS BACK IN WORLD WAR TWO. THIS WON'T TAKE A MINUTE.
OF COURSE I'M SURE. I'M LOOKING AT HIM RIGHT NOW. IT'S CAPTAIN AMERICA. AND RHINO. THEY HAVE BARTLEBY.
WHAT? NO. WE WERE SUNBATHING. WE DON'T HAVE OUR LASERS, AND I'M NOT GOING UP AGAINST CAPTAIN AMERICA AND THE RHINO--
--WITH NO WEAPONS AND WEARING NOTHING BUT A ONE-PIECE BATHING SUIT!
GET SOMEONE HERE!

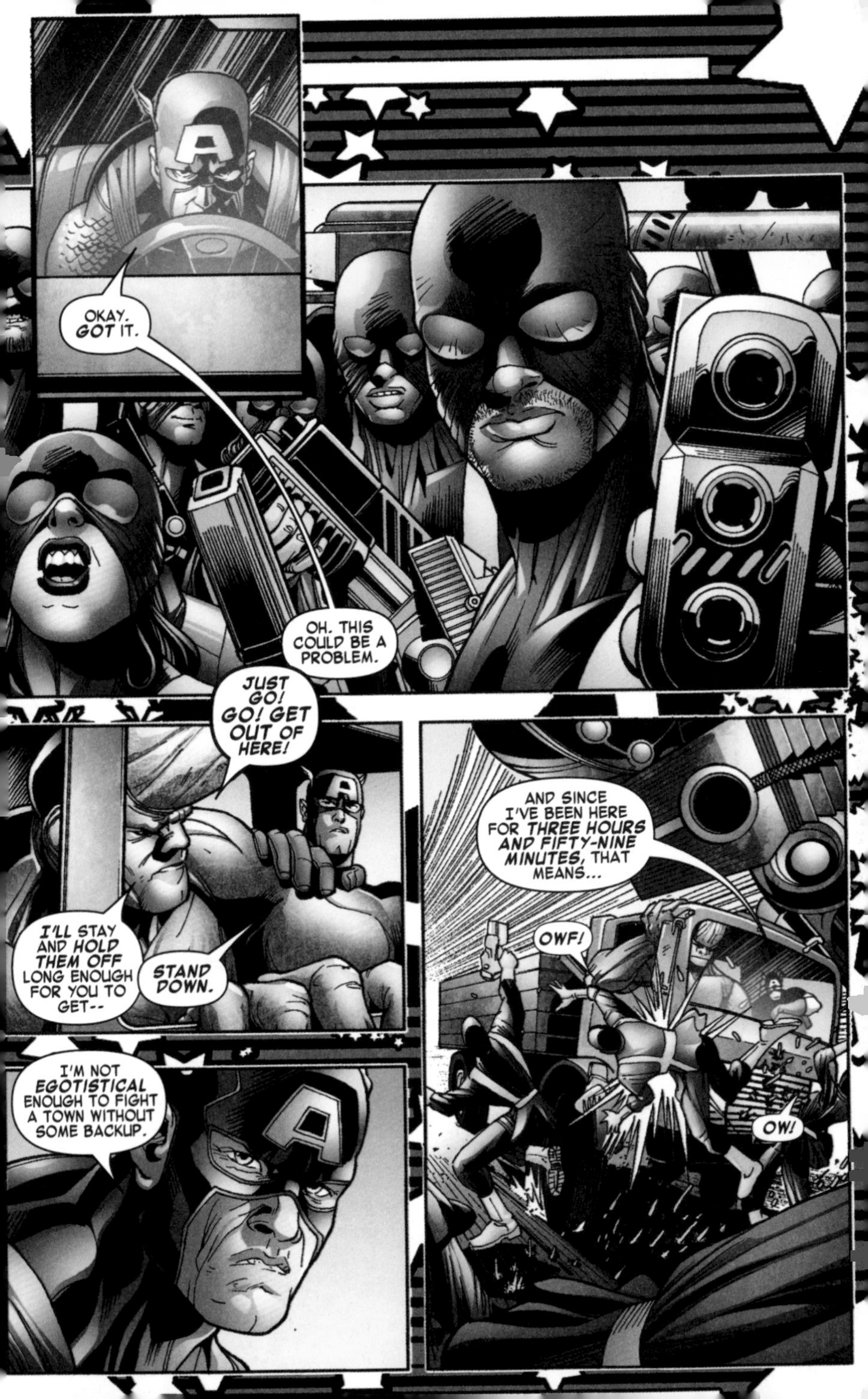
OKAY. GOT IT.
OH. THIS COULD BE A PROBLEM.
JUST GO! GO! GET OUT OF HERE!
I'LL STAY AND HOLD THEM OFF LONG ENOUGH FOR YOU TO GET--
STAND DOWN.
I'M NOT EGOTISTICAL ENOUGH TO FIGHT A TOWN WITHOUT SOME BACKUP.
AND SINCE I'VE BEEN HERE FOR THREE HOURS AND FIFTY-NINE MINUTES, THAT MEANS...
OWF!
OW!

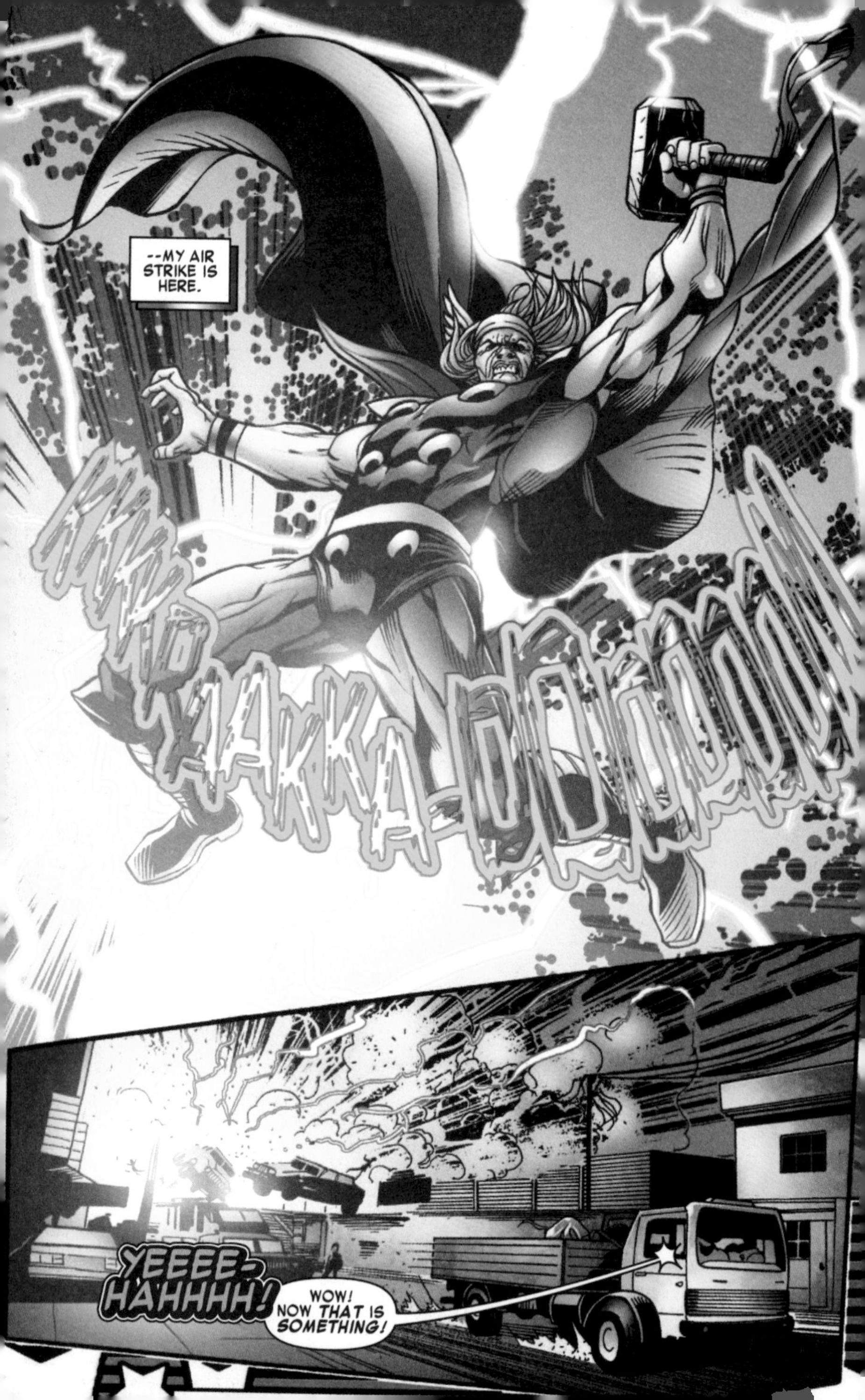
--MY AIR STRIKE IS HERE.
YEEEEE-HAHHHHH!
WOW! NOW THAT IS SOMETHING!

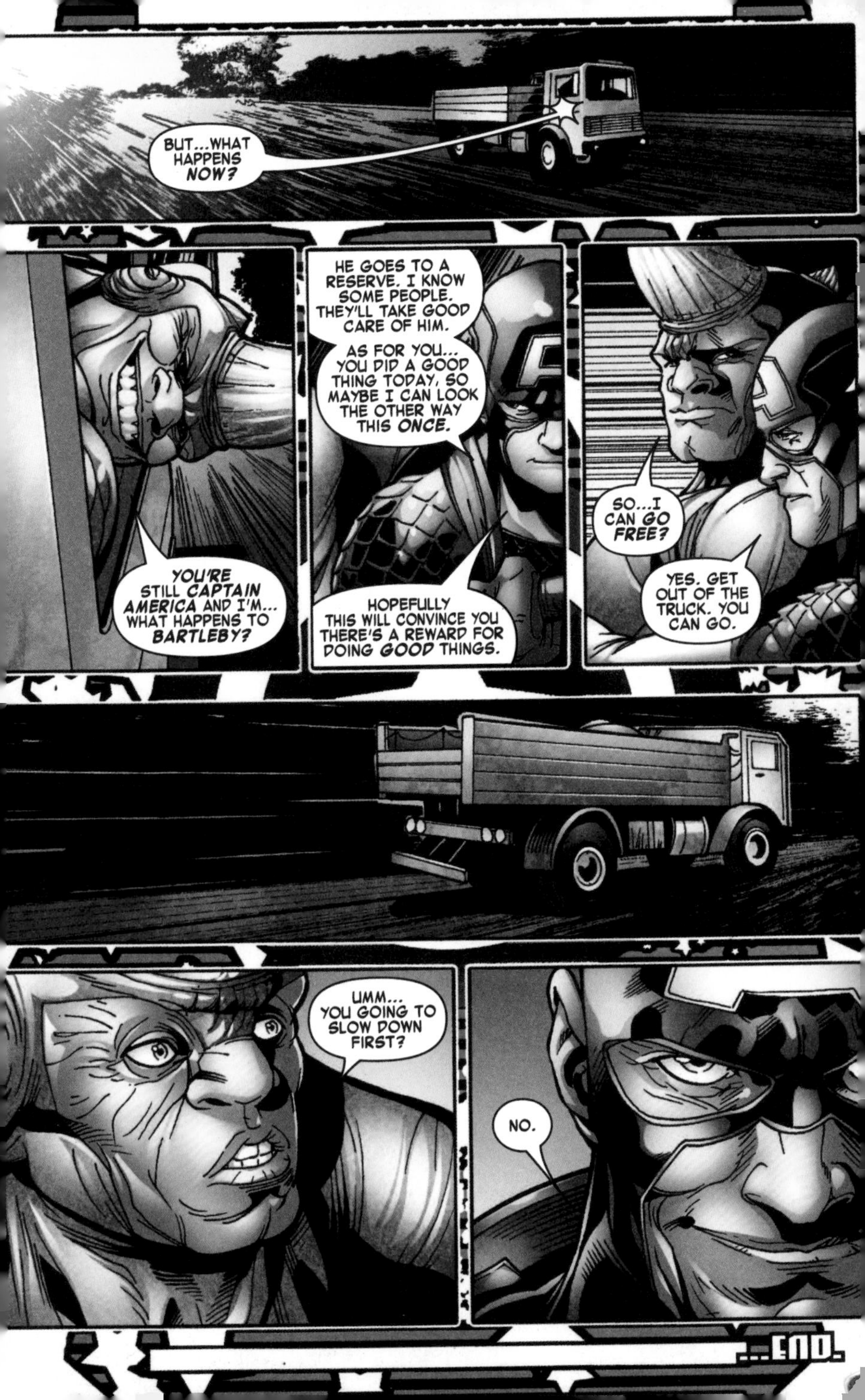
BUT...WHAT HAPPENS NOW?
YOU'RE STILL CAPTAIN AMERICA AND I'M... WHAT HAPPENS TO BARTLEBY?
HE GOES TO A RESERVE. I KNOW SOME PEOPLE. THEY'LL TAKE GOOD CARE OF HIM.
AS FOR YOU... YOU DID A GOOD THING TODAY, SO MAYBE I CAN LOOK THE OTHER WAY THIS ONCE.
HOPEFULLY THIS WILL CONVINCE YOU THERE'S A REWARD FOR DOING GOOD THINGS.
SO...I CAN GO FREE?
YES. GET OUT OF THE TRUCK. YOU CAN GO.
UMM... YOU GOING TO SLOW DOWN FIRST?
NO.
...END.

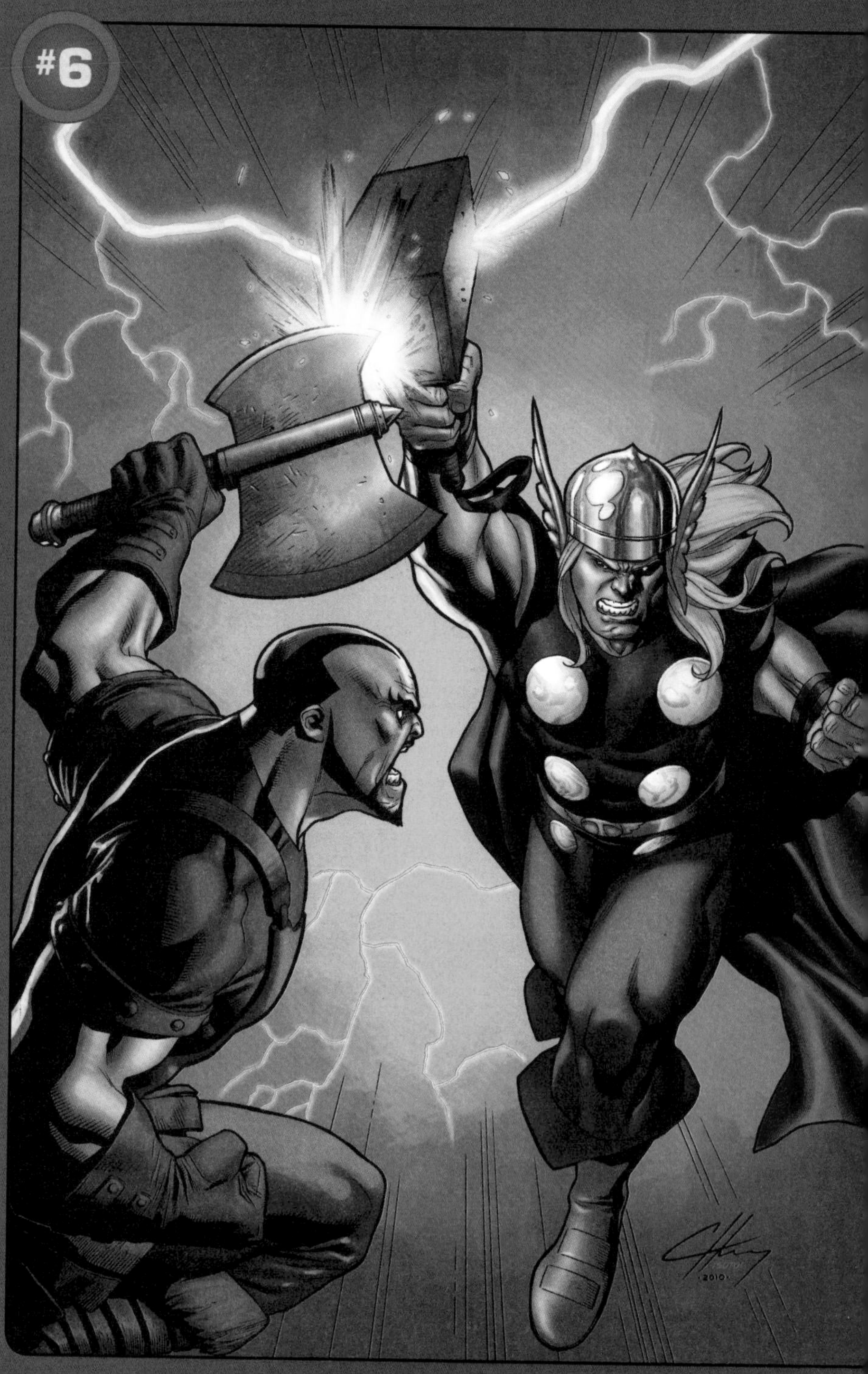
#6

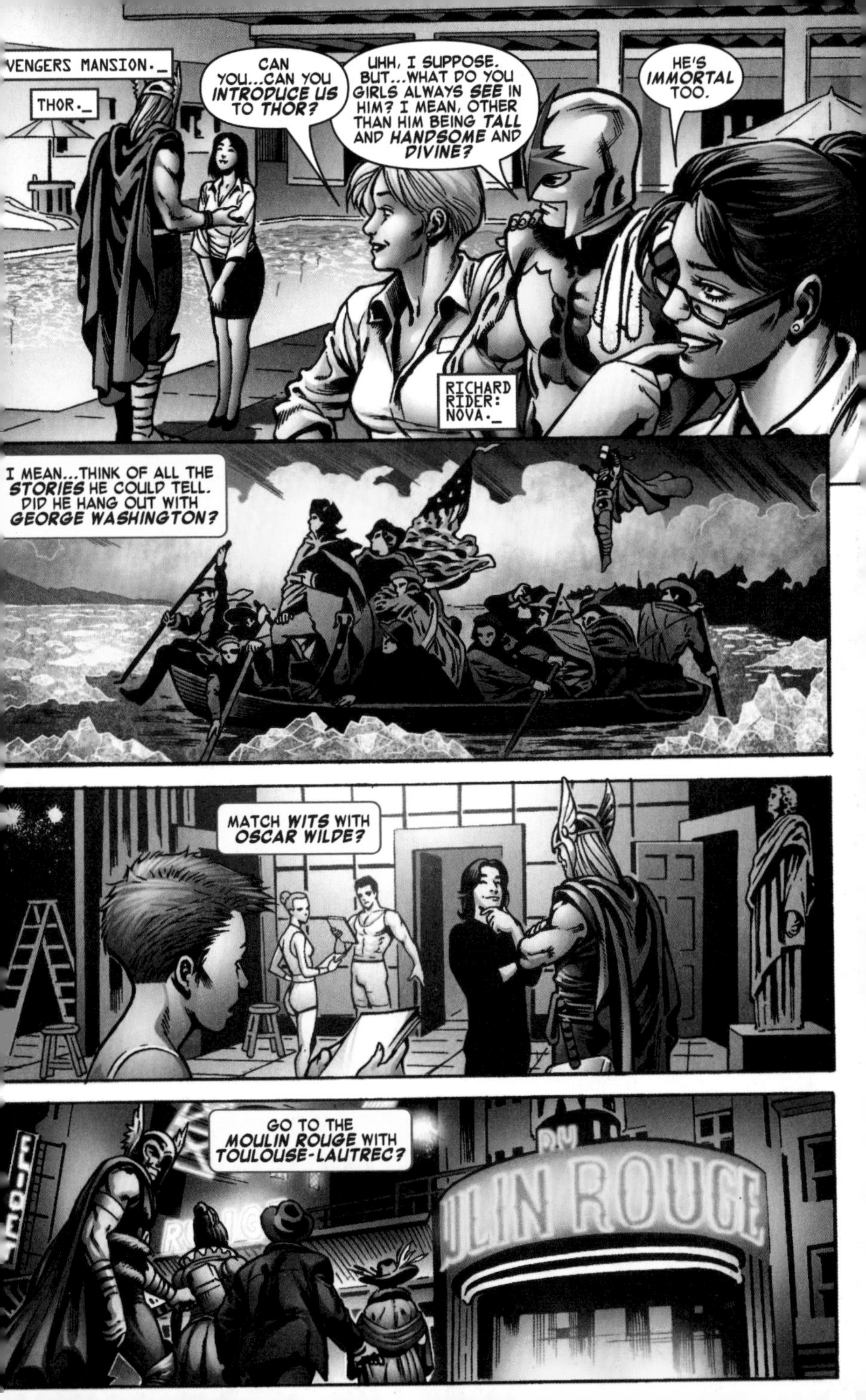
VENGERS MANSION._
THOR._
CAN YOU...CAN YOU INTRODUCE US TO THOR?
UHH, I SUPPOSE. BUT...WHAT DO YOU GIRLS ALWAYS SEE IN HIM? I MEAN, OTHER THAN HIM BEING TALL AND HANDSOME AND DIVINE?
RICHARD RIDER: NOVA._
HE'S IMMORTAL TOO.
I MEAN...THINK OF ALL THE STORIES HE COULD TELL. DID HE HANG OUT WITH GEORGE WASHINGTON?
MATCH WITS WITH OSCAR WILDE?
GO TO THE MOULIN ROUGE WITH TOULOUSE-LAUTREC?
ULIN ROUGE

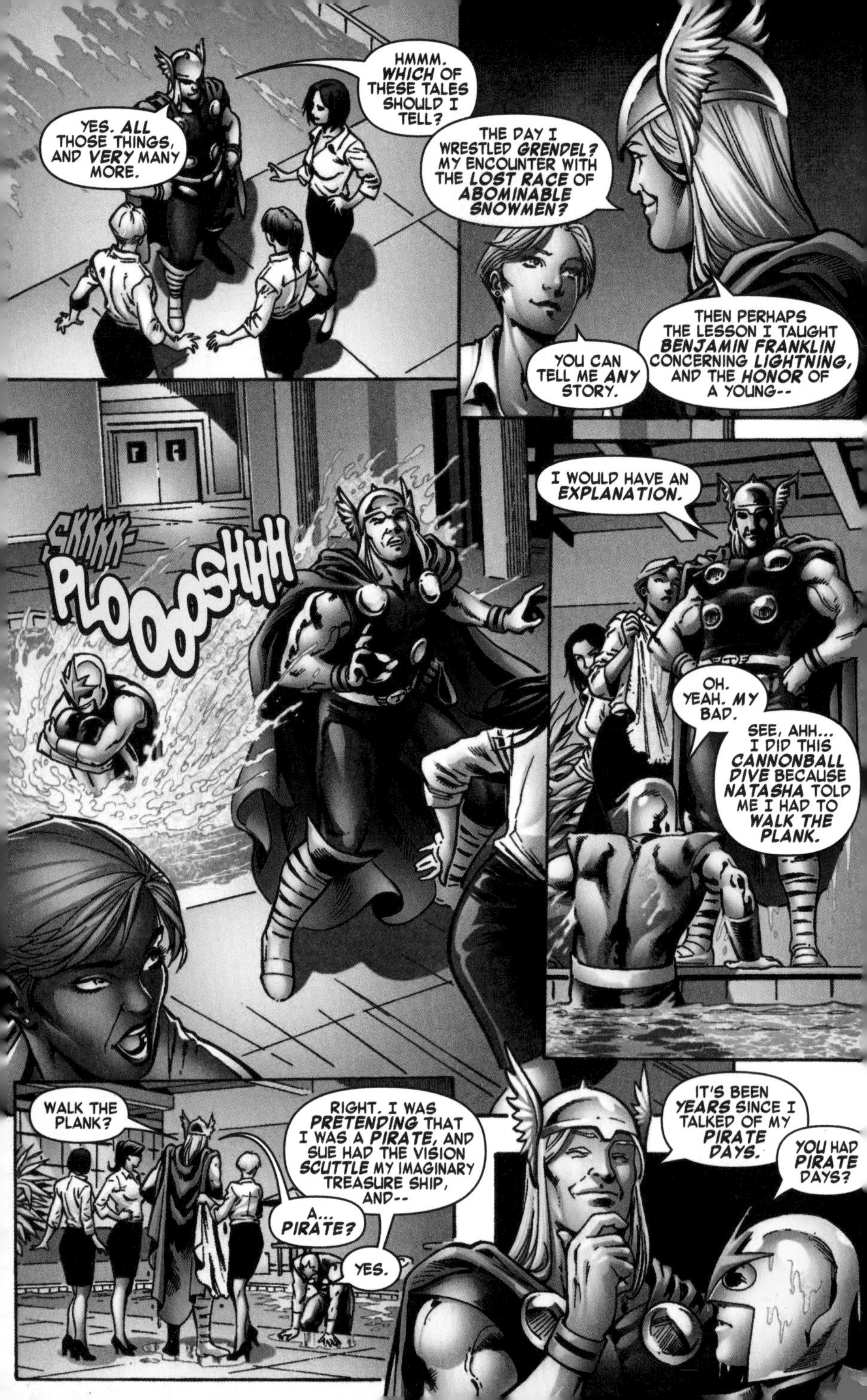
HMMM. WHICH OF THESE TALES SHOULD I TELL?
YES. ALL THOSE THINGS, AND VERY MANY MORE.
THE DAY I WRESTLED GRENDEL? MY ENCOUNTER WITH THE LOST RACE OF ABOMINABLE SNOWMEN?
YOU CAN TELL ME ANY STORY.
THEN PERHAPS THE LESSON I TAUGHT BENJAMIN FRANKLIN CONCERNING LIGHTNING, AND THE HONOR OF A YOUNG--
SKKKK-PLOOOOSHHH
I WOULD HAVE AN EXPLANATION.
OH. YEAH. MY BAD.
SEE, AHH... I DID THIS CANNONBALL DIVE BECAUSE NATASHA TOLD ME I HAD TO WALK THE PLANK.
WALK THE PLANK?
RIGHT. I WAS PRETENDING THAT I WAS A PIRATE, AND SUE HAD THE VISION SCUTTLE MY IMAGINARY TREASURE SHIP, AND--
A... PIRATE?
YES.
IT'S BEEN YEARS SINCE I TALKED OF MY PIRATE DAYS.
YOU HAD PIRATE DAYS?

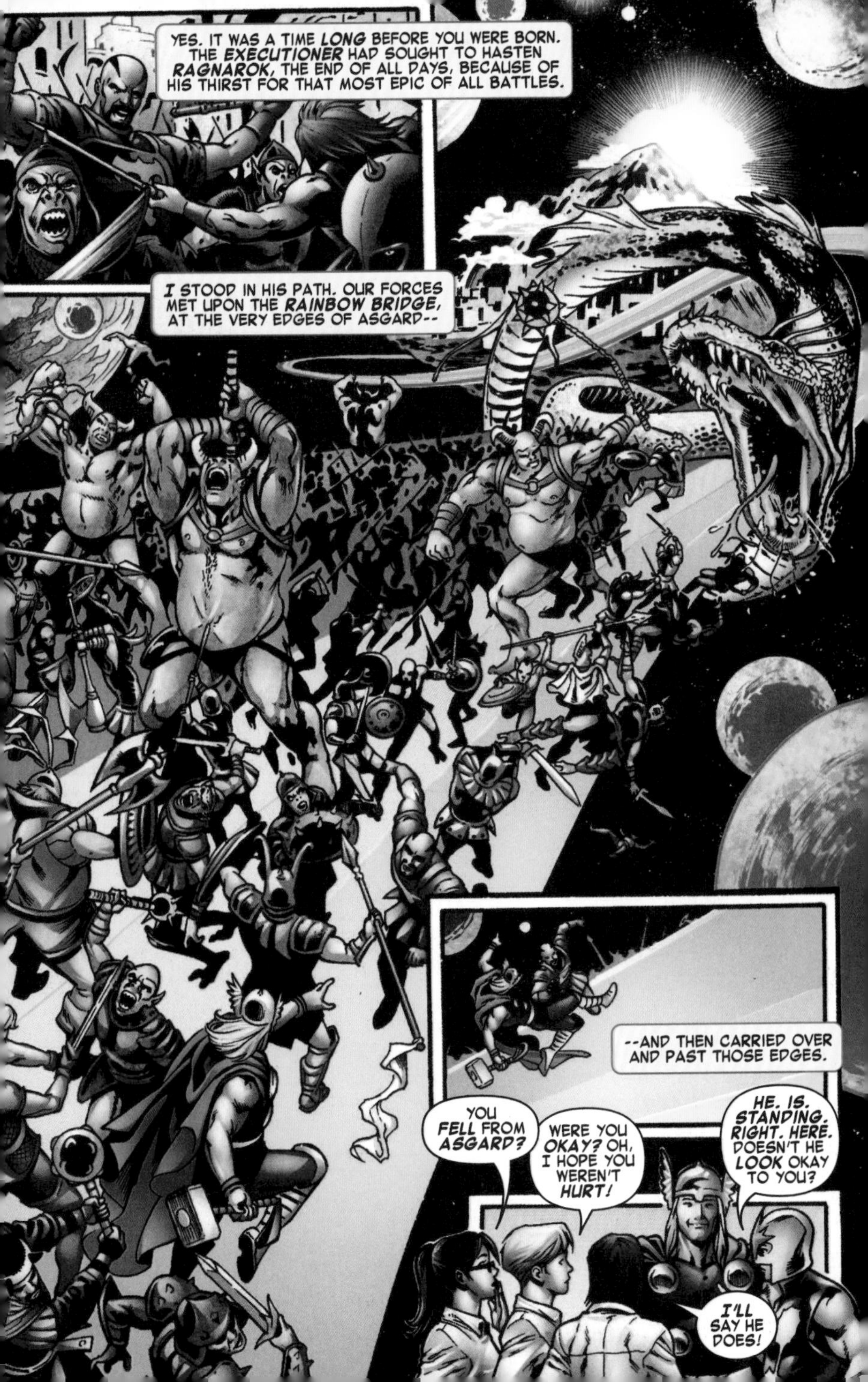

YES. IT WAS A TIME LONG BEFORE YOU WERE BORN. THE EXECUTIONER HAD SOUGHT TO HASTEN RAGNAROK, THE END OF ALL DAYS, BECAUSE OF HIS THIRST FOR THAT MOST EPIC OF ALL BATTLES.
I STOOD IN HIS PATH. OUR FORCES MET UPON THE RAINBOW BRIDGE, AT THE VERY EDGES OF ASGARD--
--AND THEN CARRIED OVER AND PAST THOSE EDGES.
YOU FELL FROM ASGARD?
WERE YOU OKAY? OH, I HOPE YOU WEREN'T HURT!
HE. IS. STANDING. RIGHT. HERE. DOESN'T HE LOOK OKAY TO YOU?
I'LL SAY HE DOES!

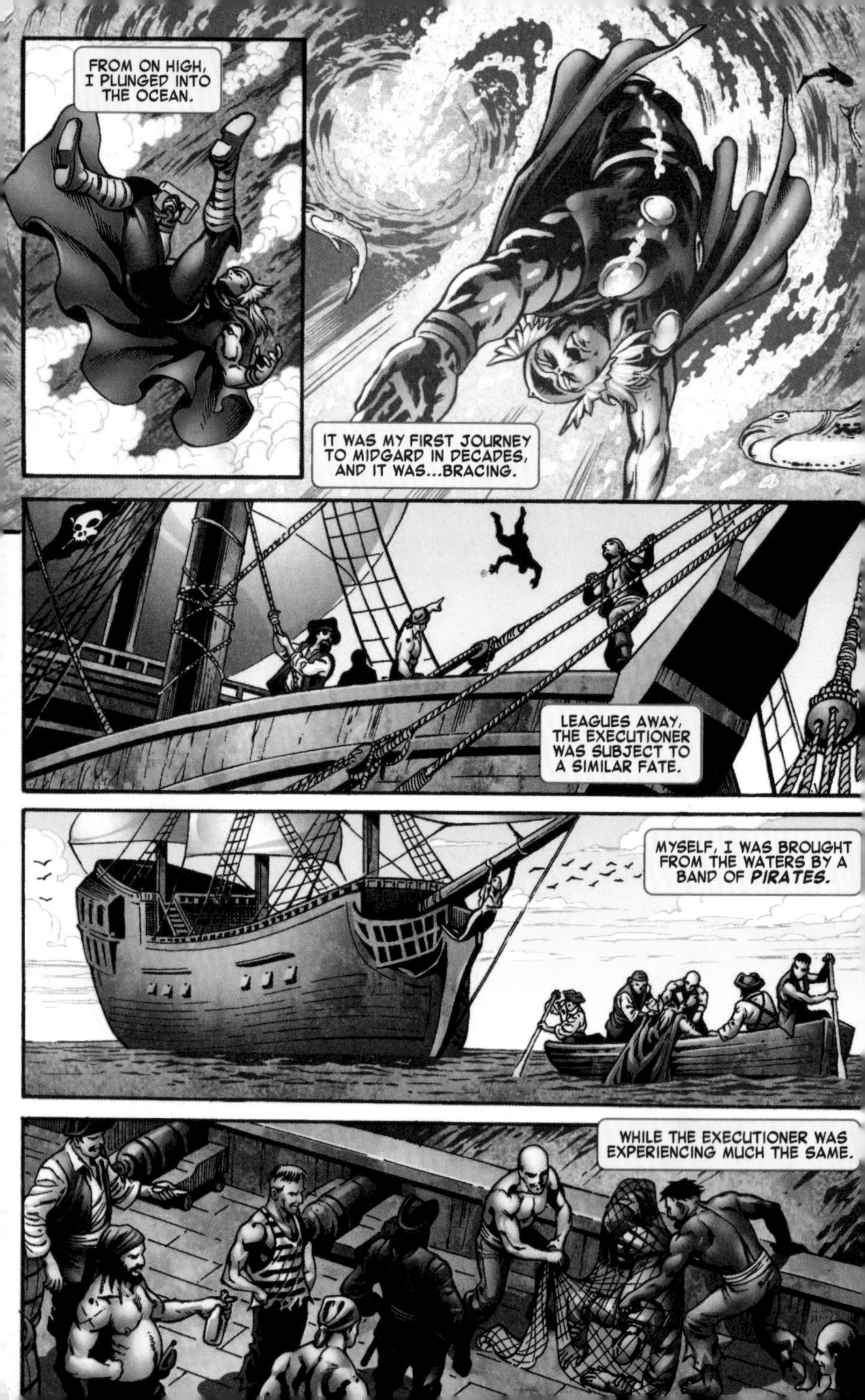
FROM ON HIGH, I PLUNGED INTO THE OCEAN.
IT WAS MY FIRST JOURNEY TO MIDGARD IN DECADES, AND IT WAS...BRACING.
LEAGUES AWAY, THE EXECUTIONER WAS SUBJECT TO A SIMILAR FATE.
MYSELF, I WAS BROUGHT FROM THE WATERS BY A BAND OF *PIRATES.*
WHILE THE EXECUTIONER WAS EXPERIENCING MUCH THE SAME.

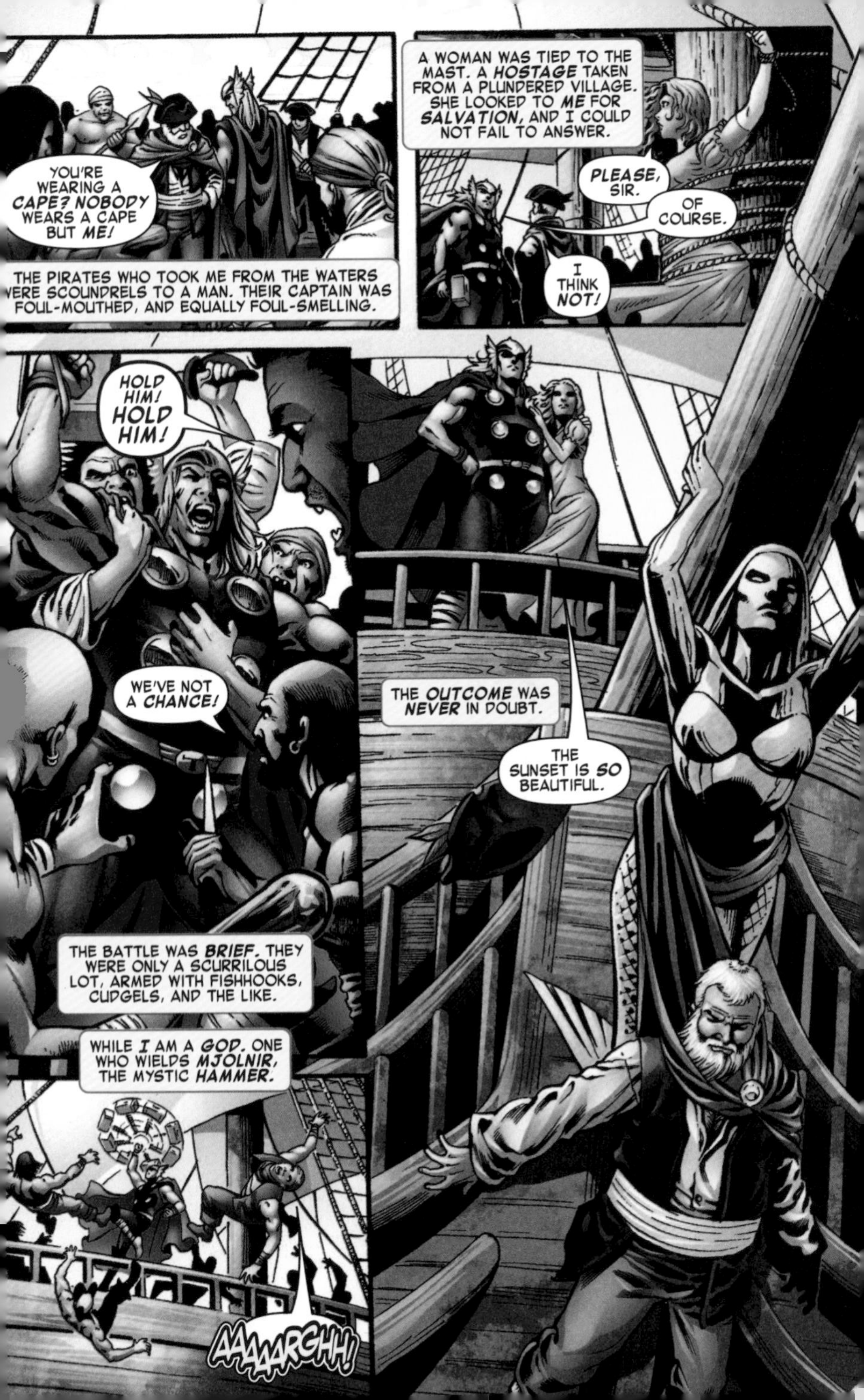
YOU'RE WEARING A CAPE? NOBODY WEARS A CAPE BUT ME!
THE PIRATES WHO TOOK ME FROM THE WATERS WERE SCOUNDRELS TO A MAN. THEIR CAPTAIN WAS FOUL-MOUTHED, AND EQUALLY FOUL-SMELLING.
A WOMAN WAS TIED TO THE MAST. A HOSTAGE TAKEN FROM A PLUNDERED VILLAGE. SHE LOOKED TO ME FOR SALVATION, AND I COULD NOT FAIL TO ANSWER.
PLEASE, SIR.
OF COURSE.
I THINK NOT!
HOLD HIM! HOLD HIM!
WE'VE NOT A CHANCE!
THE BATTLE WAS BRIEF. THEY WERE ONLY A SCURRILOUS LOT, ARMED WITH FISHHOOKS, CUDGELS, AND THE LIKE.
WHILE I AM A GOD. ONE WHO WIELDS MJOLNIR, THE MYSTIC HAMMER.
AAAAARGHH!
THE OUTCOME WAS NEVER IN DOUBT.
THE SUNSET IS SO BEAUTIFUL.

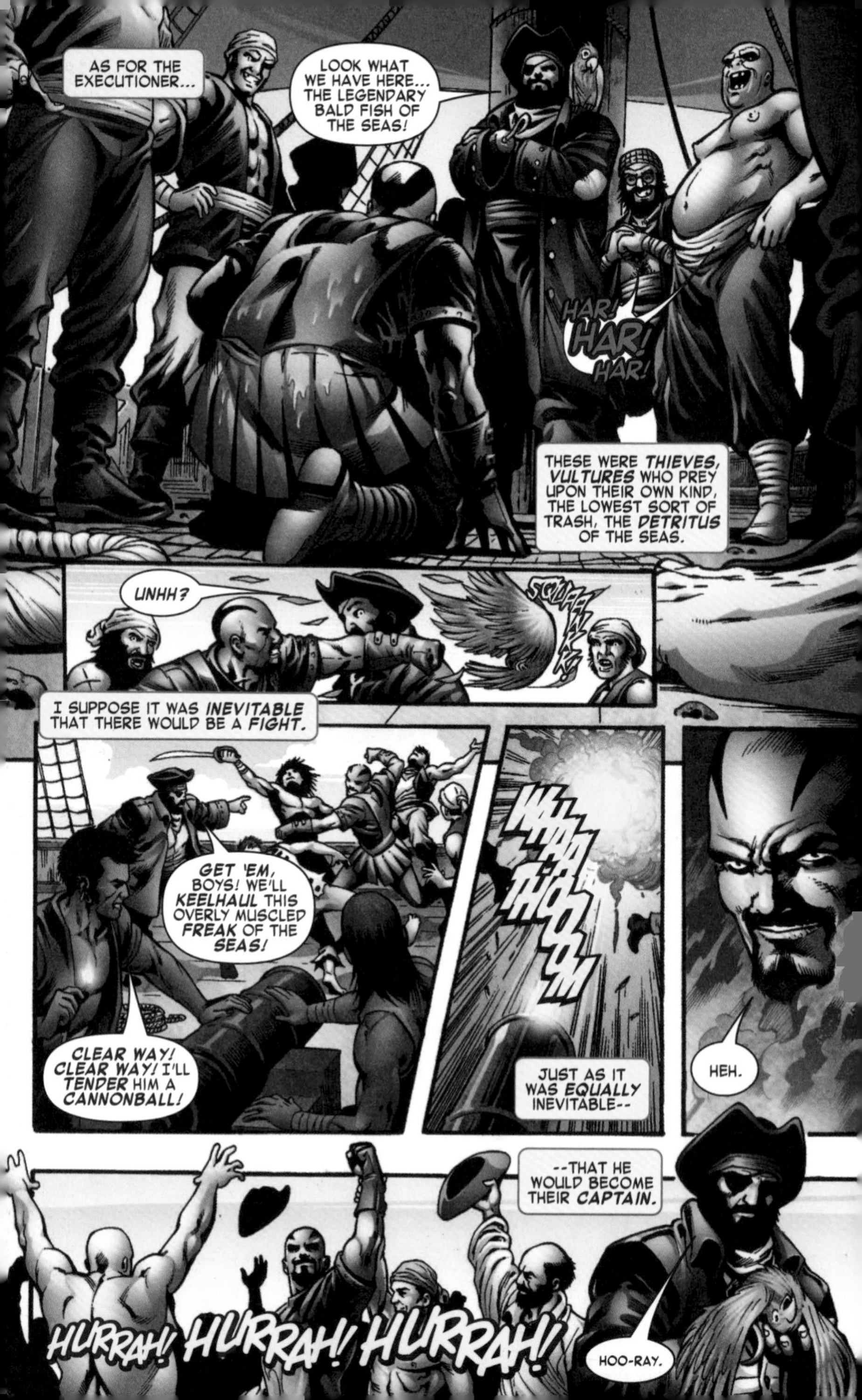
AS FOR THE EXECUTIONER...
LOOK WHAT WE HAVE HERE... THE LEGENDARY BALD FISH OF THE SEAS!
HAR! HAR! HAR!
THESE WERE THIEVES, VULTURES WHO PREY UPON THEIR OWN KIND, THE LOWEST SORT OF TRASH, THE DETRITUS OF THE SEAS.
UNHH?
SQUAAWK!
I SUPPOSE IT WAS INEVITABLE THAT THERE WOULD BE A FIGHT.
GET 'EM, BOYS! WE'LL KEELHAUL THIS OVERLY MUSCLED FREAK OF THE SEAS!
CLEAR WAY! CLEAR WAY! I'LL TENDER HIM A CANNONBALL!
WHA-THOOOM
JUST AS IT WAS EQUALLY INEVITABLE--
HEH.
--THAT HE WOULD BECOME THEIR CAPTAIN.
HURRAH! HURRAH! HURRAH!
HOO-RAY.

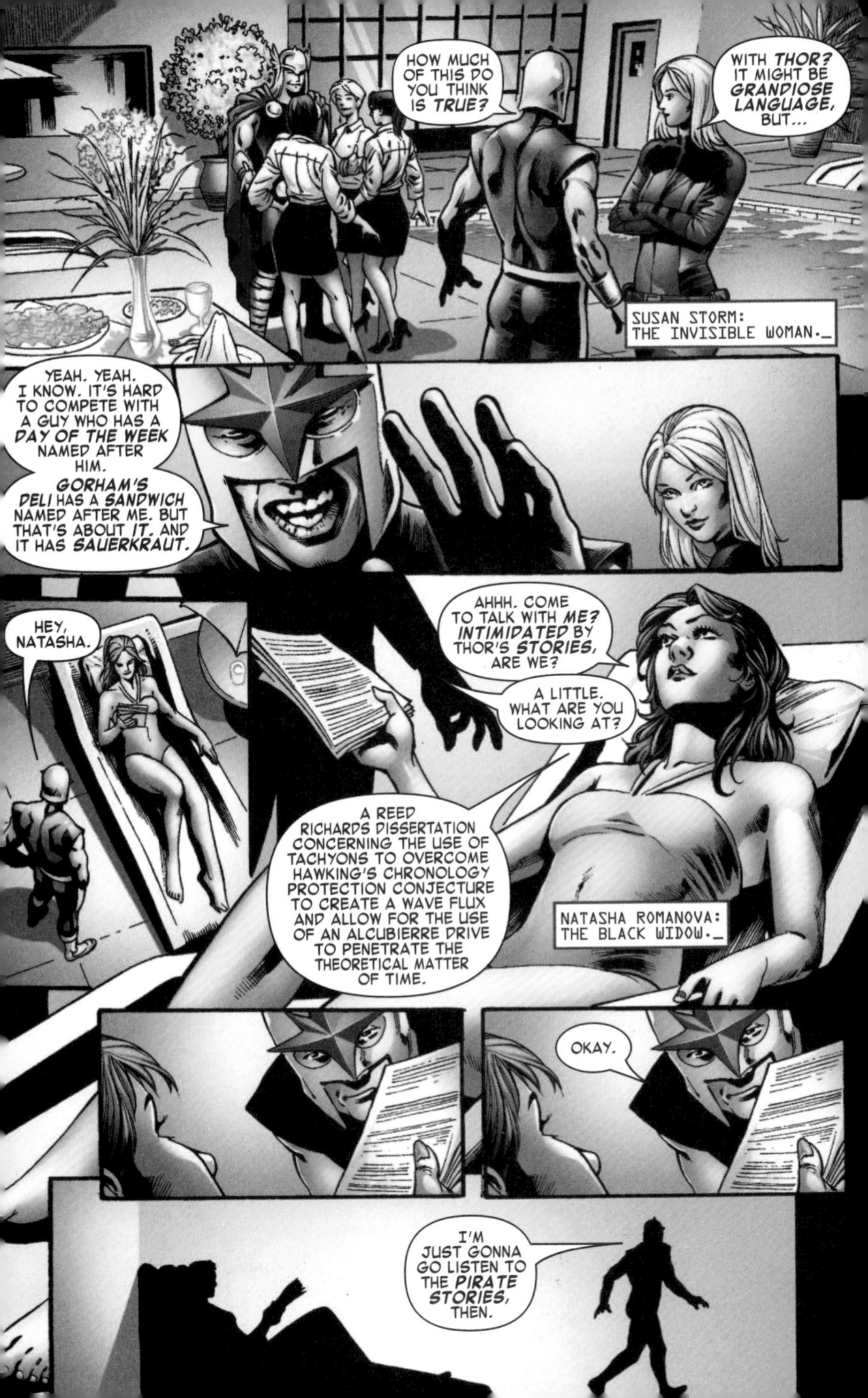
HOW MUCH OF THIS DO YOU THINK IS TRUE?
WITH THOR? IT MIGHT BE GRANDIOSE LANGUAGE, BUT...
SUSAN STORM: THE INVISIBLE WOMAN.
YEAH. YEAH. I KNOW. IT'S HARD TO COMPETE WITH A GUY WHO HAS A DAY OF THE WEEK NAMED AFTER HIM.
GORHAM'S DELI HAS A SANDWICH NAMED AFTER ME. BUT THAT'S ABOUT IT. AND IT HAS SAUERKRAUT.
HEY, NATASHA.
AHHH. COME TO TALK WITH ME? INTIMIDATED BY THOR'S STORIES, ARE WE?
A LITTLE. WHAT ARE YOU LOOKING AT?
A REED RICHARDS DISSERTATION CONCERNING THE USE OF TACHYONS TO OVERCOME HAWKING'S CHRONOLOGY PROTECTION CONJECTURE TO CREATE A WAVE FLUX AND ALLOW FOR THE USE OF AN ALCUBIERRE DRIVE TO PENETRATE THE THEORETICAL MATTER OF TIME.
NATASHA ROMANOVA: THE BLACK WIDOW.
OKAY.
I'M JUST GONNA GO LISTEN TO THE PIRATE STORIES, THEN.

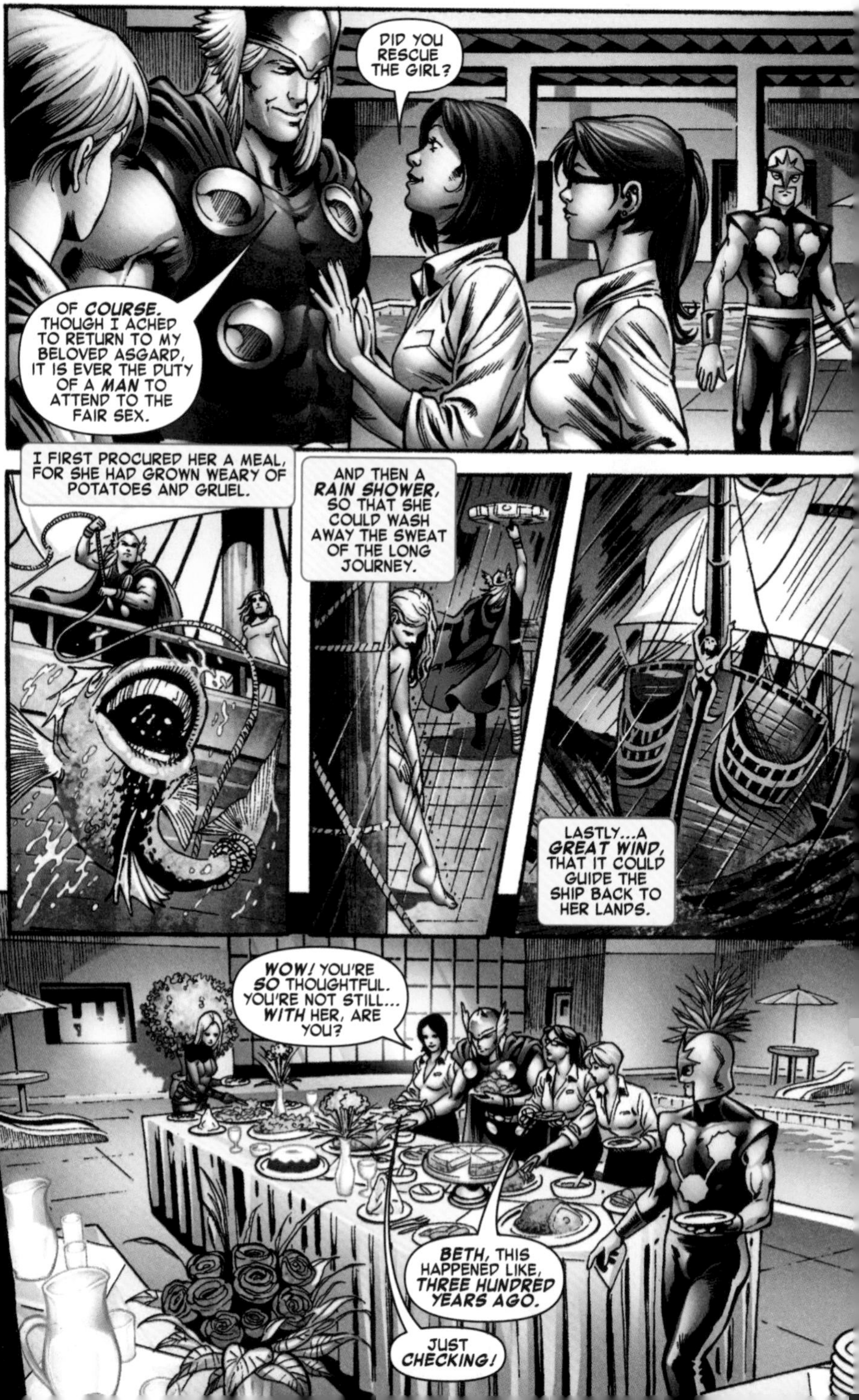
DID YOU RESCUE THE GIRL?
OF COURSE. THOUGH I ACHED TO RETURN TO MY BELOVED ASGARD, IT IS EVER THE DUTY OF A MAN TO ATTEND TO THE FAIR SEX.
I FIRST PROCURED HER A MEAL, FOR SHE HAD GROWN WEARY OF POTATOES AND GRUEL.
AND THEN A RAIN SHOWER, SO THAT SHE COULD WASH AWAY THE SWEAT OF THE LONG JOURNEY.
LASTLY...A GREAT WIND, THAT IT COULD GUIDE THE SHIP BACK TO HER LANDS.
WOW! YOU'RE SO THOUGHTFUL. YOU'RE NOT STILL... WITH HER, ARE YOU?
BETH, THIS HAPPENED LIKE, THREE HUNDRED YEARS AGO.
JUST CHECKING!

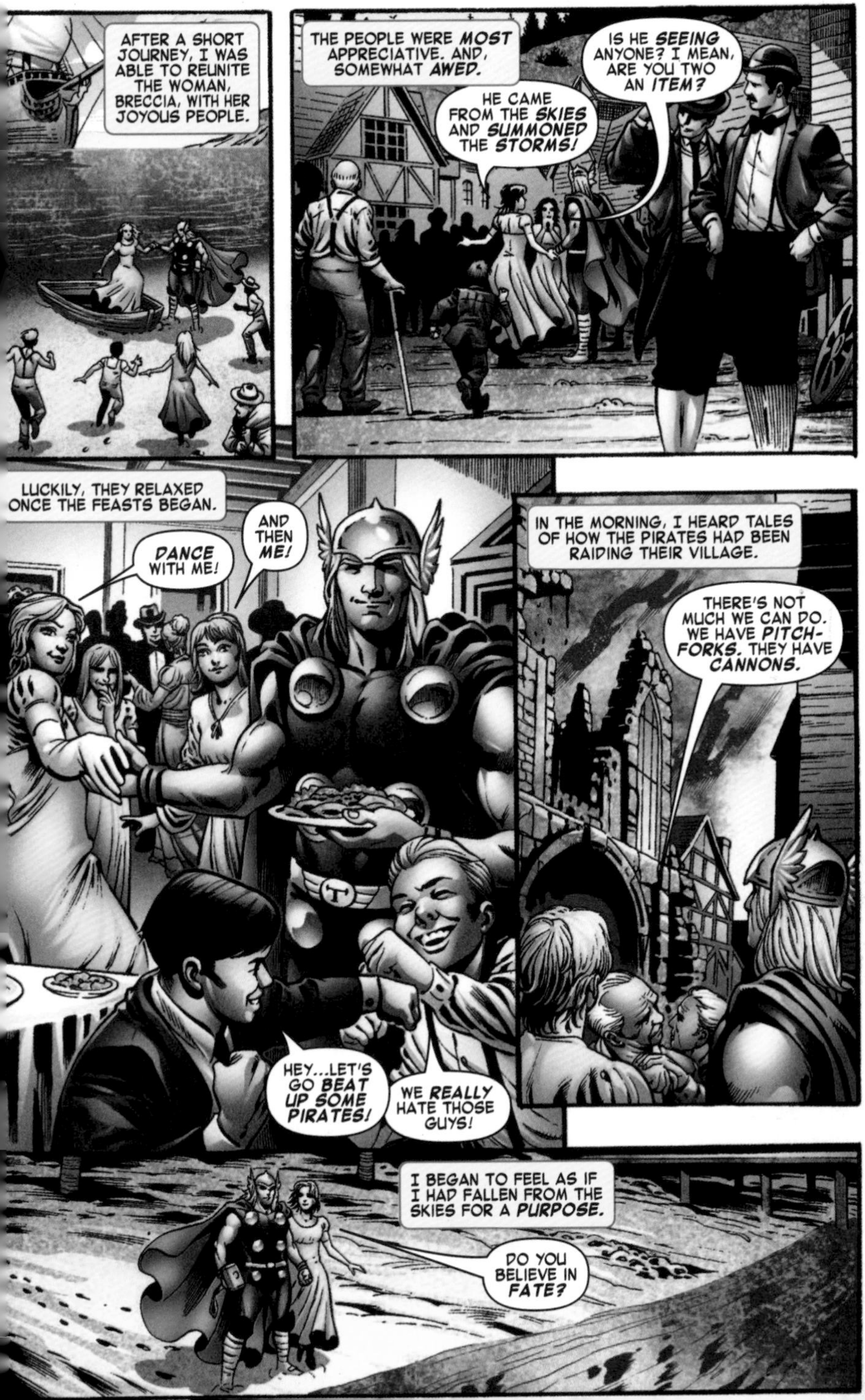
AFTER A SHORT JOURNEY, I WAS ABLE TO REUNITE THE WOMAN, BRECCIA, WITH HER JOYOUS PEOPLE.
THE PEOPLE WERE MOST APPRECIATIVE. AND, SOMEWHAT AWED.
HE CAME FROM THE SKIES AND SUMMONED THE STORMS!
IS HE SEEING ANYONE? I MEAN, ARE YOU TWO AN ITEM?
LUCKILY, THEY RELAXED ONCE THE FEASTS BEGAN.
DANCE WITH ME!
AND THEN ME!
HEY...LET'S GO BEAT UP SOME PIRATES!
WE REALLY HATE THOSE GUYS!
IN THE MORNING, I HEARD TALES OF HOW THE PIRATES HAD BEEN RAIDING THEIR VILLAGE.
THERE'S NOT MUCH WE CAN DO. WE HAVE PITCH-FORKS. THEY HAVE CANNONS.
I BEGAN TO FEEL AS IF I HAD FALLEN FROM THE SKIES FOR A PURPOSE.
DO YOU BELIEVE IN FATE?

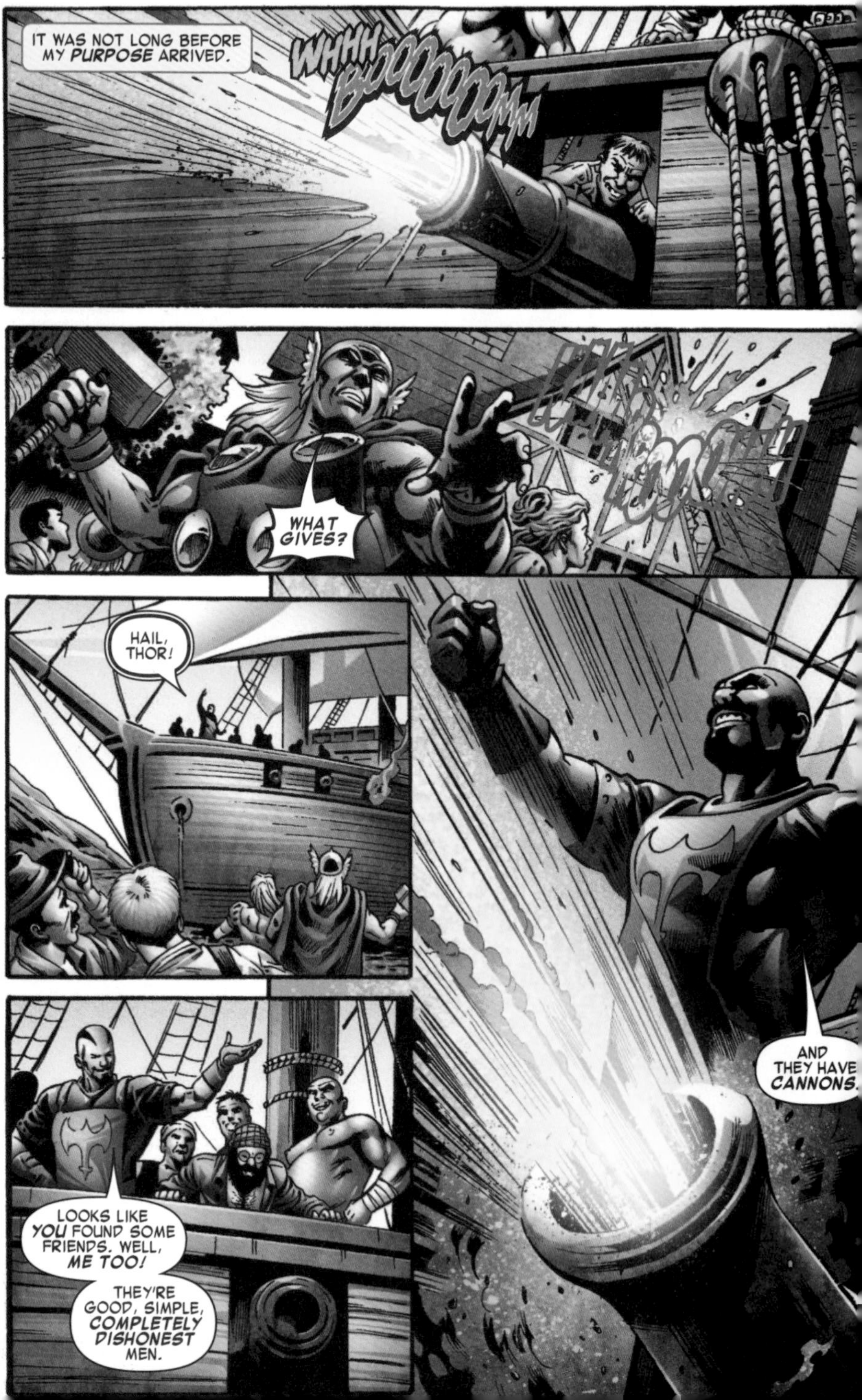
IT WAS NOT LONG BEFORE MY PURPOSE ARRIVED.
WHHH BOOOOOOOMM
WHAT GIVES?
HAIL, THOR!
AND THEY HAVE CANNONS.
LOOKS LIKE YOU FOUND SOME FRIENDS. WELL, ME TOO!
THEY'RE GOOD, SIMPLE, COMPLETELY DISHONEST MEN.

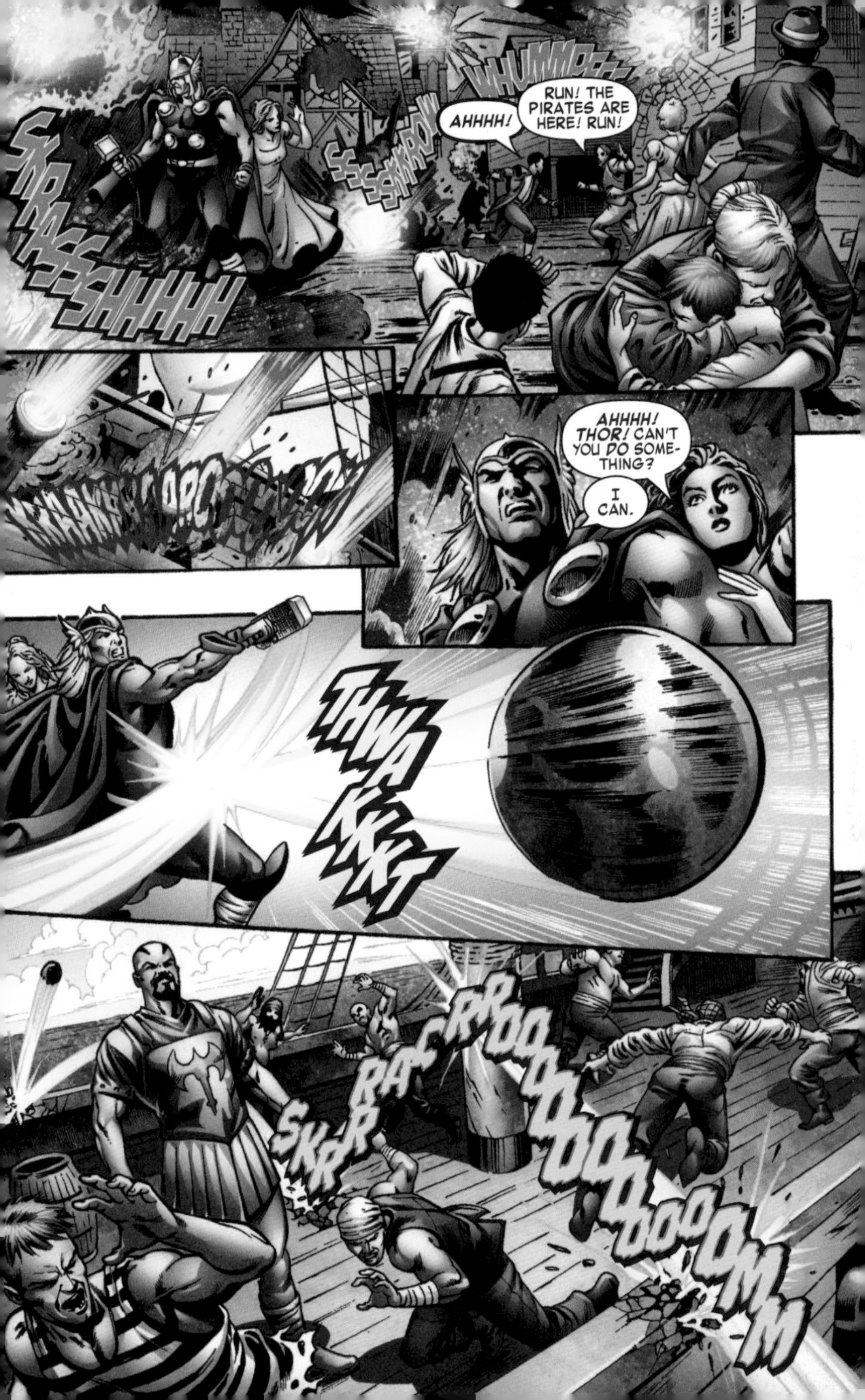
AHHHH!
RUN! THE PIRATES ARE HERE! RUN!
AHHHH! *THOR!* CAN'T YOU *DO* SOMETHING?
I CAN.
THWAKKKT

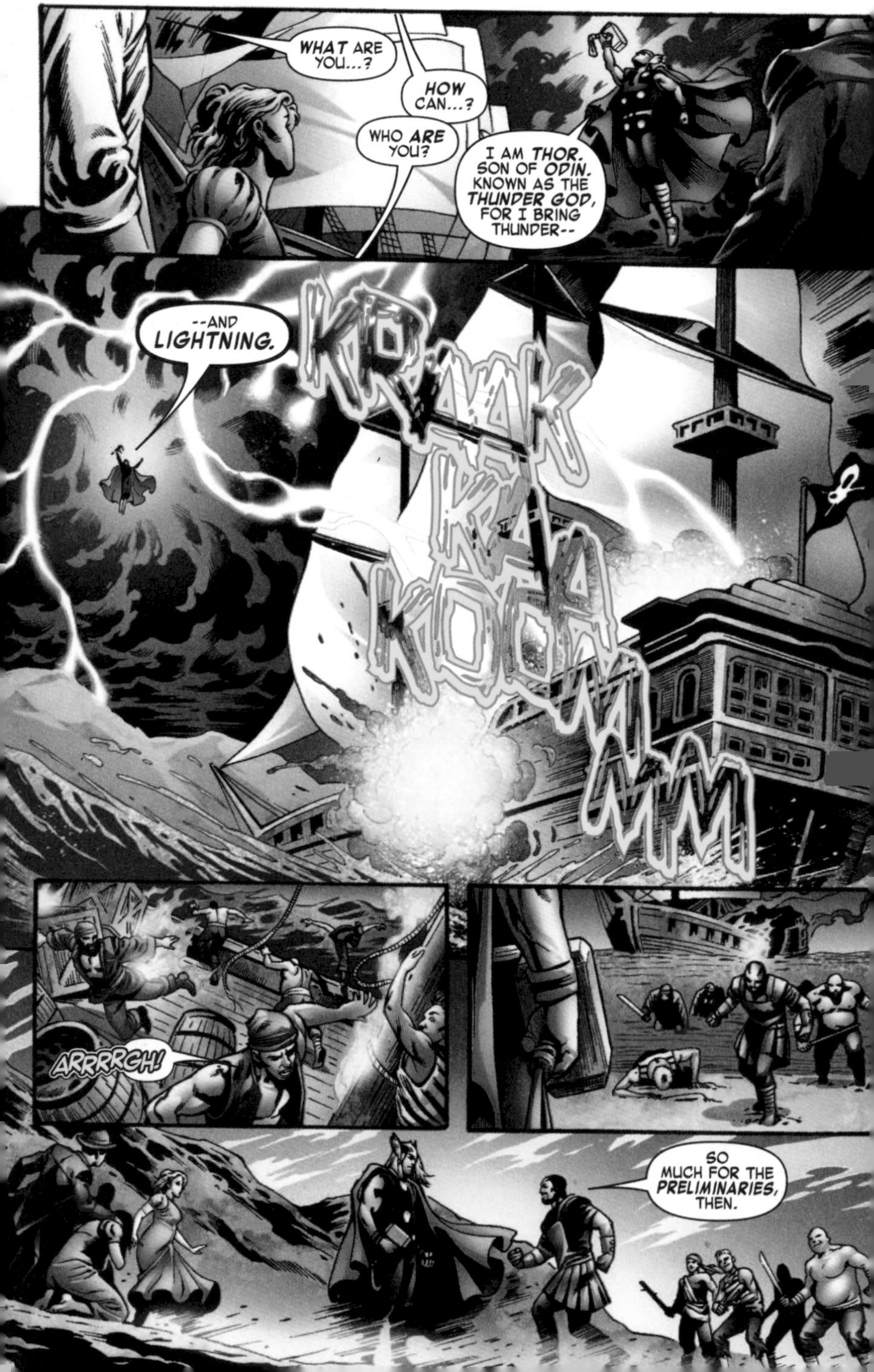

WHAT ARE YOU...?
HOW CAN...?
WHO ARE YOU?
I AM THOR. SON OF ODIN. KNOWN AS THE THUNDER GOD, FOR I BRING THUNDER--
--AND LIGHTNING.
ARRRRGH!
SO MUCH FOR THE PRELIMINARIES, THEN.

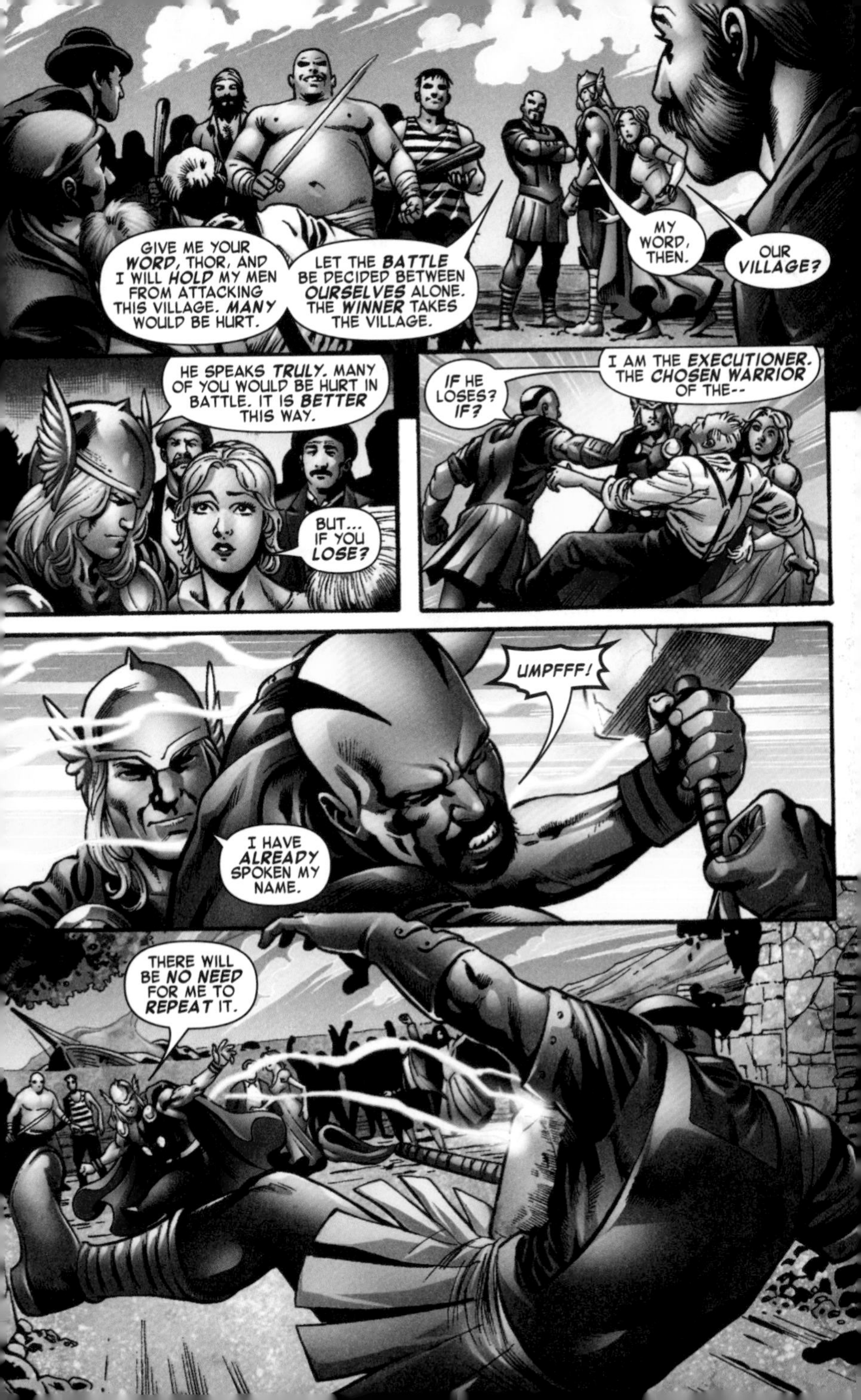
GIVE ME YOUR WORD, THOR, AND I WILL HOLD MY MEN FROM ATTACKING THIS VILLAGE. MANY WOULD BE HURT.
LET THE BATTLE BE DECIDED BETWEEN OURSELVES ALONE. THE WINNER TAKES THE VILLAGE.
MY WORD, THEN.
OUR VILLAGE?
HE SPEAKS TRULY. MANY OF YOU WOULD BE HURT IN BATTLE. IT IS BETTER THIS WAY.
BUT... IF YOU LOSE?
IF HE LOSES? IF?
I AM THE EXECUTIONER. THE CHOSEN WARRIOR OF THE--
UMPFFF!
I HAVE ALREADY SPOKEN MY NAME.
THERE WILL BE NO NEED FOR ME TO REPEAT IT.

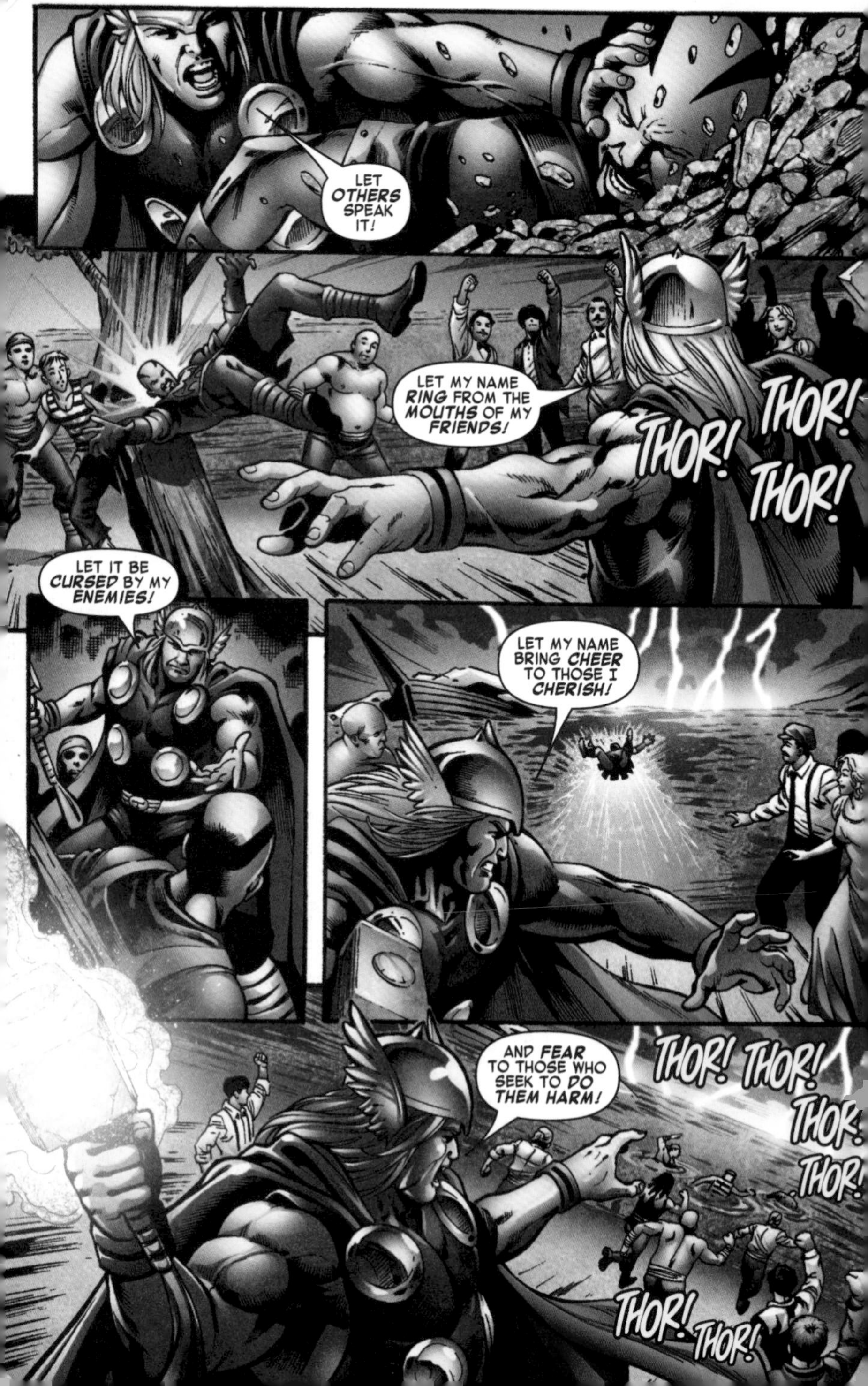
LET OTHERS SPEAK IT!
LET MY NAME RING FROM THE MOUTHS OF MY FRIENDS!
THOR! THOR! THOR!
LET IT BE CURSED BY MY ENEMIES!
LET MY NAME BRING CHEER TO THOSE I CHERISH!
AND FEAR TO THOSE WHO SEEK TO DO THEM HARM!
THOR! THOR! THOR! THOR!
THOR! THOR!

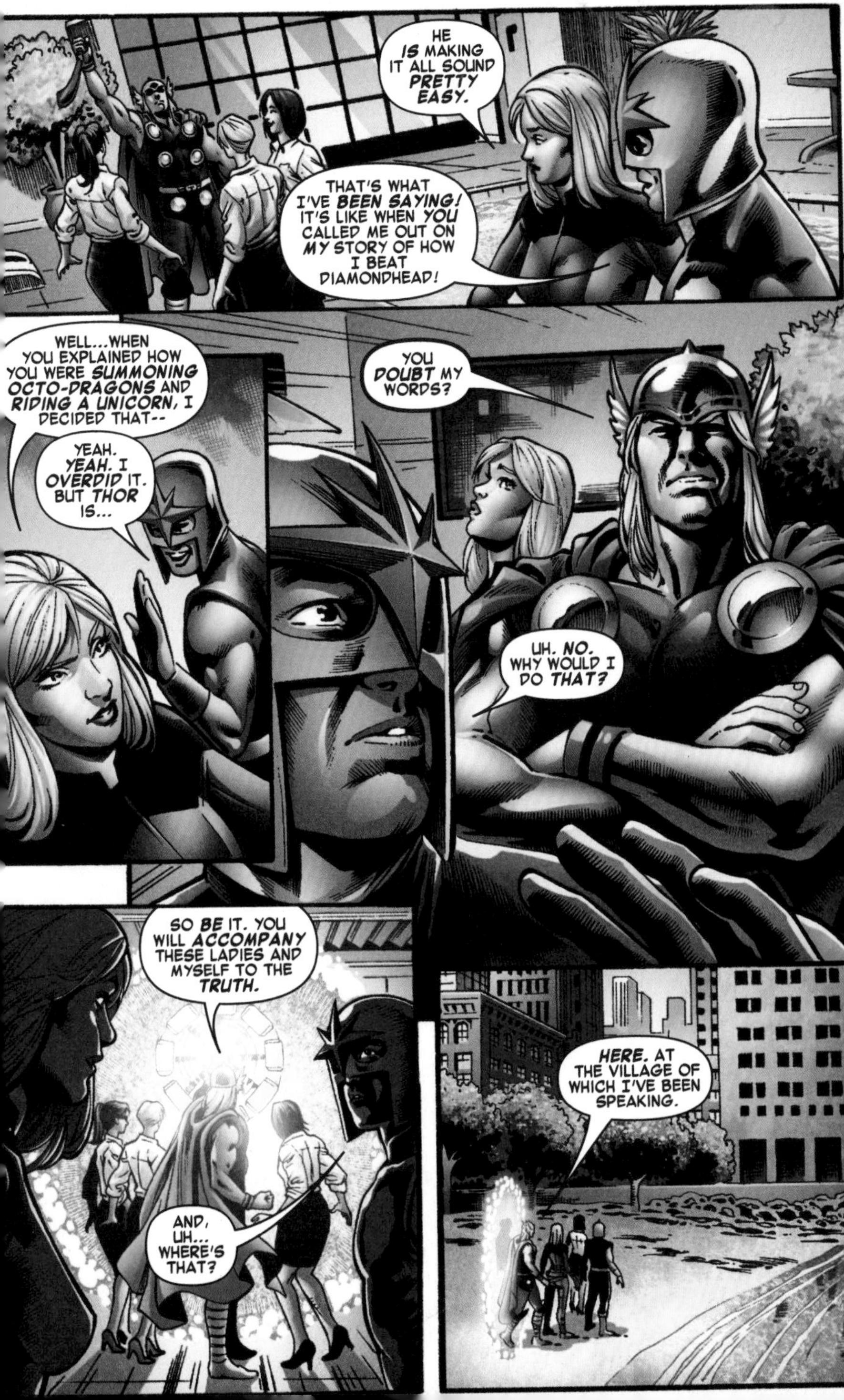
HE IS MAKING IT ALL SOUND PRETTY EASY.
THAT'S WHAT I'VE BEEN SAYING! IT'S LIKE WHEN YOU CALLED ME OUT ON MY STORY OF HOW I BEAT DIAMONDHEAD!
WELL...WHEN YOU EXPLAINED HOW YOU WERE SUMMONING OCTO-DRAGONS AND RIDING A UNICORN, I DECIDED THAT--
YEAH. YEAH. I OVERDID IT. BUT THOR IS...
YOU DOUBT MY WORDS?
UH. NO. WHY WOULD I DO THAT?
SO BE IT. YOU WILL ACCOMPANY THESE LADIES AND MYSELF TO THE TRUTH.
AND, UH... WHERE'S THAT?
HERE. AT THE VILLAGE OF WHICH I'VE BEEN SPEAKING.

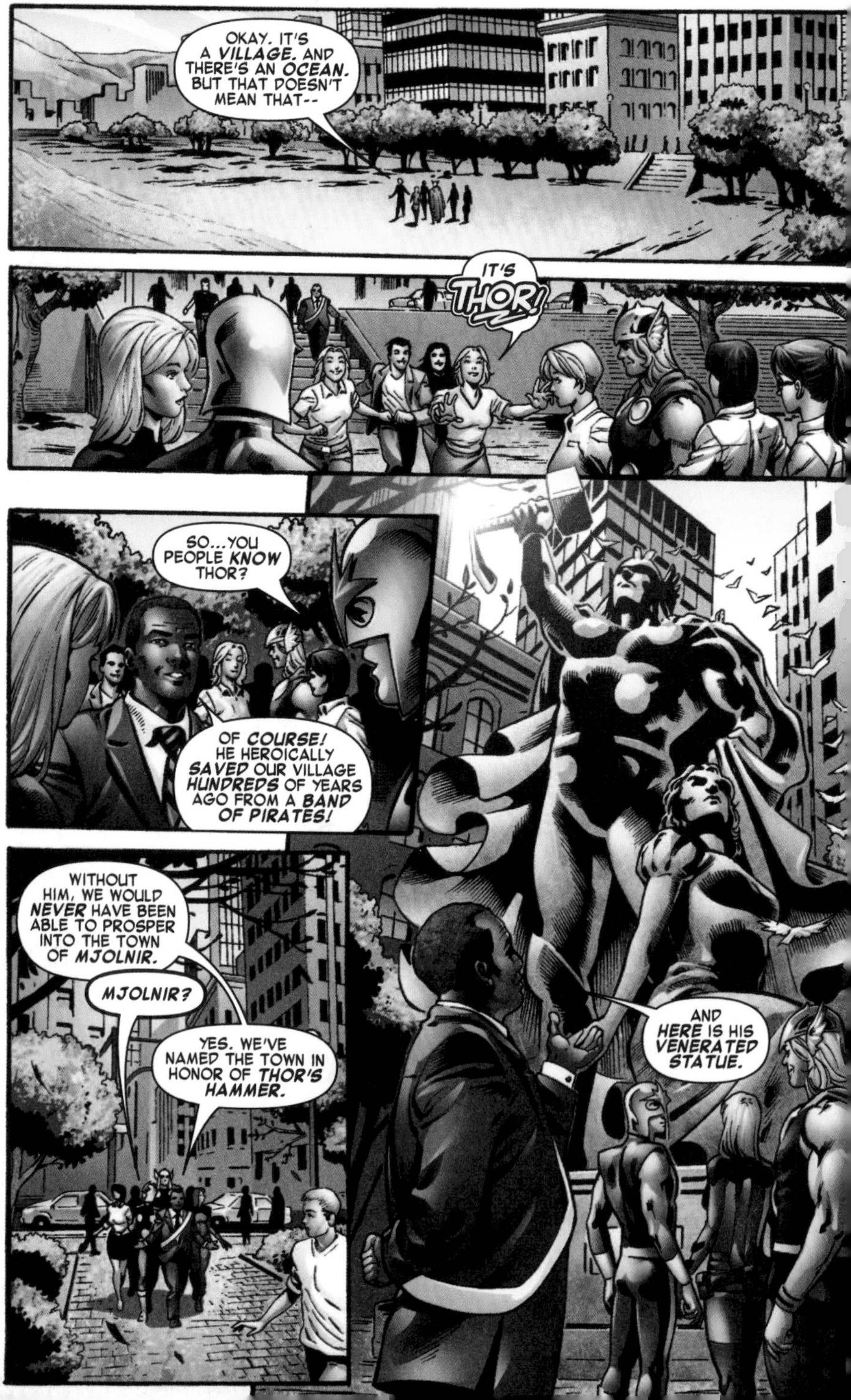
OKAY. IT'S A VILLAGE. AND THERE'S AN OCEAN. BUT THAT DOESN'T MEAN THAT--
IT'S THOR!
SO...YOU PEOPLE KNOW THOR?
OF COURSE! HE HEROICALLY SAVED OUR VILLAGE HUNDREDS OF YEARS AGO FROM A BAND OF PIRATES!
WITHOUT HIM, WE WOULD NEVER HAVE BEEN ABLE TO PROSPER INTO THE TOWN OF MJOLNIR.
MJOLNIR?
YES. WE'VE NAMED THE TOWN IN HONOR OF THOR'S HAMMER.
AND HERE IS HIS VENERATED STATUE.

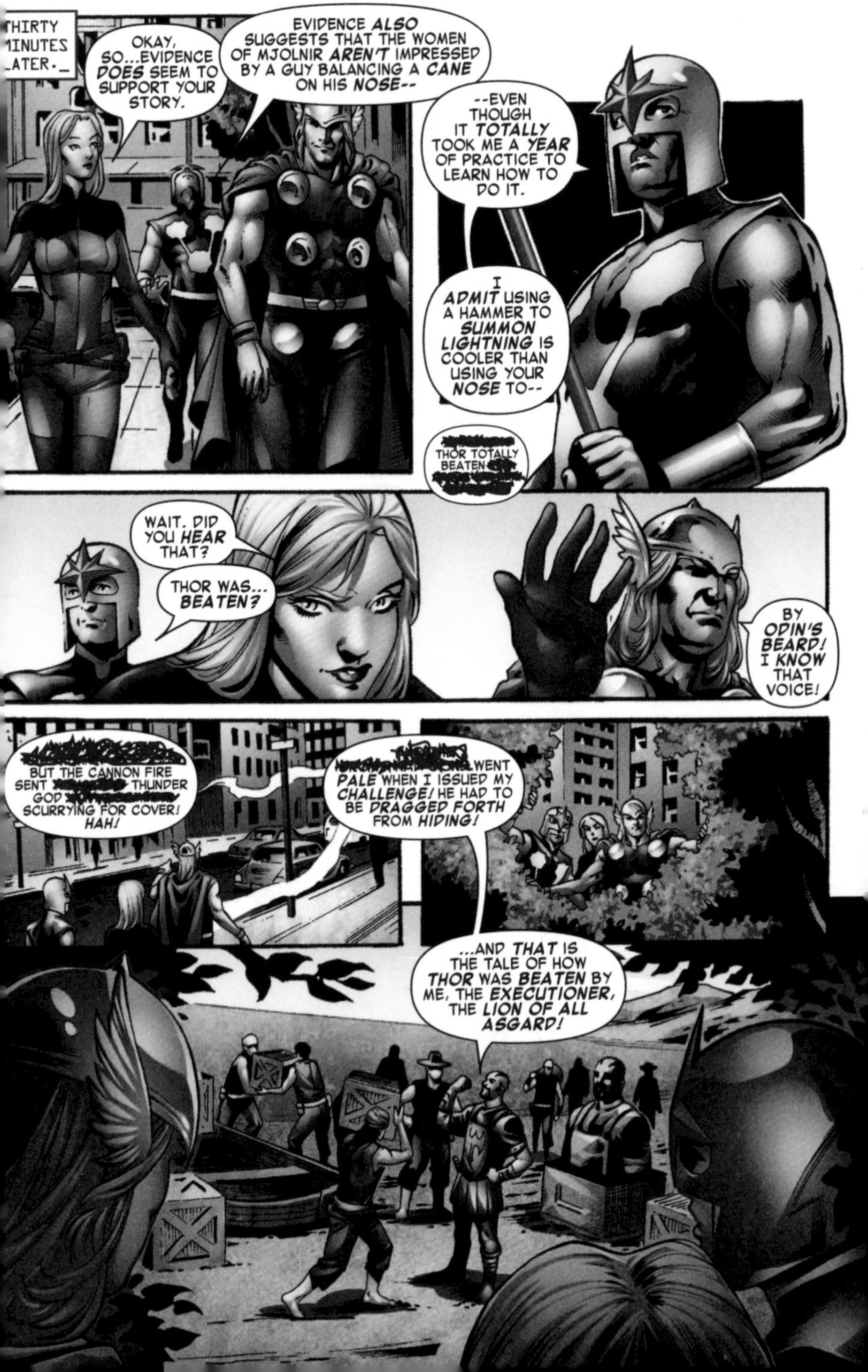
HIRTY INUTES ATER.
OKAY, SO...EVIDENCE DOES SEEM TO SUPPORT YOUR STORY.
EVIDENCE ALSO SUGGESTS THAT THE WOMEN OF MJOLNIR AREN'T IMPRESSED BY A GUY BALANCING A CANE ON HIS NOSE--
--EVEN THOUGH IT TOTALLY TOOK ME A YEAR OF PRACTICE TO LEARN HOW TO DO IT.
I ADMIT USING A HAMMER TO SUMMON LIGHTNING IS COOLER THAN USING YOUR NOSE TO--
[redacted] THOR TOTALLY BEATEN [redacted]
WAIT. DID YOU HEAR THAT?
THOR WAS... BEATEN?
BY ODIN'S BEARD! I KNOW THAT VOICE!
[redacted] BUT THE CANNON FIRE SENT [redacted] THUNDER GOD SCURRYING FOR COVER! HAH!
[redacted] WENT PALE WHEN I ISSUED MY CHALLENGE! HE HAD TO BE DRAGGED FORTH FROM HIDING!
...AND THAT IS THE TALE OF HOW THOR WAS BEATEN BY ME, THE EXECUTIONER, THE LION OF ALL ASGARD!

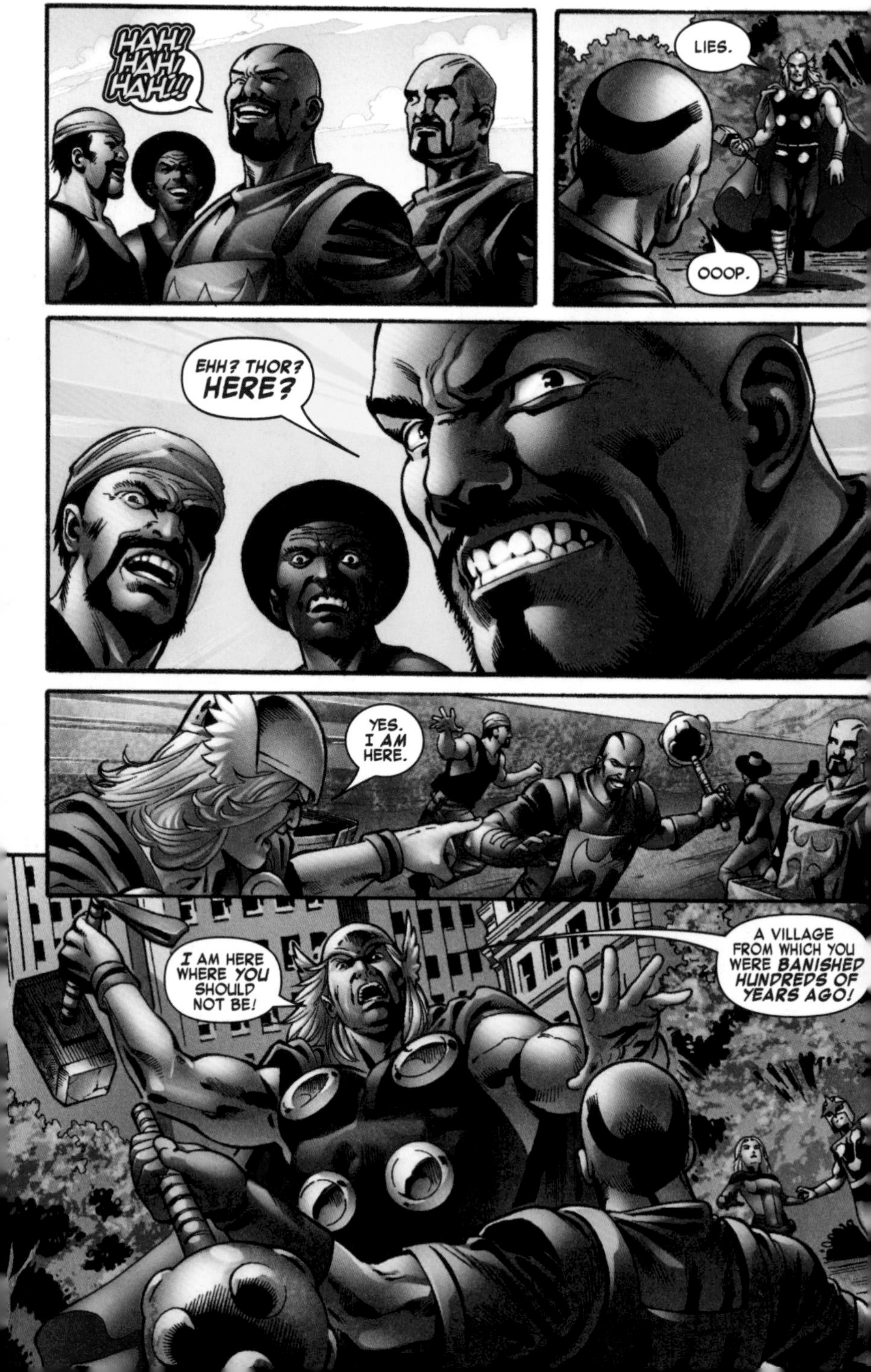
HAH! HAH! HAH!!!
LIES.
OOOP.
EHH? THOR? HERE?
YES. I AM HERE.
I AM HERE WHERE YOU SHOULD NOT BE!
A VILLAGE FROM WHICH YOU WERE BANISHED HUNDREDS OF YEARS AGO!

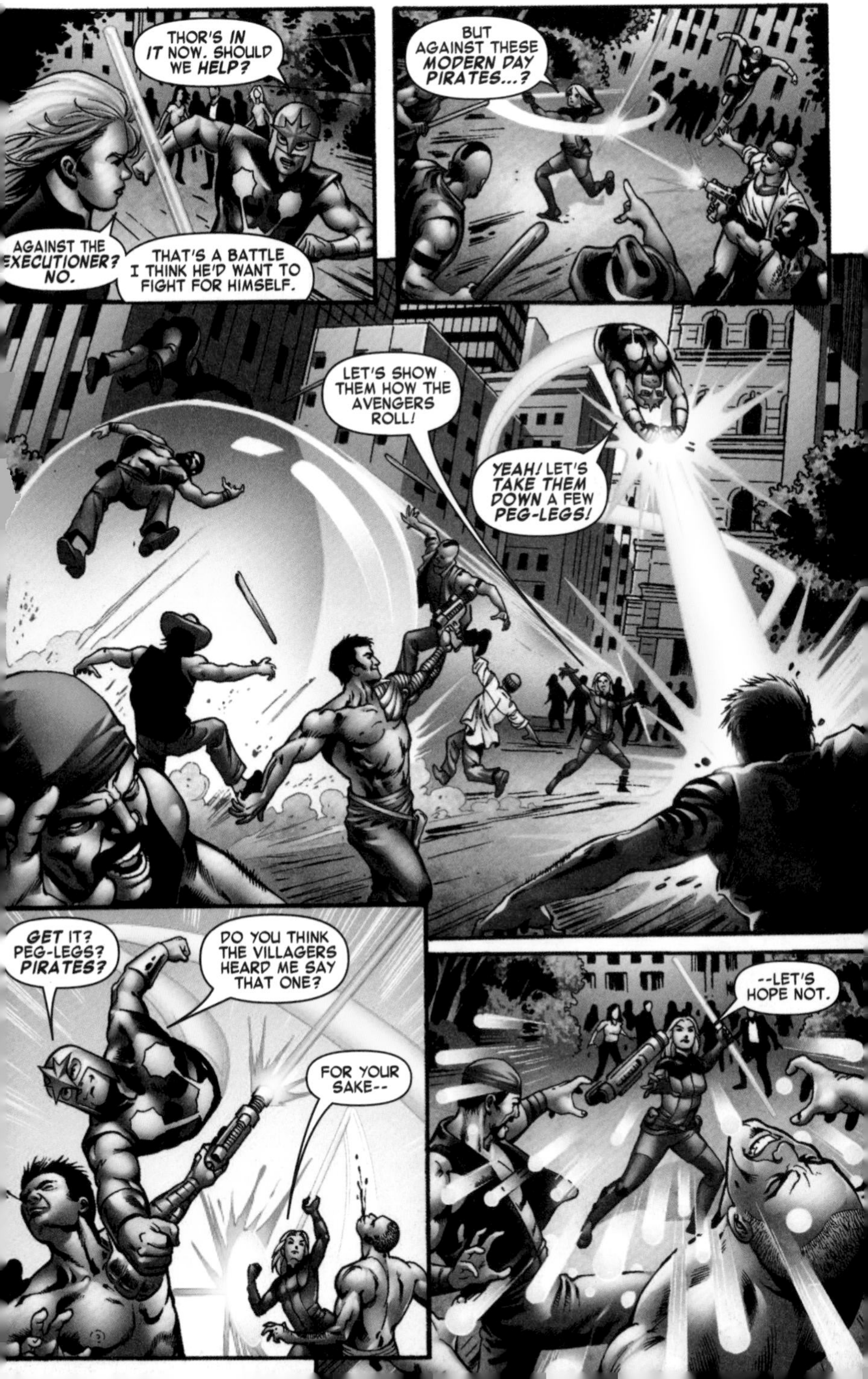
THOR'S IN IT NOW. SHOULD WE HELP?
AGAINST THE EXECUTIONER? NO.
THAT'S A BATTLE I THINK HE'D WANT TO FIGHT FOR HIMSELF.
BUT AGAINST THESE MODERN DAY PIRATES...?
LET'S SHOW THEM HOW THE AVENGERS ROLL!
YEAH! LET'S TAKE THEM DOWN A FEW PEG-LEGS!
GET IT? PEG-LEGS? PIRATES?
DO YOU THINK THE VILLAGERS HEARD ME SAY THAT ONE?
FOR YOUR SAKE--
--LET'S HOPE NOT.

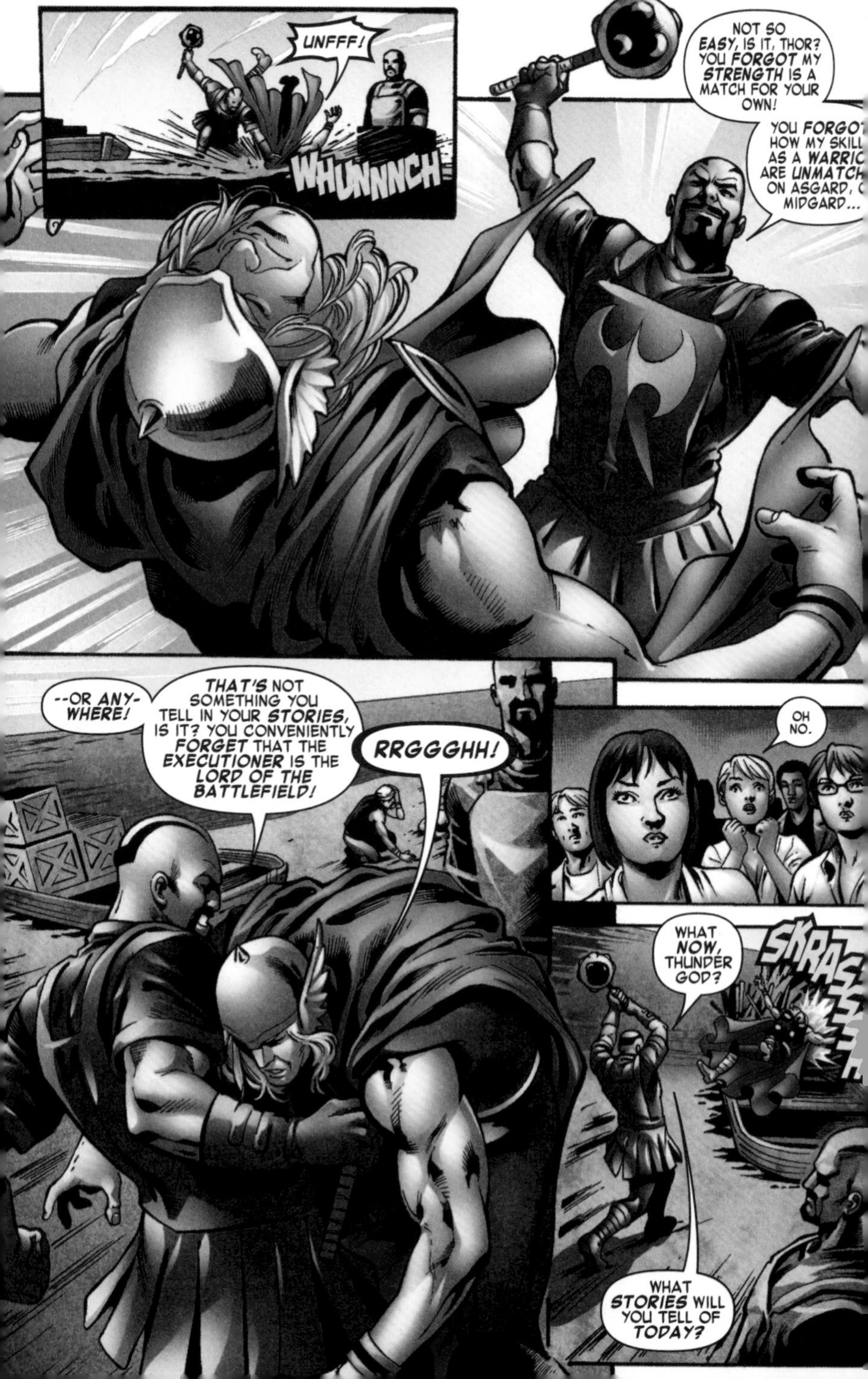
UNFFF!
WHUNNNCH
NOT SO EASY, IS IT, THOR? YOU FORGOT MY STRENGTH IS A MATCH FOR YOUR OWN!
YOU FORGOT HOW MY SKILL AS A WARRIC ARE UNMATCH ON ASGARD, MIDGARD...
--OR ANYWHERE!
THAT'S NOT SOMETHING YOU TELL IN YOUR STORIES, IS IT? YOU CONVENIENTLY FORGET THAT THE EXECUTIONER IS THE LORD OF THE BATTLEFIELD!
RRGGGHH!
OH NO.
WHAT NOW, THUNDER GOD?
WHAT STORIES WILL YOU TELL OF TODAY?

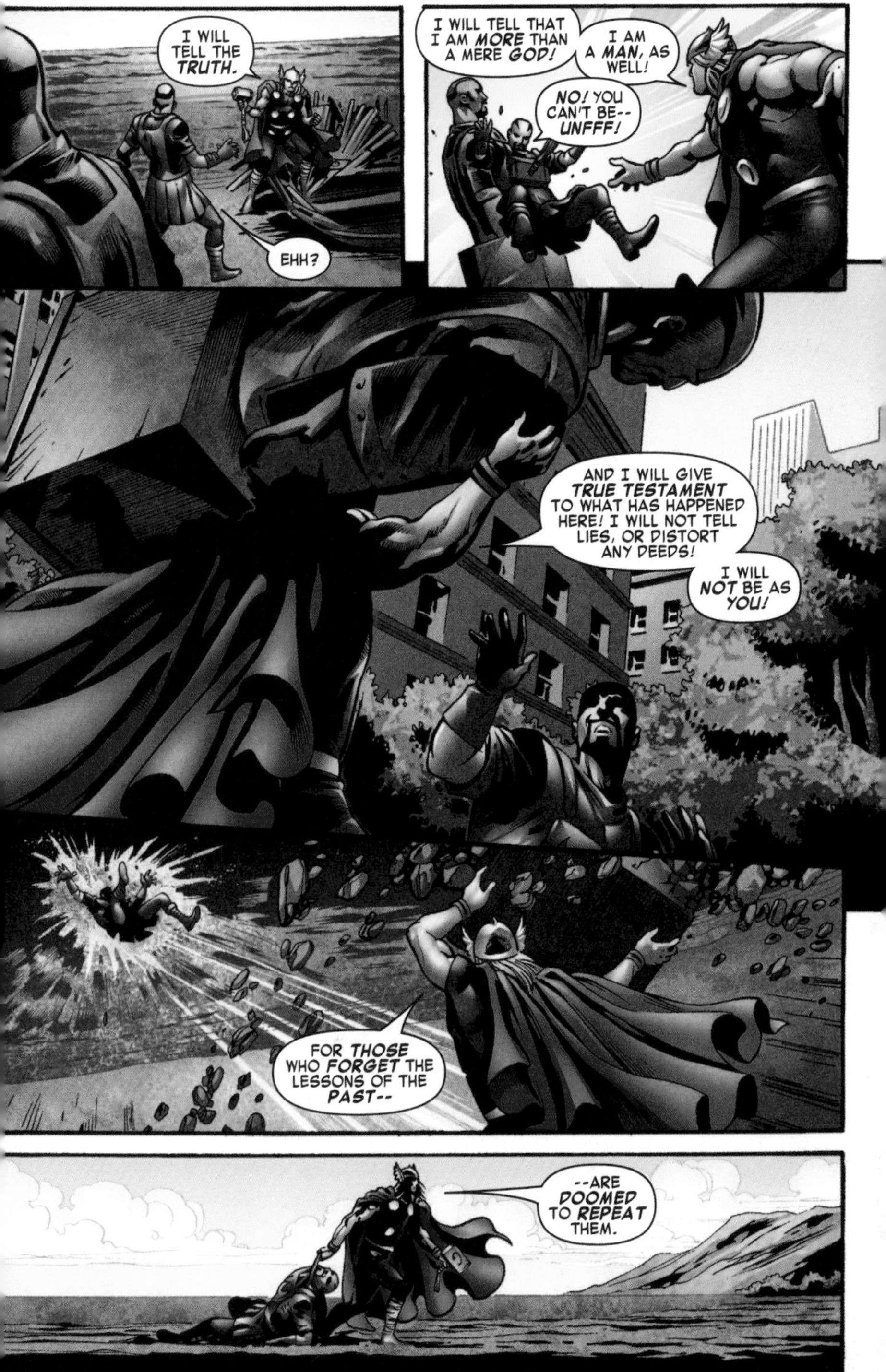
I WILL TELL THE TRUTH.
EHH?
I WILL TELL THAT I AM MORE THAN A MERE GOD!
I AM A MAN, AS WELL!
NO! YOU CAN'T BE-- UNFFF!
AND I WILL GIVE TRUE TESTAMENT TO WHAT HAS HAPPENED HERE! I WILL NOT TELL LIES, OR DISTORT ANY DEEDS!
I WILL NOT BE AS YOU!
FOR THOSE WHO FORGET THE LESSONS OF THE PAST--
--ARE DOOMED TO REPEAT THEM.

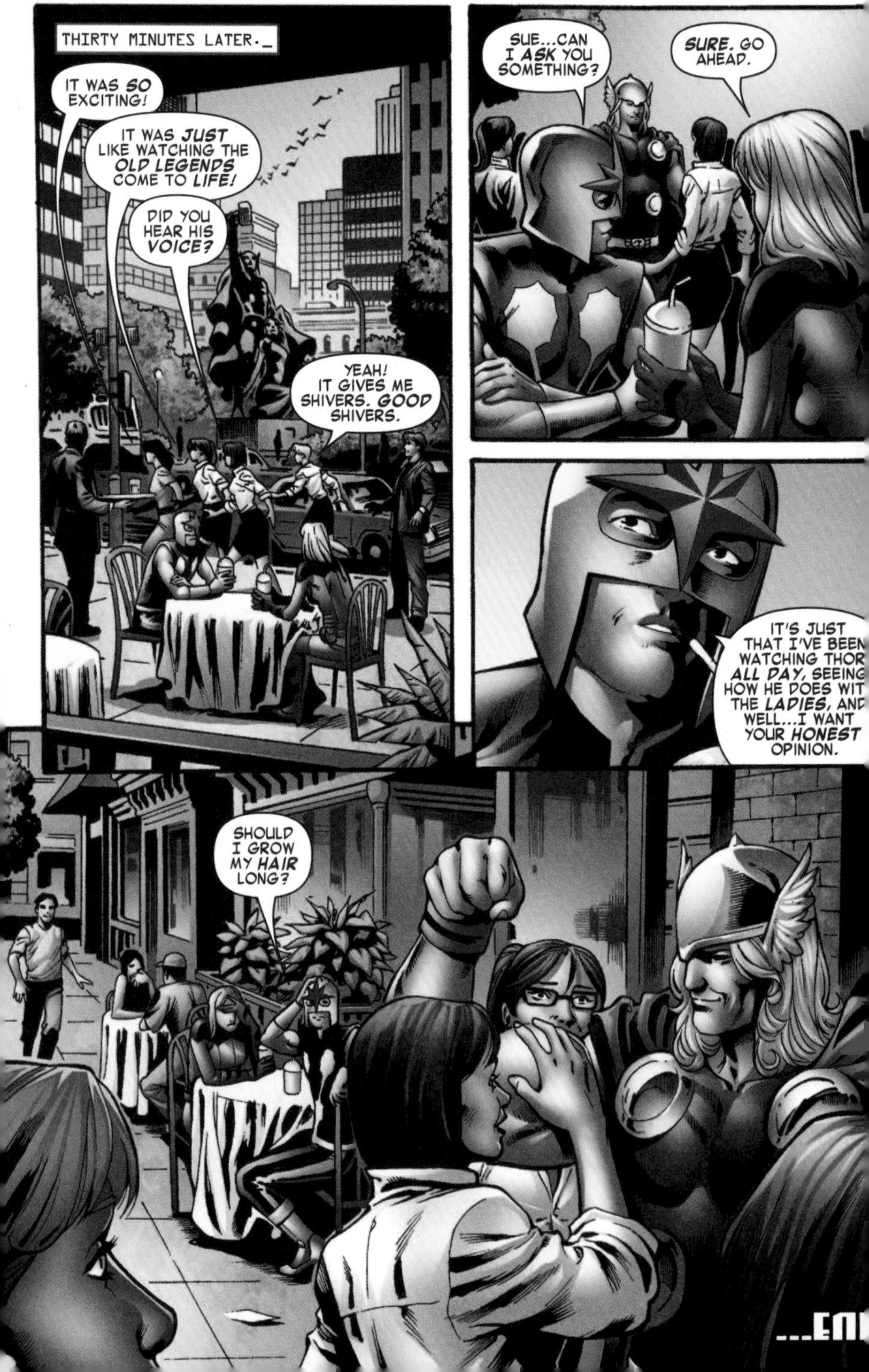

THIRTY MINUTES LATER._
IT WAS SO EXCITING!
IT WAS JUST LIKE WATCHING THE OLD LEGENDS COME TO LIFE!
DID YOU HEAR HIS VOICE?
YEAH! IT GIVES ME SHIVERS. GOOD SHIVERS.
SUE...CAN I ASK YOU SOMETHING?
SURE. GO AHEAD.
IT'S JUST THAT I'VE BEEN WATCHING THOR ALL DAY, SEEING HOW HE DOES WIT THE LADIES, AND WELL...I WANT YOUR HONEST OPINION.
SHOULD I GROW MY HAIR LONG?
...EN

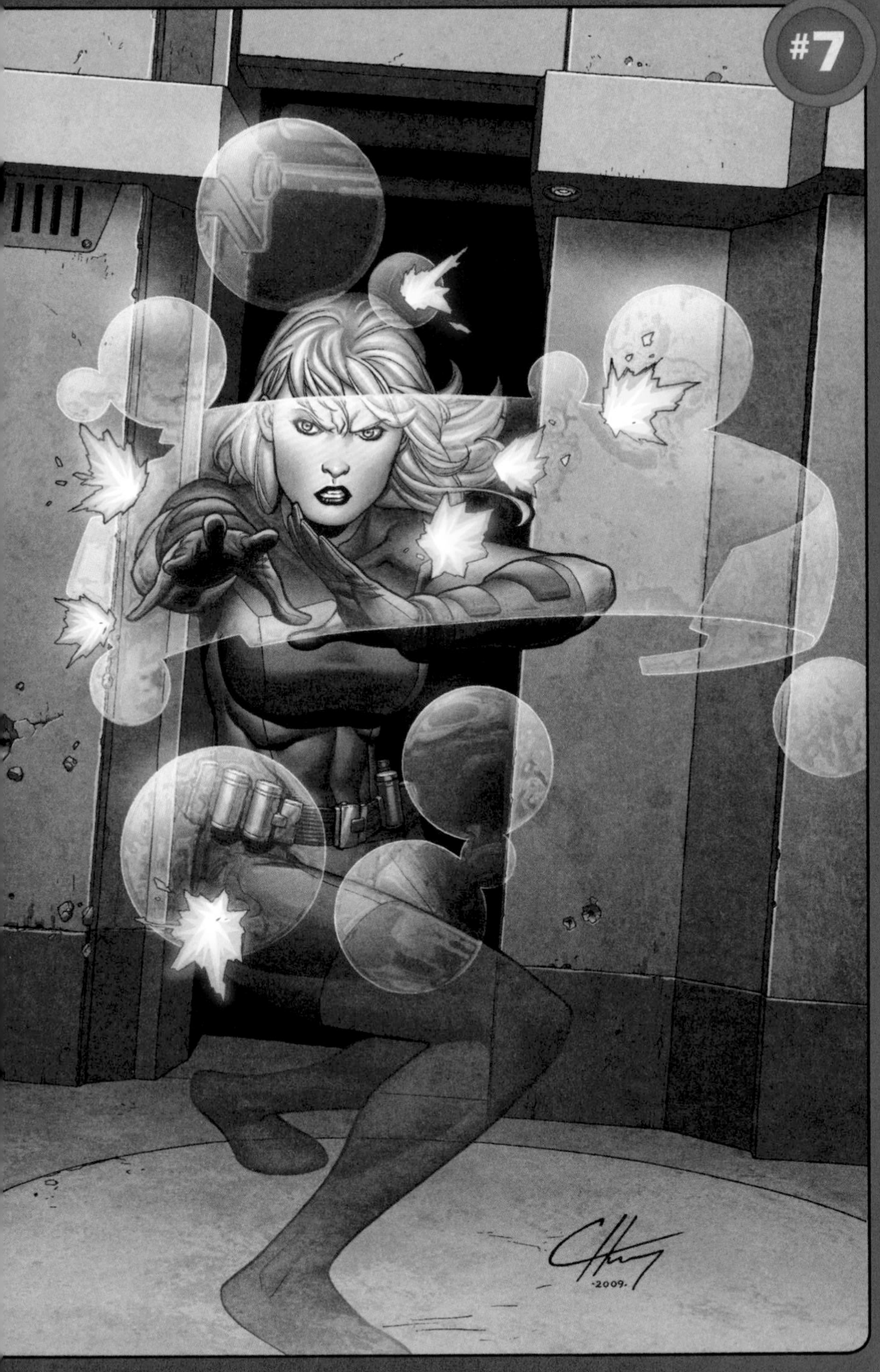
#7
-2009-

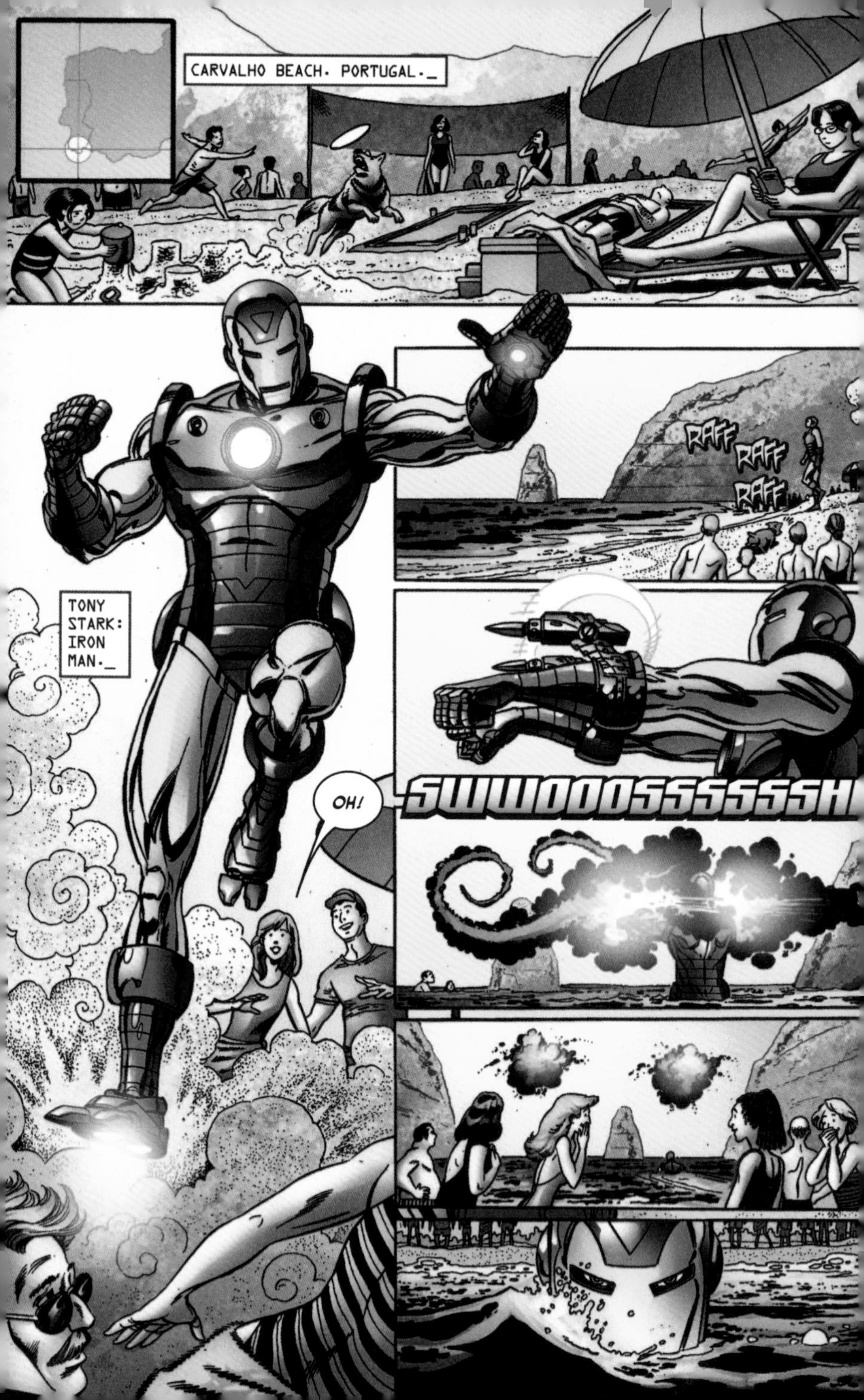
CARVALHO BEACH. PORTUGAL._
TONY STARK: IRON MAN._
RAFF RAFF RAFF
OH!
SWWOOOSSSSSSSH

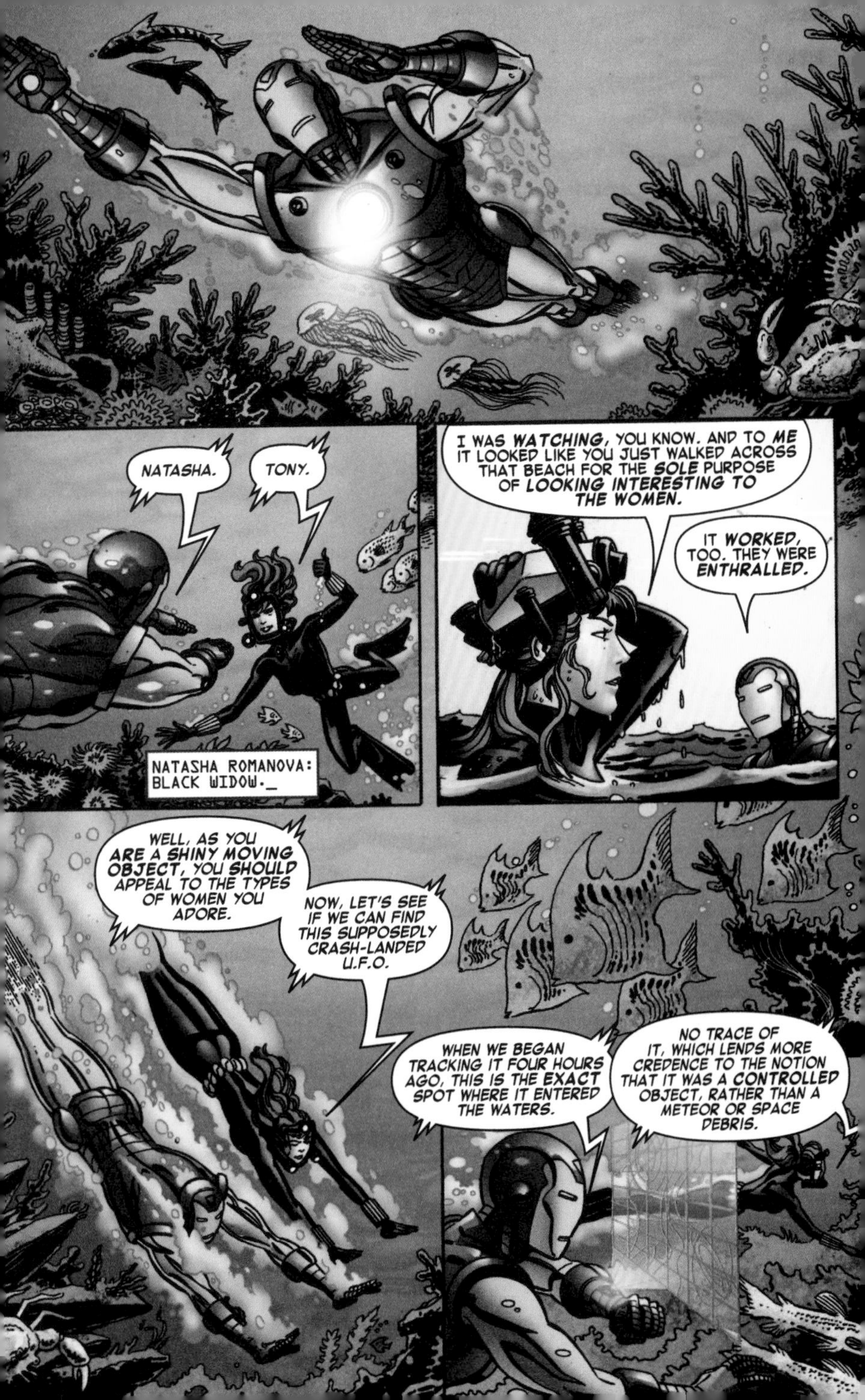

NATASHA.
TONY.
NATASHA ROMANOVA: BLACK WIDOW._
I WAS WATCHING, YOU KNOW. AND TO ME IT LOOKED LIKE YOU JUST WALKED ACROSS THAT BEACH FOR THE SOLE PURPOSE OF LOOKING INTERESTING TO THE WOMEN.
IT WORKED, TOO. THEY WERE ENTHRALLED.
WELL, AS YOU ARE A SHINY MOVING OBJECT, YOU SHOULD APPEAL TO THE TYPES OF WOMEN YOU ADORE.
NOW, LET'S SEE IF WE CAN FIND THIS SUPPOSEDLY CRASH-LANDED U.F.O.
WHEN WE BEGAN TRACKING IT FOUR HOURS AGO, THIS IS THE EXACT SPOT WHERE IT ENTERED THE WATERS.
NO TRACE OF IT, WHICH LENDS MORE CREDENCE TO THE NOTION THAT IT WAS A CONTROLLED OBJECT, RATHER THAN A METEOR OR SPACE DEBRIS.

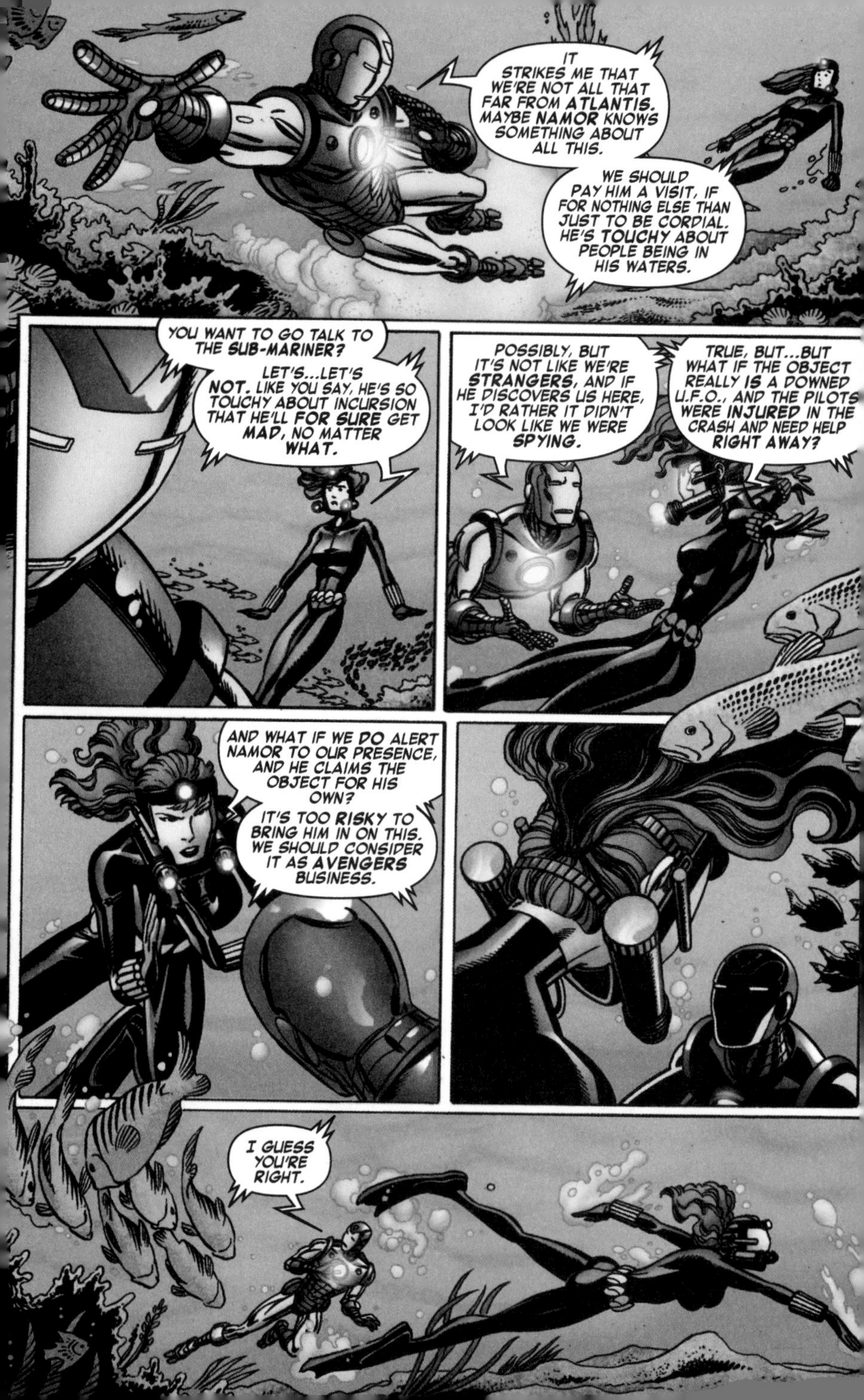

IT STRIKES ME THAT WE'RE NOT ALL THAT FAR FROM ATLANTIS. MAYBE NAMOR KNOWS SOMETHING ABOUT ALL THIS.
WE SHOULD PAY HIM A VISIT, IF FOR NOTHING ELSE THAN JUST TO BE CORDIAL. HE'S TOUCHY ABOUT PEOPLE BEING IN HIS WATERS.
YOU WANT TO GO TALK TO THE SUB-MARINER?
LET'S...LET'S NOT. LIKE YOU SAY, HE'S SO TOUCHY ABOUT INCURSION THAT HE'LL FOR SURE GET MAD, NO MATTER WHAT.
POSSIBLY, BUT IT'S NOT LIKE WE'RE STRANGERS, AND IF HE DISCOVERS US HERE, I'D RATHER IT DIDN'T LOOK LIKE WE WERE SPYING.
TRUE, BUT...BUT WHAT IF THE OBJECT REALLY IS A DOWNED U.F.O., AND THE PILOTS WERE INJURED IN THE CRASH AND NEED HELP RIGHT AWAY?
AND WHAT IF WE DO ALERT NAMOR TO OUR PRESENCE, AND HE CLAIMS THE OBJECT FOR HIS OWN?
IT'S TOO RISKY TO BRING HIM IN ON THIS. WE SHOULD CONSIDER IT AS AVENGERS BUSINESS.
I GUESS YOU'RE RIGHT.

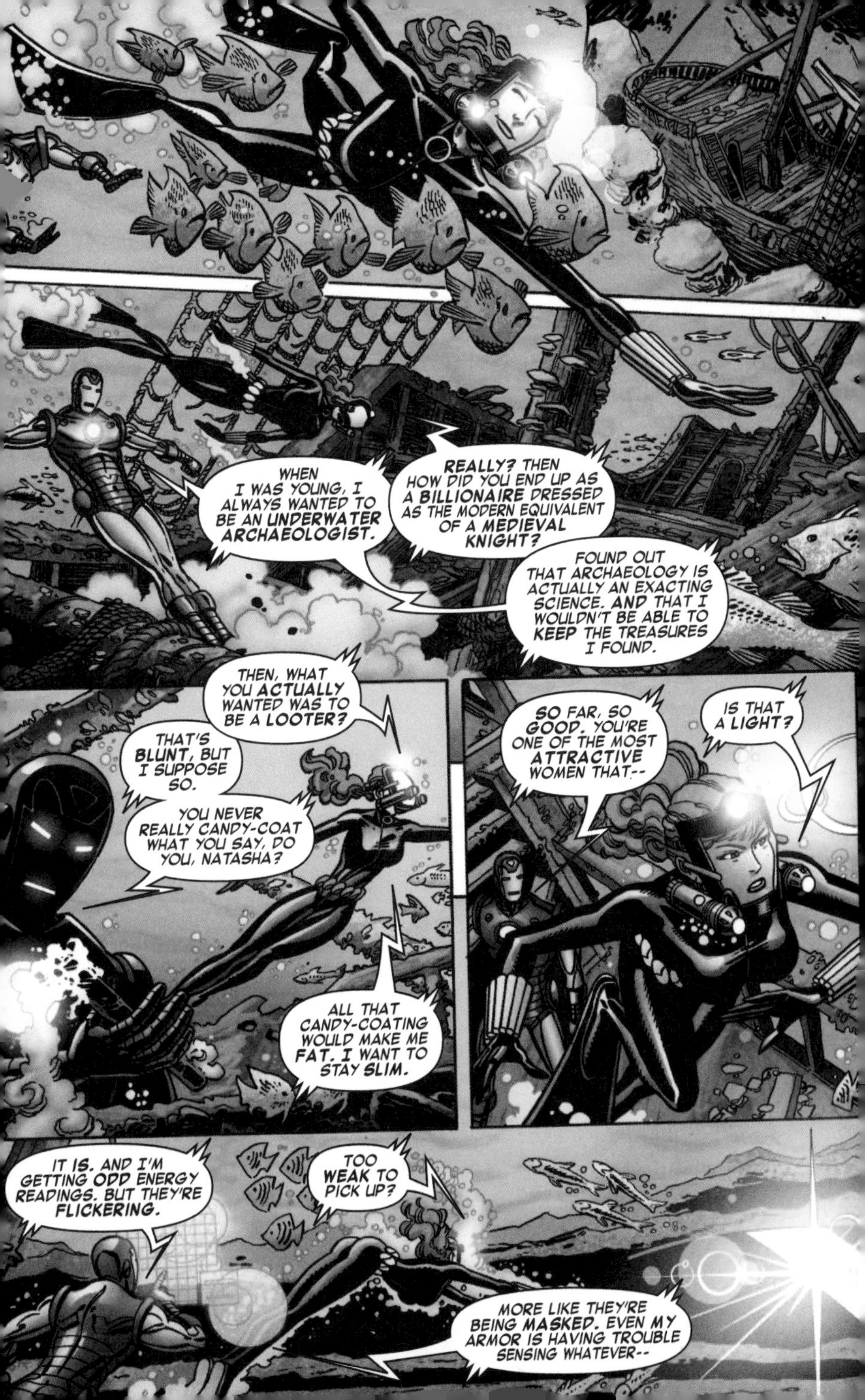
WHEN I WAS YOUNG, I ALWAYS WANTED TO BE AN UNDERWATER ARCHAEOLOGIST.
REALLY? THEN HOW DID YOU END UP AS A BILLIONAIRE DRESSED AS THE MODERN EQUIVALENT OF A MEDIEVAL KNIGHT?
FOUND OUT THAT ARCHAEOLOGY IS ACTUALLY AN EXACTING SCIENCE. AND THAT I WOULDN'T BE ABLE TO KEEP THE TREASURES I FOUND.
THEN, WHAT YOU ACTUALLY WANTED WAS TO BE A LOOTER?
THAT'S BLUNT, BUT I SUPPOSE SO.
YOU NEVER REALLY CANDY-COAT WHAT YOU SAY, DO YOU, NATASHA?
ALL THAT CANDY-COATING WOULD MAKE ME FAT. I WANT TO STAY SLIM.
SO FAR, SO GOOD. YOU'RE ONE OF THE MOST ATTRACTIVE WOMEN THAT--
IS THAT A LIGHT?
IT IS. AND I'M GETTING ODD ENERGY READINGS. BUT THEY'RE FLICKERING.
TOO WEAK TO PICK UP?
MORE LIKE THEY'RE BEING MASKED. EVEN MY ARMOR IS HAVING TROUBLE SENSING WHATEVER--

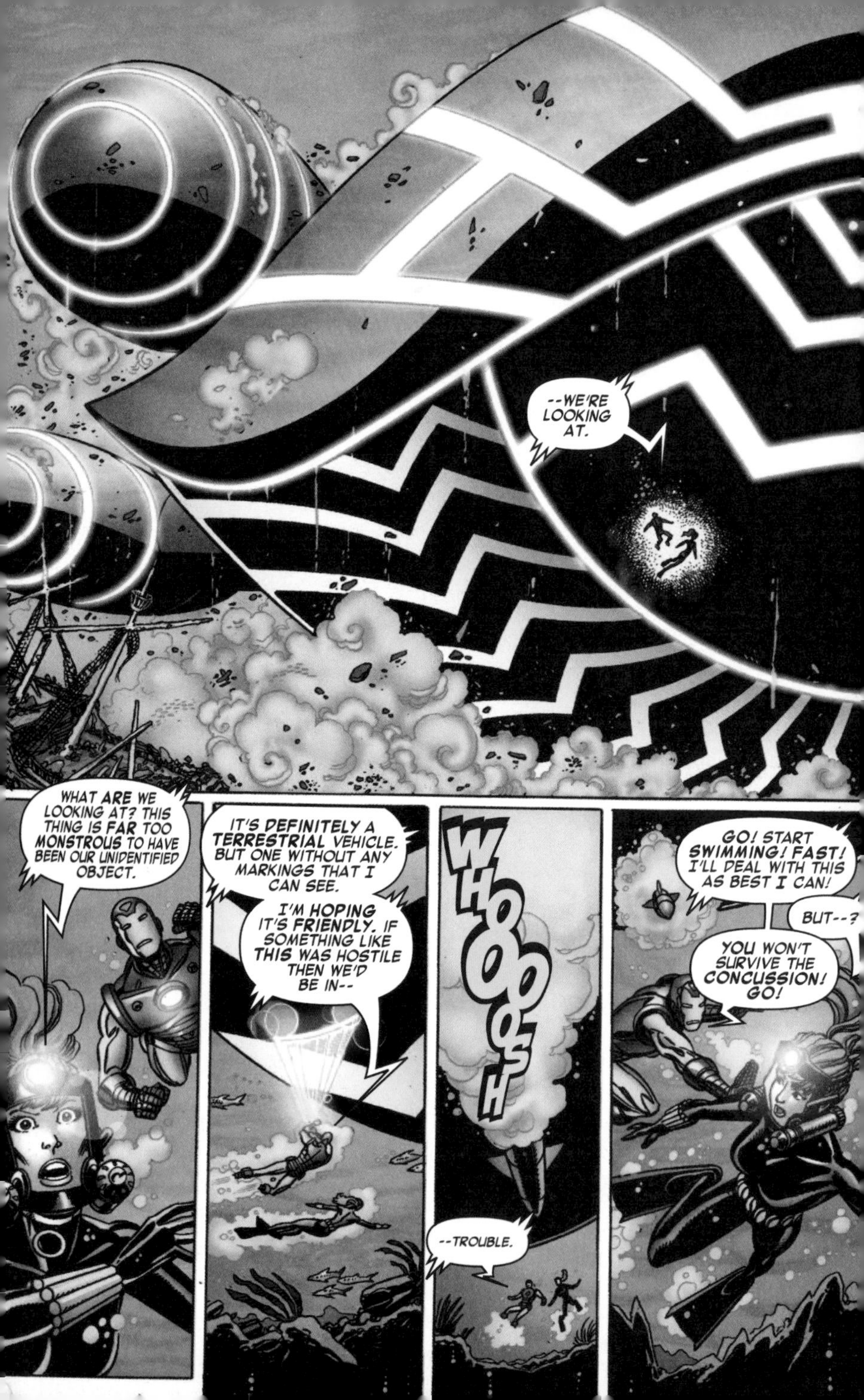
--WE'RE LOOKING AT.
WHAT ARE WE LOOKING AT? THIS THING IS FAR TOO MONSTROUS TO HAVE BEEN OUR UNIDENTIFIED OBJECT.
IT'S DEFINITELY A TERRESTRIAL VEHICLE. BUT ONE WITHOUT ANY MARKINGS THAT I CAN SEE.
I'M HOPING IT'S FRIENDLY. IF SOMETHING LIKE THIS WAS HOSTILE THEN WE'D BE IN--
WHOOOOSH
--TROUBLE.
GO! START SWIMMING! FAST! I'LL DEAL WITH THIS AS BEST I CAN!
BUT--?
YOU WON'T SURVIVE THE CONCUSSION! GO!

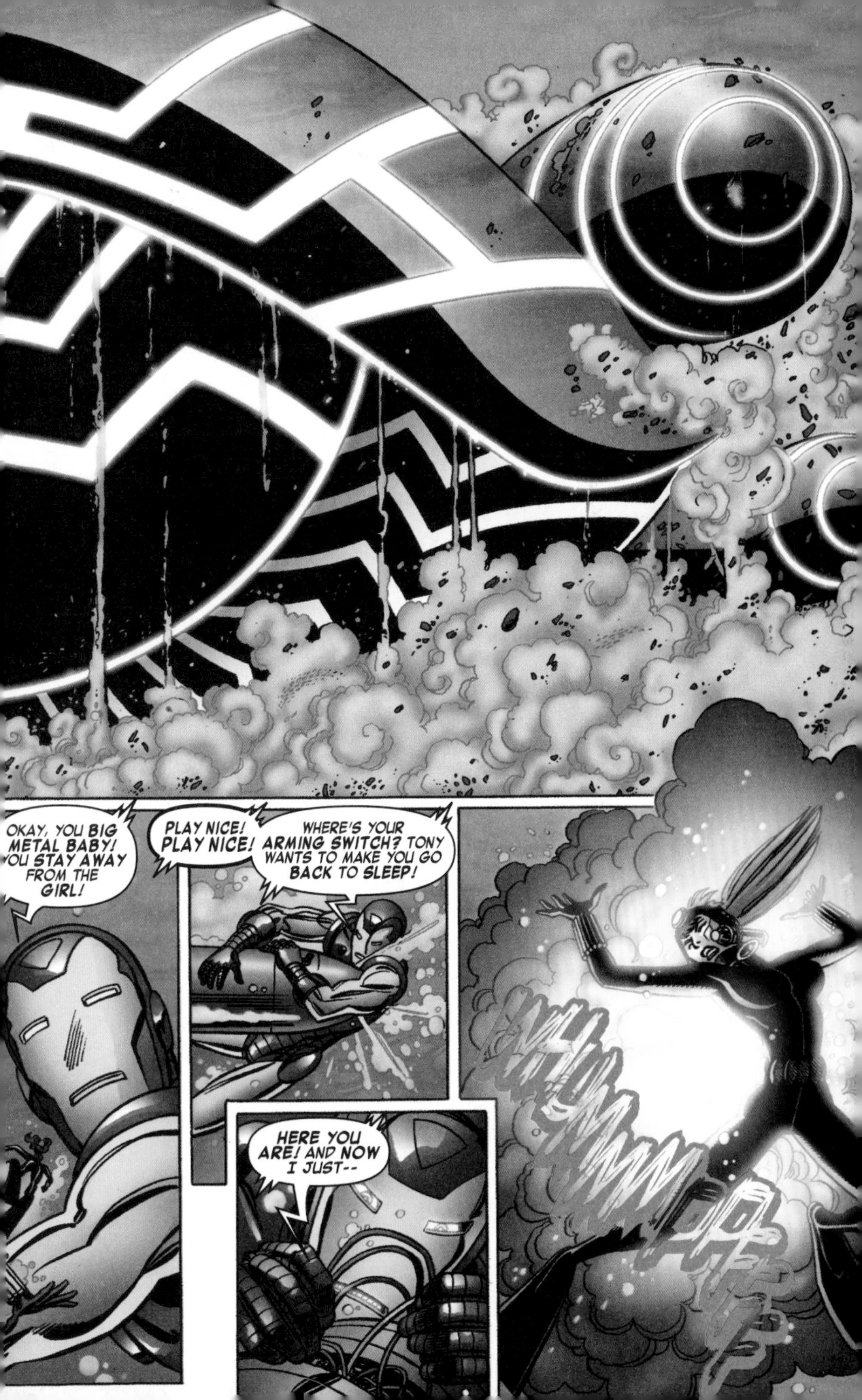

OKAY, YOU BIG METAL BABY! OU STAY AWAY FROM THE GIRL!
PLAY NICE! PLAY NICE!
WHERE'S YOUR ARMING SWITCH? TONY WANTS TO MAKE YOU GO BACK TO SLEEP!
HERE YOU ARE! AND NOW I JUST--

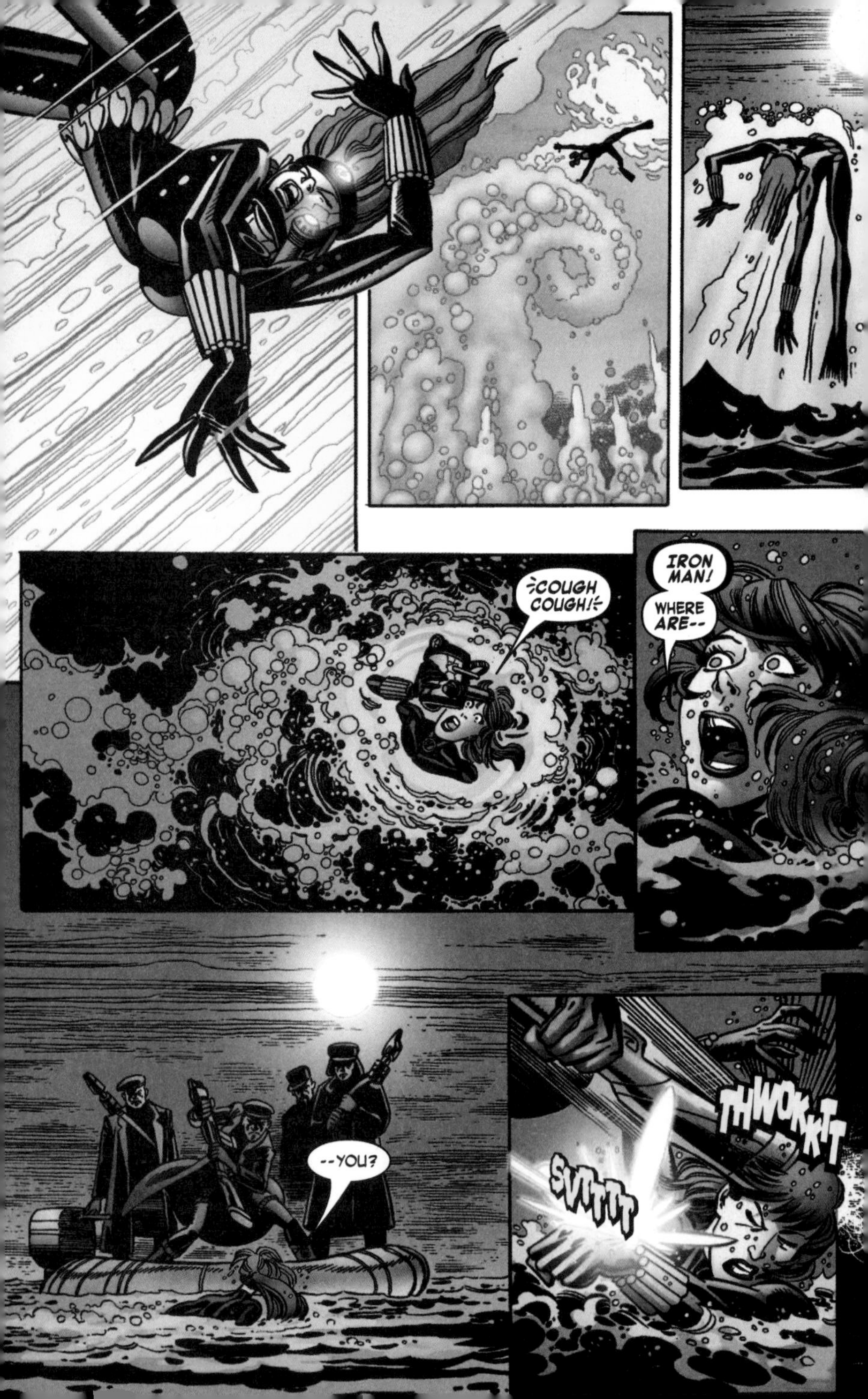

COUGH COUGH!
IRON MAN!
WHERE ARE--
--YOU?
THWOKKTT
SVTTTT

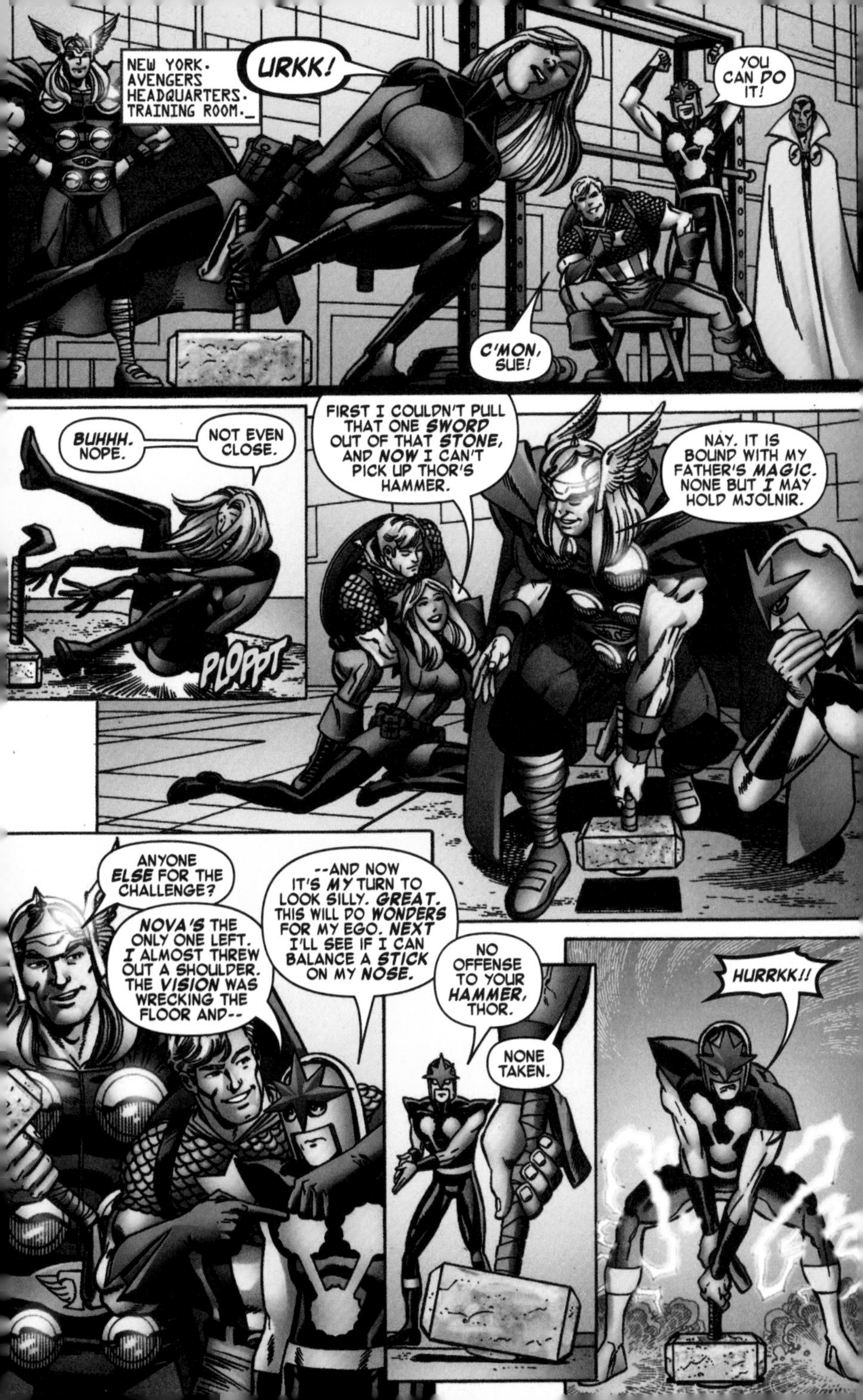
NEW YORK. AVENGERS HEADQUARTERS. TRAINING ROOM._
URKK!
YOU CAN DO IT!
C'MON, SUE!
BUHHH. NOPE.
NOT EVEN CLOSE.
PLOPPT
FIRST I COULDN'T PULL THAT ONE SWORD OUT OF THAT STONE, AND NOW I CAN'T PICK UP THOR'S HAMMER.
NAY. IT IS BOUND WITH MY FATHER'S MAGIC. NONE BUT I MAY HOLD MJOLNIR.
ANYONE ELSE FOR THE CHALLENGE?
NOVA'S THE ONLY ONE LEFT. I ALMOST THREW OUT A SHOULDER. THE VISION WAS WRECKING THE FLOOR AND--
--AND NOW IT'S MY TURN TO LOOK SILLY. GREAT. THIS WILL DO WONDERS FOR MY EGO. NEXT I'LL SEE IF I CAN BALANCE A STICK ON MY NOSE.
NO OFFENSE TO YOUR HAMMER, THOR.
NONE TAKEN.
HURRKK!!

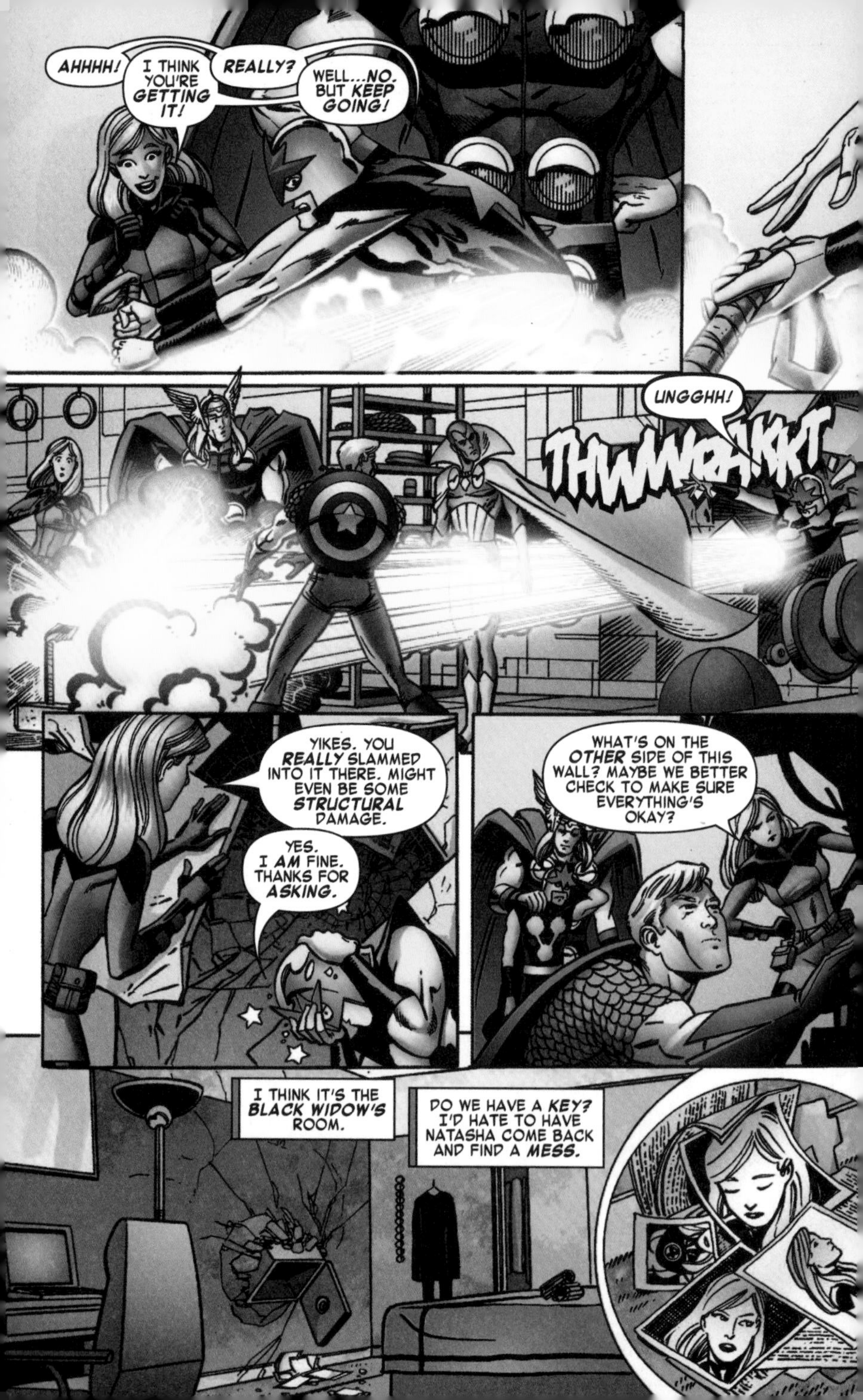
AHHHH!
I THINK YOU'RE GETTING IT!
REALLY?
WELL...NO. BUT KEEP GOING!
UNGGHH!
THWWRAKKT
YIKES. YOU REALLY SLAMMED INTO IT THERE. MIGHT EVEN BE SOME STRUCTURAL DAMAGE.
YES. I AM FINE. THANKS FOR ASKING.
WHAT'S ON THE OTHER SIDE OF THIS WALL? MAYBE WE BETTER CHECK TO MAKE SURE EVERYTHING'S OKAY?
I THINK IT'S THE BLACK WIDOW'S ROOM.
DO WE HAVE A KEY? I'D HATE TO HAVE NATASHA COME BACK AND FIND A MESS.

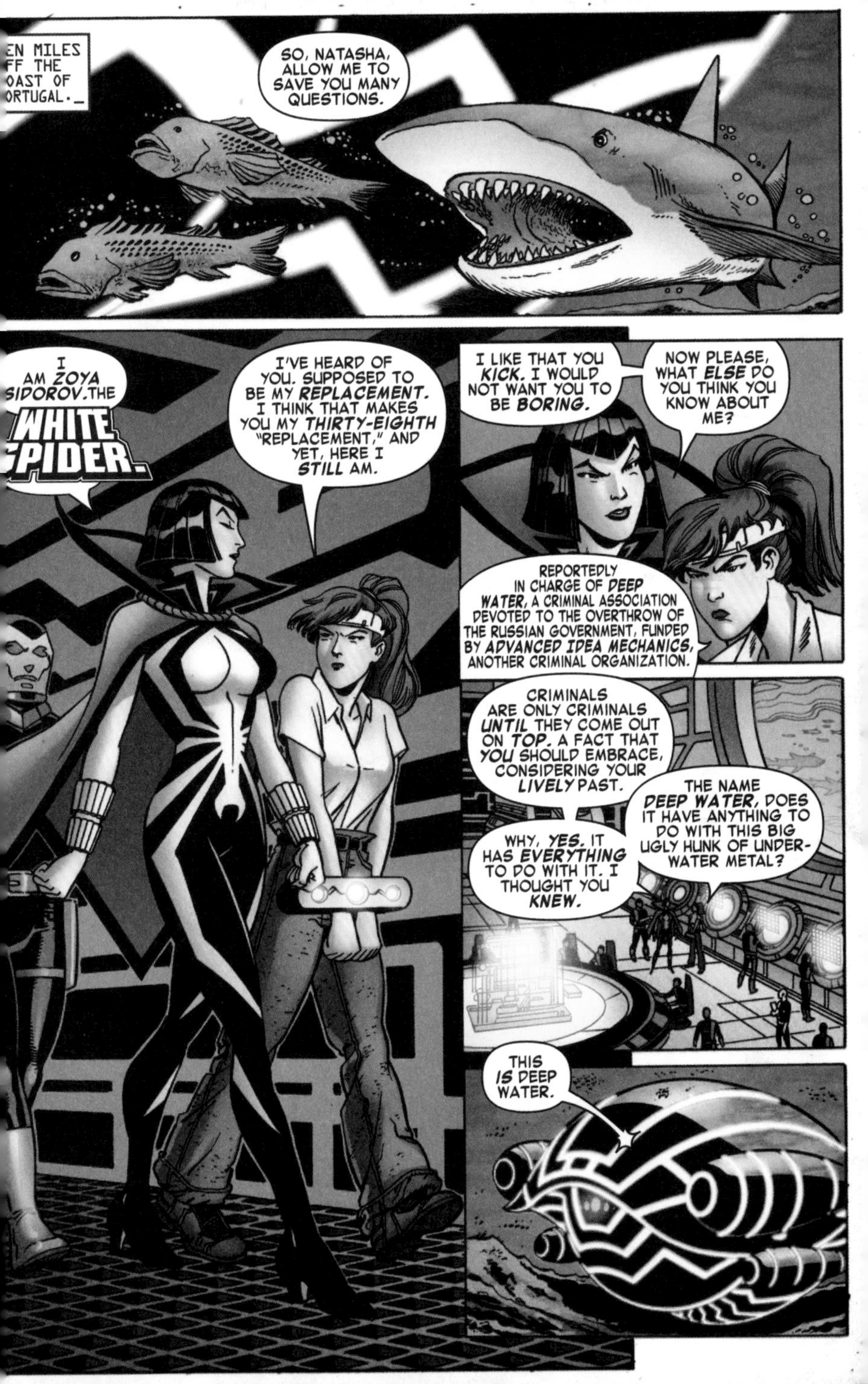
EN MILES
FF THE
OAST OF
ORTUGAL._
SO, NATASHA, ALLOW ME TO SAVE YOU MANY QUESTIONS.
I AM ZOYA SIDOROV. THE WHITE SPIDER.
I'VE HEARD OF YOU. SUPPOSED TO BE MY REPLACEMENT. I THINK THAT MAKES YOU MY THIRTY-EIGHTH "REPLACEMENT," AND YET, HERE I STILL AM.
I LIKE THAT YOU KICK. I WOULD NOT WANT YOU TO BE BORING.
NOW PLEASE, WHAT ELSE DO YOU THINK YOU KNOW ABOUT ME?
REPORTEDLY IN CHARGE OF DEEP WATER, A CRIMINAL ASSOCIATION DEVOTED TO THE OVERTHROW OF THE RUSSIAN GOVERNMENT, FUNDED BY ADVANCED IDEA MECHANICS, ANOTHER CRIMINAL ORGANIZATION.
CRIMINALS ARE ONLY CRIMINALS UNTIL THEY COME OUT ON TOP. A FACT THAT YOU SHOULD EMBRACE, CONSIDERING YOUR LIVELY PAST.
THE NAME DEEP WATER, DOES IT HAVE ANYTHING TO DO WITH THIS BIG UGLY HUNK OF UNDER-WATER METAL?
WHY, YES. IT HAS EVERYTHING TO DO WITH IT. I THOUGHT YOU KNEW.
THIS IS DEEP WATER.

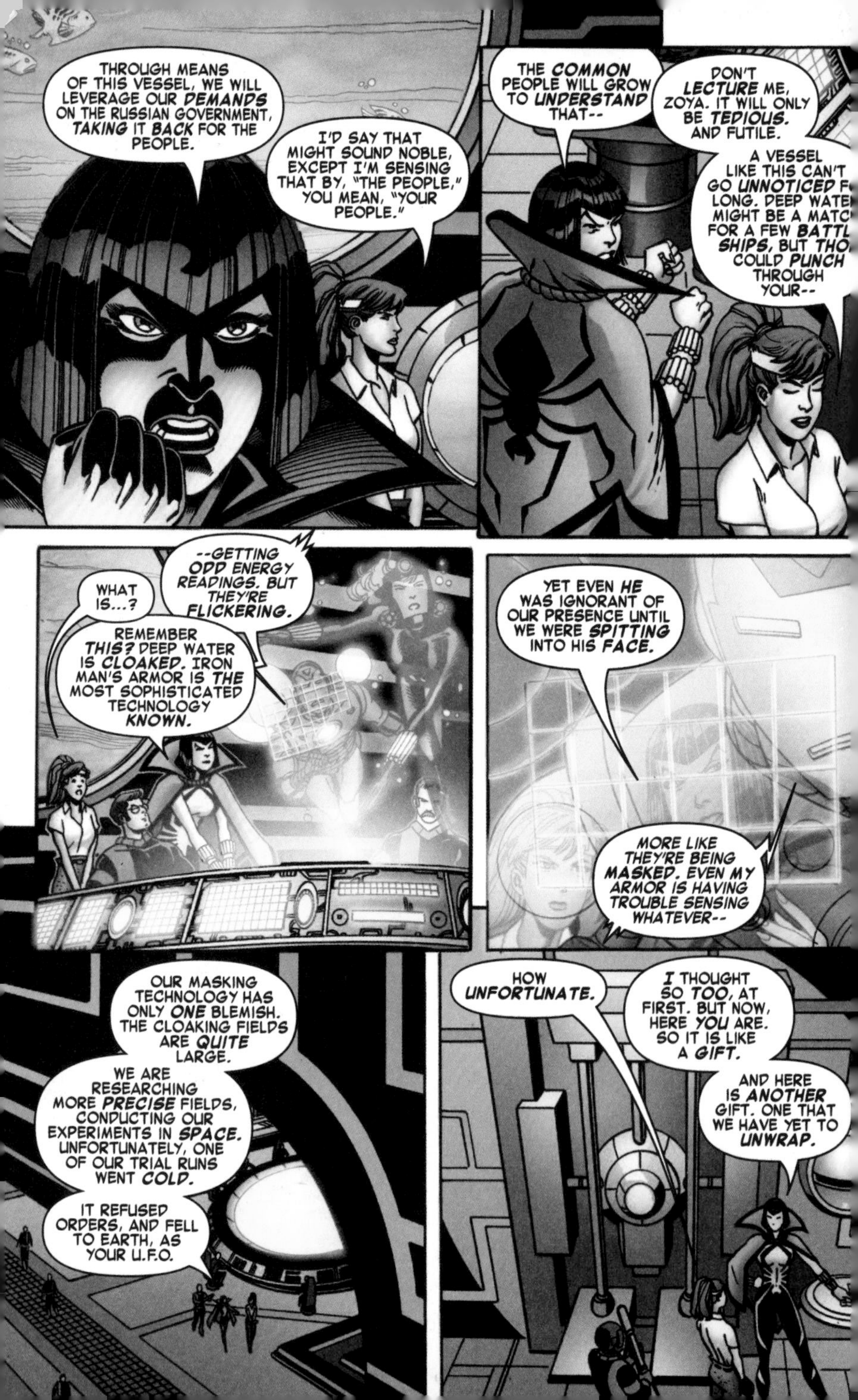
THROUGH MEANS OF THIS VESSEL, WE WILL LEVERAGE OUR DEMANDS ON THE RUSSIAN GOVERNMENT, TAKING IT BACK FOR THE PEOPLE.
I'D SAY THAT MIGHT SOUND NOBLE, EXCEPT I'M SENSING THAT BY, "THE PEOPLE," YOU MEAN, "YOUR PEOPLE."
THE COMMON PEOPLE WILL GROW TO UNDERSTAND THAT--
DON'T LECTURE ME, ZOYA. IT WILL ONLY BE TEDIOUS. AND FUTILE.
A VESSEL LIKE THIS CAN'T GO UNNOTICED F LONG. DEEP WATE MIGHT BE A MATC FOR A FEW BATTL SHIPS, BUT THO COULD PUNCH THROUGH YOUR--
WHAT IS...?
--GETTING ODD ENERGY READINGS. BUT THEY'RE FLICKERING.
REMEMBER THIS? DEEP WATER IS CLOAKED. IRON MAN'S ARMOR IS THE MOST SOPHISTICATED TECHNOLOGY KNOWN.
YET EVEN HE WAS IGNORANT OF OUR PRESENCE UNTIL WE WERE SPITTING INTO HIS FACE.
MORE LIKE THEY'RE BEING MASKED. EVEN MY ARMOR IS HAVING TROUBLE SENSING WHATEVER--
OUR MASKING TECHNOLOGY HAS ONLY ONE BLEMISH. THE CLOAKING FIELDS ARE QUITE LARGE.
WE ARE RESEARCHING MORE PRECISE FIELDS, CONDUCTING OUR EXPERIMENTS IN SPACE. UNFORTUNATELY, ONE OF OUR TRIAL RUNS WENT COLD.
IT REFUSED ORDERS, AND FELL TO EARTH, AS YOUR U.F.O.
HOW UNFORTUNATE.
I THOUGHT SO TOO, AT FIRST. BUT NOW, HERE YOU ARE. SO IT IS LIKE A GIFT.
AND HERE IS ANOTHER GIFT. ONE THAT WE HAVE YET TO UNWRAP.

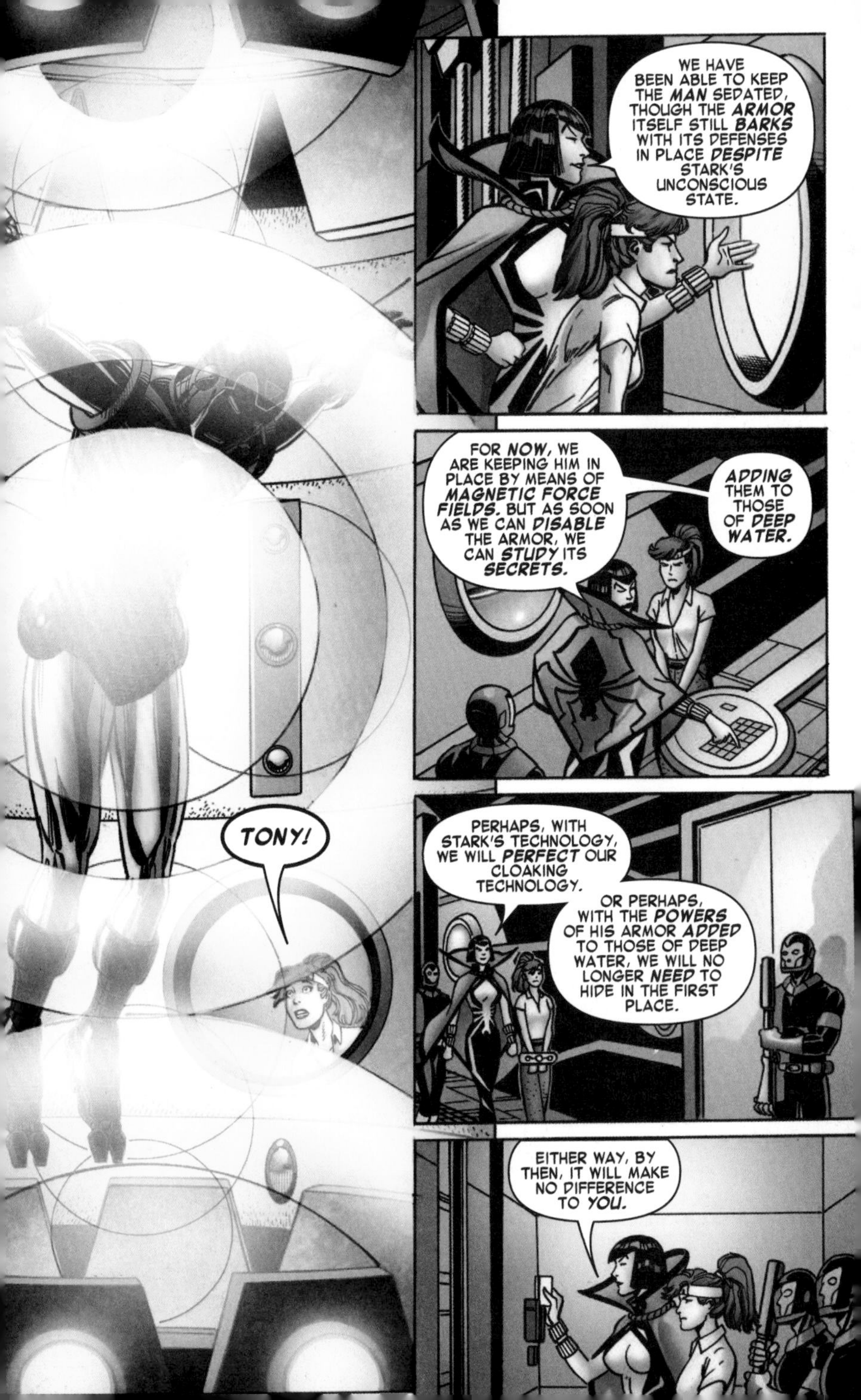
WE HAVE BEEN ABLE TO KEEP THE MAN SEDATED, THOUGH THE ARMOR ITSELF STILL BARKS WITH ITS DEFENSES IN PLACE DESPITE STARK'S UNCONSCIOUS STATE.
FOR NOW, WE ARE KEEPING HIM IN PLACE BY MEANS OF MAGNETIC FORCE FIELDS. BUT AS SOON AS WE CAN DISABLE THE ARMOR, WE CAN STUDY ITS SECRETS.
ADDING THEM TO THOSE OF DEEP WATER.
PERHAPS, WITH STARK'S TECHNOLOGY, WE WILL PERFECT OUR CLOAKING TECHNOLOGY.
OR PERHAPS, WITH THE POWERS OF HIS ARMOR ADDED TO THOSE OF DEEP WATER, WE WILL NO LONGER NEED TO HIDE IN THE FIRST PLACE.
EITHER WAY, BY THEN, IT WILL MAKE NO DIFFERENCE TO YOU.
TONY!

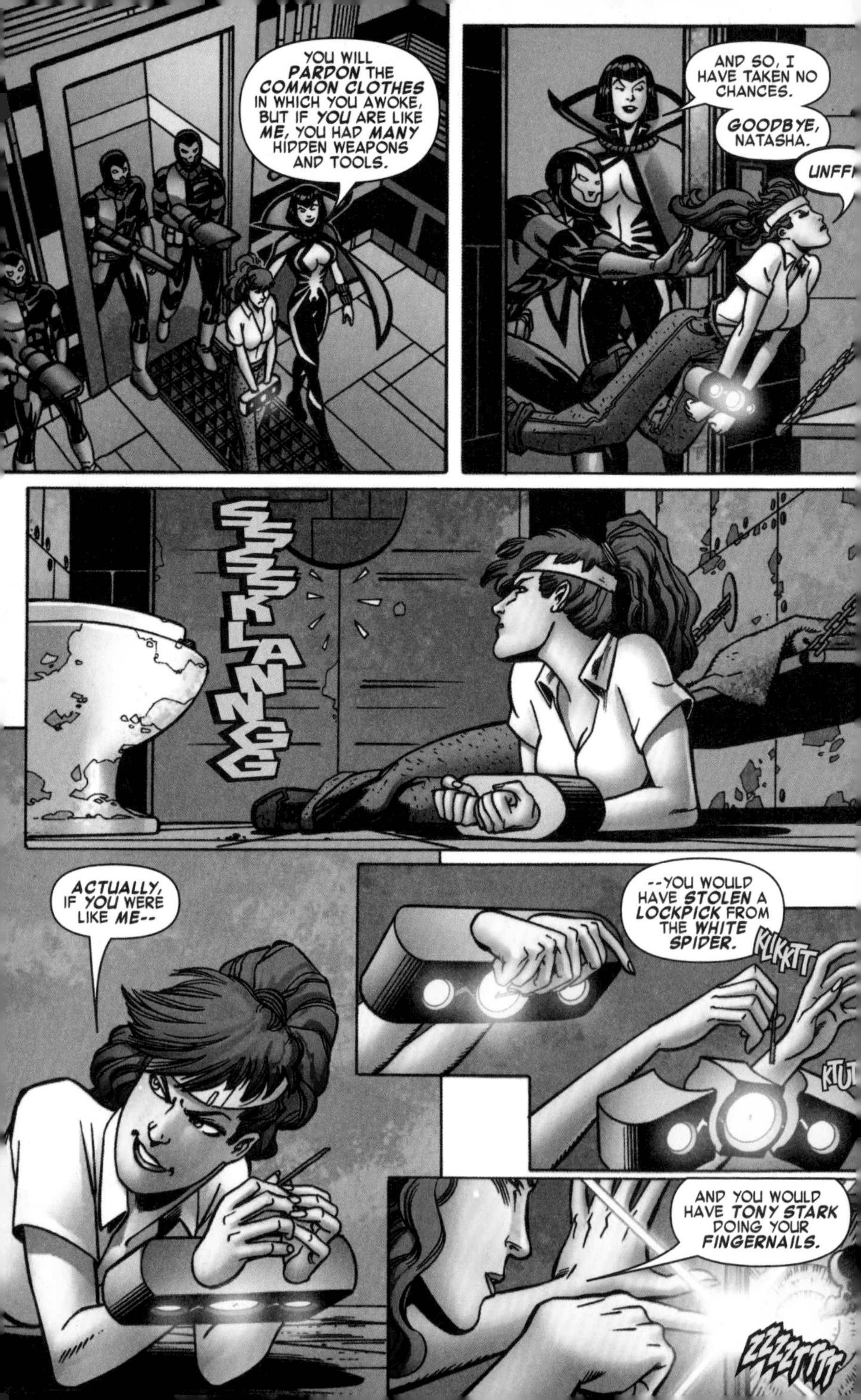
YOU WILL PARDON THE COMMON CLOTHES IN WHICH YOU AWOKE, BUT IF YOU ARE LIKE ME, YOU HAD MANY HIDDEN WEAPONS AND TOOLS.
AND SO, I HAVE TAKEN NO CHANCES.
GOODBYE, NATASHA.
UNFF!
SSSKLANNGG
ACTUALLY, IF YOU WERE LIKE ME--
--YOU WOULD HAVE STOLEN A LOCKPICK FROM THE WHITE SPIDER.
KLIKKTT
KTUT
AND YOU WOULD HAVE TONY STARK DOING YOUR FINGERNAILS.
ZZZZTTTT

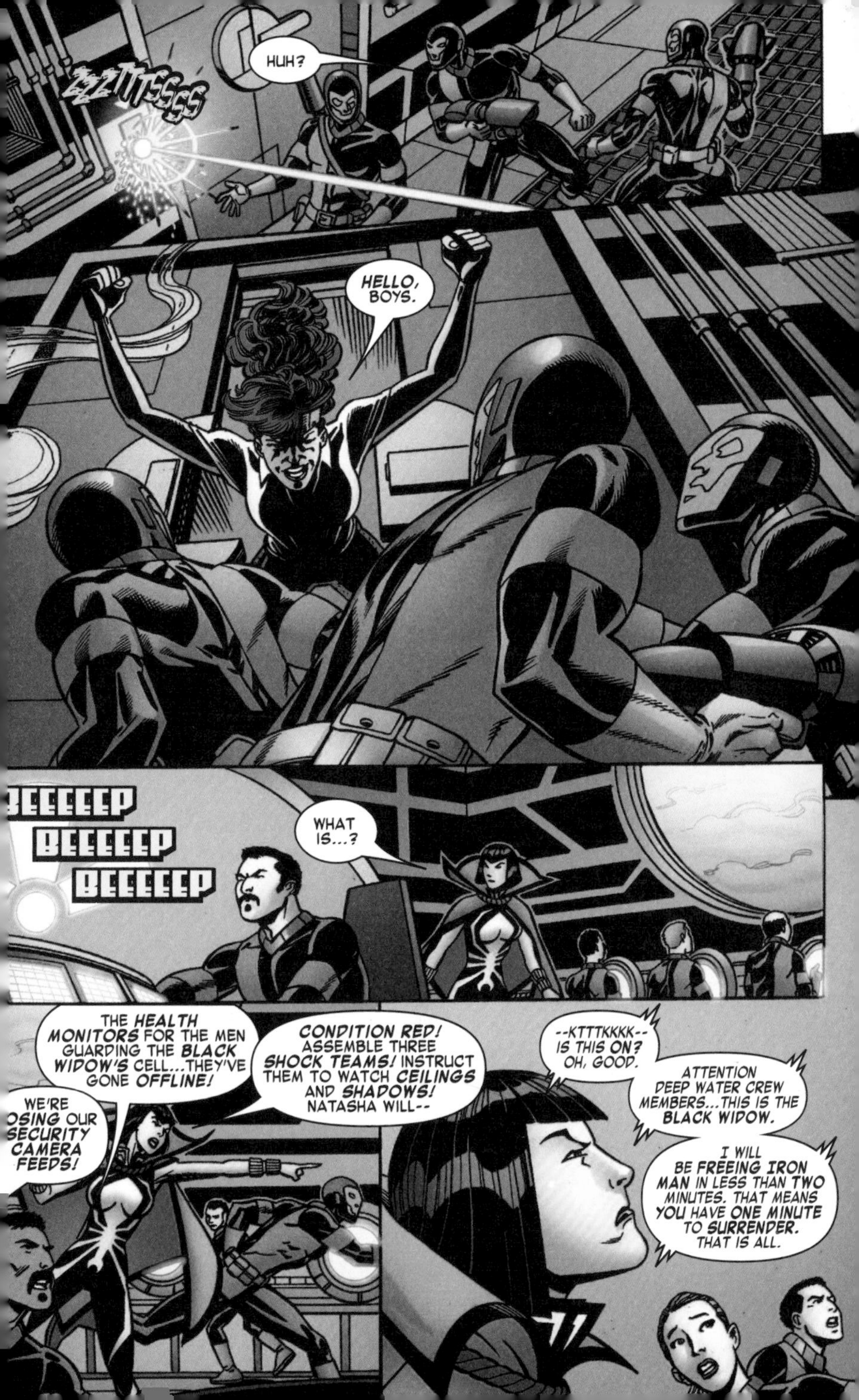
ZZZTTTSSSS
HUH?
HELLO, BOYS.
BEEEEEP
BEEEEEP
BEEEEEP
WHAT IS...?
THE HEALTH MONITORS FOR THE MEN GUARDING THE BLACK WIDOW'S CELL...THEY'VE GONE OFFLINE!
WE'RE OSING OUR SECURITY CAMERA FEEDS!
CONDITION RED! ASSEMBLE THREE SHOCK TEAMS! INSTRUCT THEM TO WATCH CEILINGS AND SHADOWS! NATASHA WILL--
--KTTTKKKK-- IS THIS ON? OH, GOOD.
ATTENTION DEEP WATER CREW MEMBERS...THIS IS THE BLACK WIDOW.
I WILL BE FREEING IRON MAN IN LESS THAN TWO MINUTES. THAT MEANS YOU HAVE ONE MINUTE TO SURRENDER. THAT IS ALL.

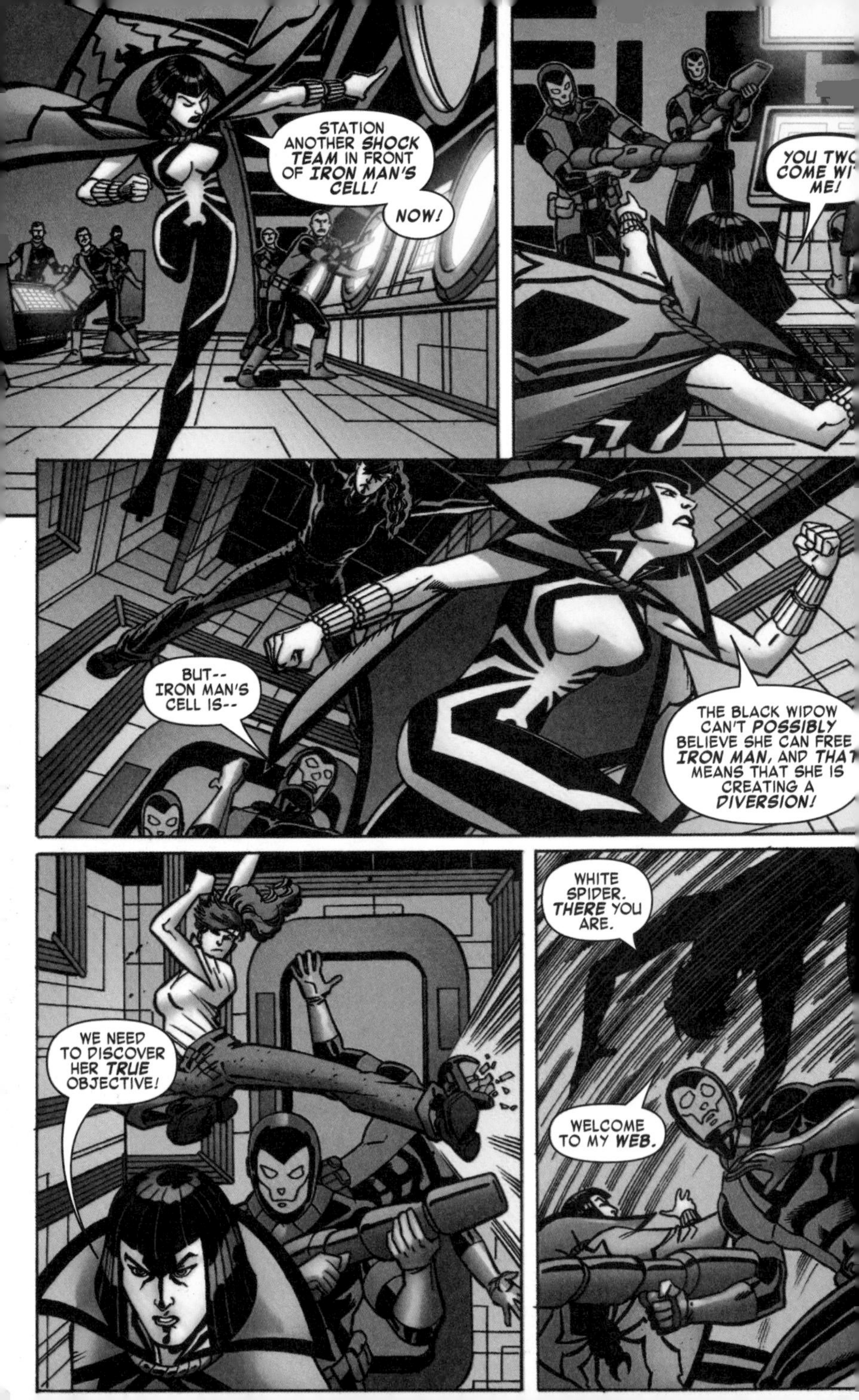
STATION ANOTHER SHOCK TEAM IN FRONT OF IRON MAN'S CELL!
NOW!
YOU TWO COME WITH ME!
BUT-- IRON MAN'S CELL IS--
THE BLACK WIDOW CAN'T POSSIBLY BELIEVE SHE CAN FREE IRON MAN, AND THAT MEANS THAT SHE IS CREATING A DIVERSION!
WE NEED TO DISCOVER HER TRUE OBJECTIVE!
WHITE SPIDER. THERE YOU ARE.
WELCOME TO MY WEB.

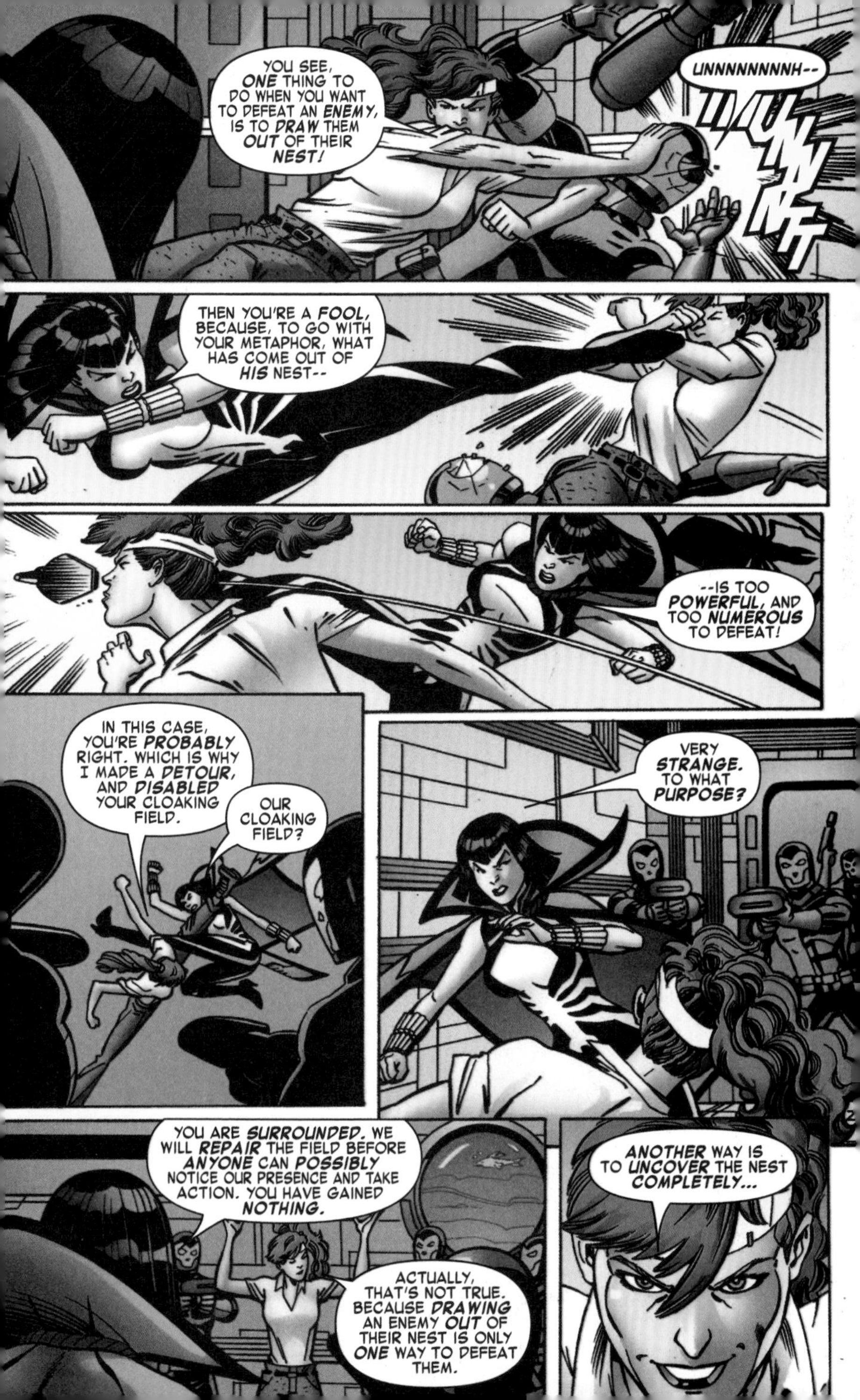

YOU SEE, ONE THING TO DO WHEN YOU WANT TO DEFEAT AN ENEMY, IS TO DRAW THEM OUT OF THEIR NEST!
UNNNNNNNNH--
THEN YOU'RE A FOOL, BECAUSE, TO GO WITH YOUR METAPHOR, WHAT HAS COME OUT OF HIS NEST--
--IS TOO POWERFUL, AND TOO NUMEROUS TO DEFEAT!
IN THIS CASE, YOU'RE PROBABLY RIGHT. WHICH IS WHY I MADE A DETOUR, AND DISABLED YOUR CLOAKING FIELD.
OUR CLOAKING FIELD?
VERY STRANGE. TO WHAT PURPOSE?
YOU ARE SURROUNDED. WE WILL REPAIR THE FIELD BEFORE ANYONE CAN POSSIBLY NOTICE OUR PRESENCE AND TAKE ACTION. YOU HAVE GAINED NOTHING.
ACTUALLY, THAT'S NOT TRUE. BECAUSE DRAWING AN ENEMY OUT OF THEIR NEST IS ONLY ONE WAY TO DEFEAT THEM.
ANOTHER WAY IS TO UNCOVER THE NEST COMPLETELY...

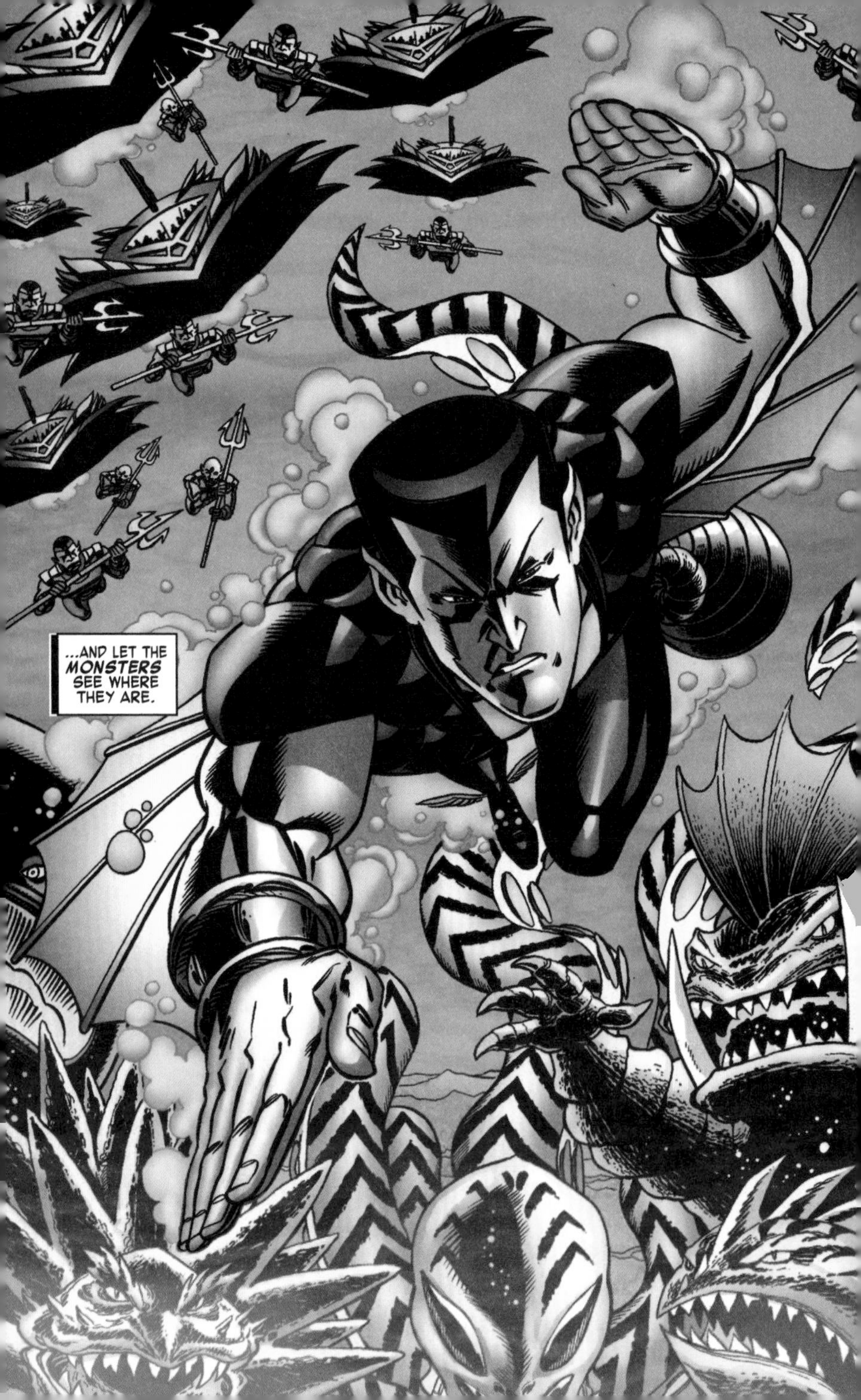
...AND LET THE MONSTERS SEE WHERE THEY ARE.

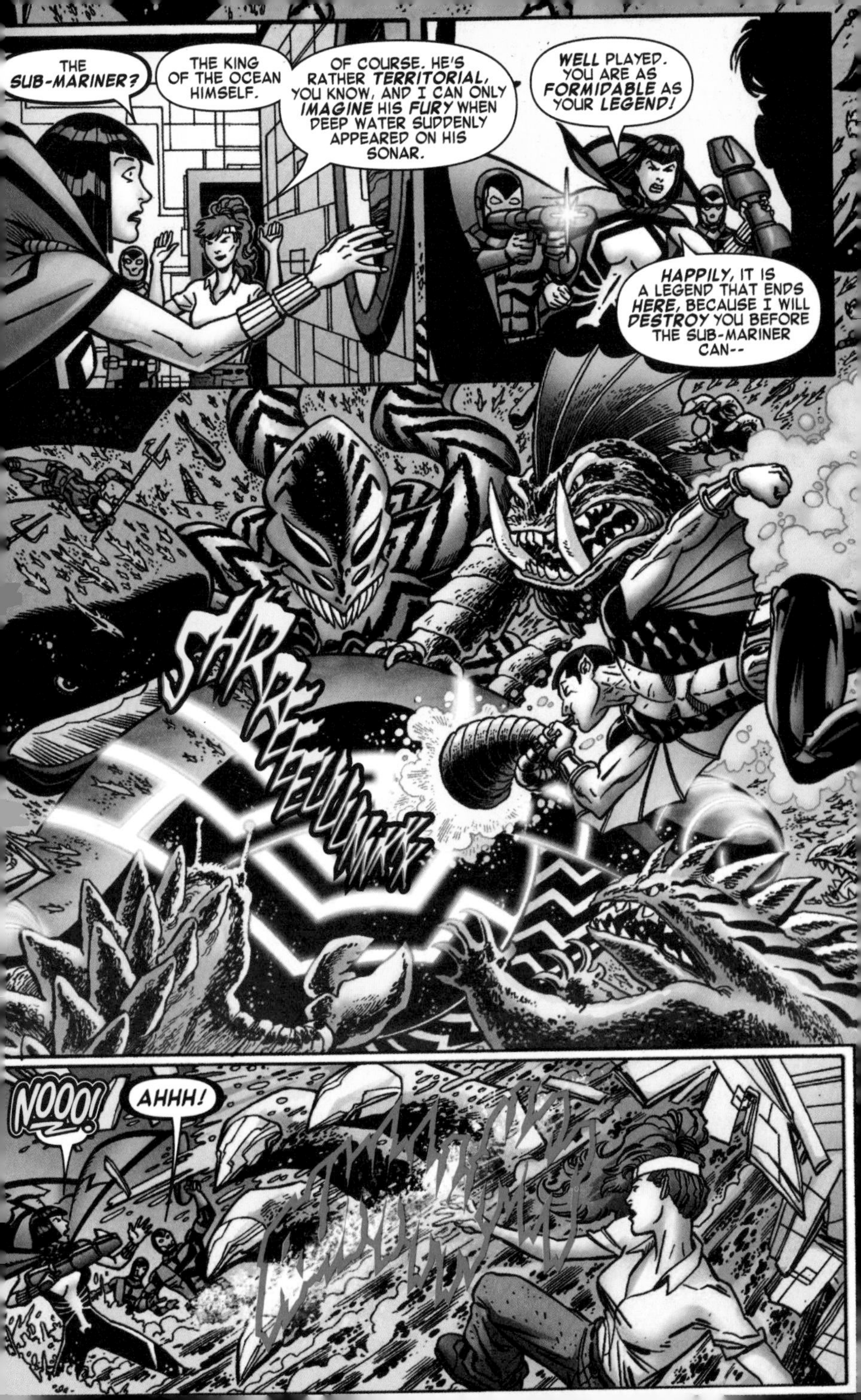
THE SUB-MARINER?
THE KING OF THE OCEAN HIMSELF.
OF COURSE. HE'S RATHER TERRITORIAL, YOU KNOW, AND I CAN ONLY IMAGINE HIS FURY WHEN DEEP WATER SUDDENLY APPEARED ON HIS SONAR.
WELL PLAYED. YOU ARE AS FORMIDABLE AS YOUR LEGEND!
HAPPILY, IT IS A LEGEND THAT ENDS HERE, BECAUSE I WILL DESTROY YOU BEFORE THE SUB-MARINER CAN--
NOOO!
AHHH!

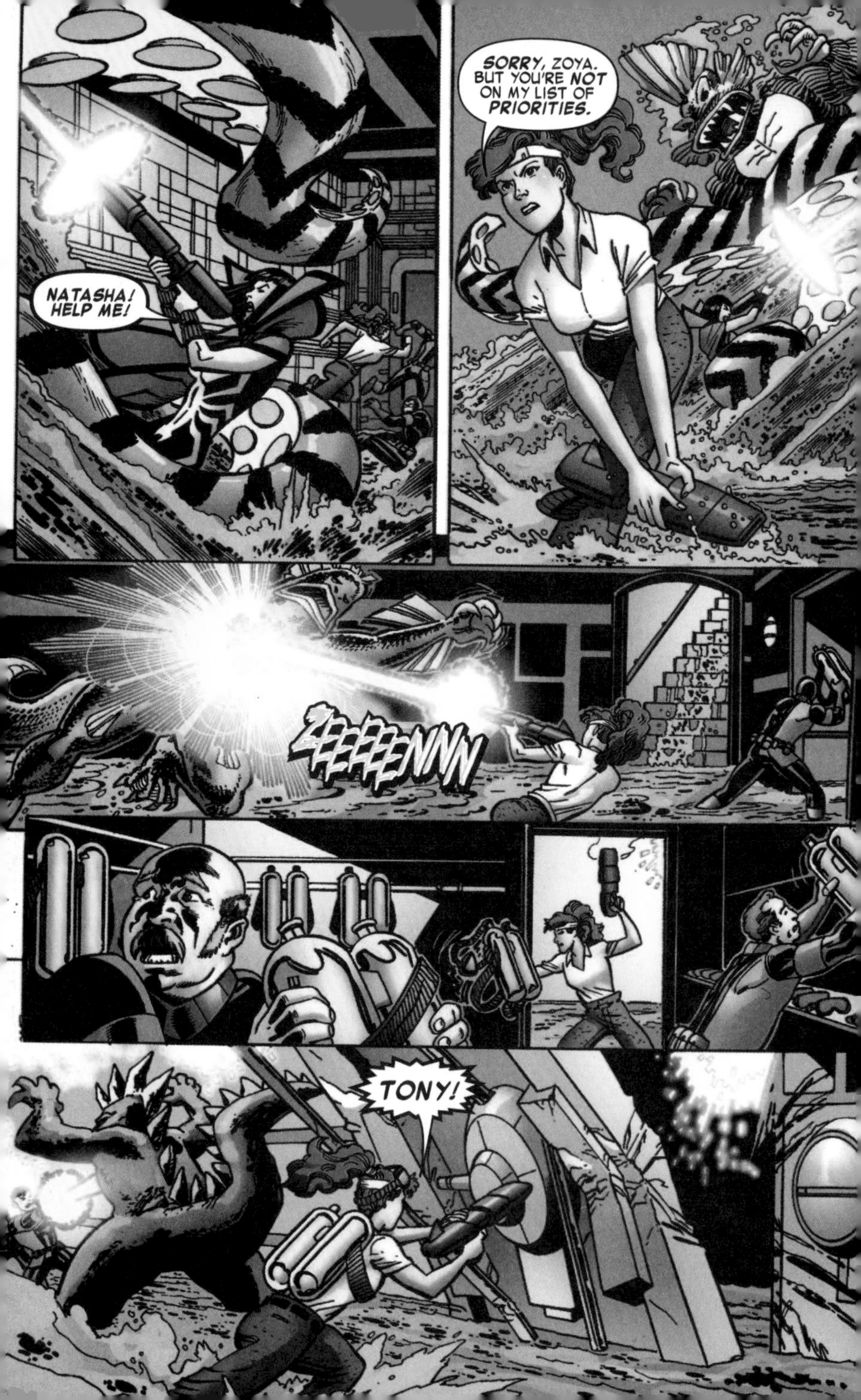

NATASHA! HELP ME!
SORRY, ZOYA. BUT YOU'RE NOT ON MY LIST OF PRIORITIES.
ZEEEEEENNNN
TONY!

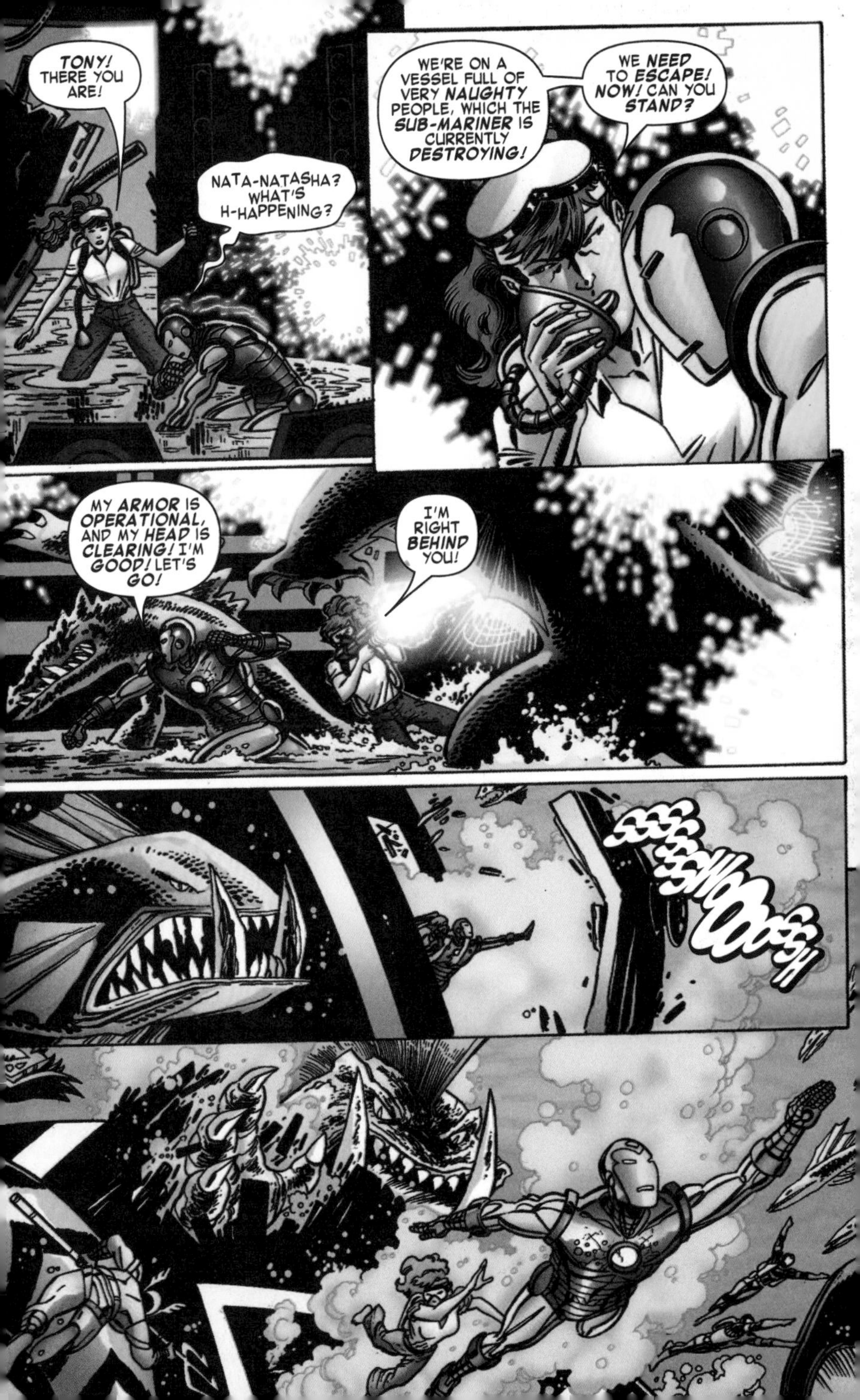
TONY! THERE YOU ARE!
NATA-NATASHA? WHAT'S H-HAPPENING?
WE'RE ON A VESSEL FULL OF VERY NAUGHTY PEOPLE, WHICH THE SUB-MARINER IS CURRENTLY DESTROYING!
WE NEED TO ESCAPE! NOW! CAN YOU STAND?
MY ARMOR IS OPERATIONAL, AND MY HEAD IS CLEARING! I'M GOOD! LET'S GO!
I'M RIGHT BEHIND YOU!
SSSSSWOOOSSH

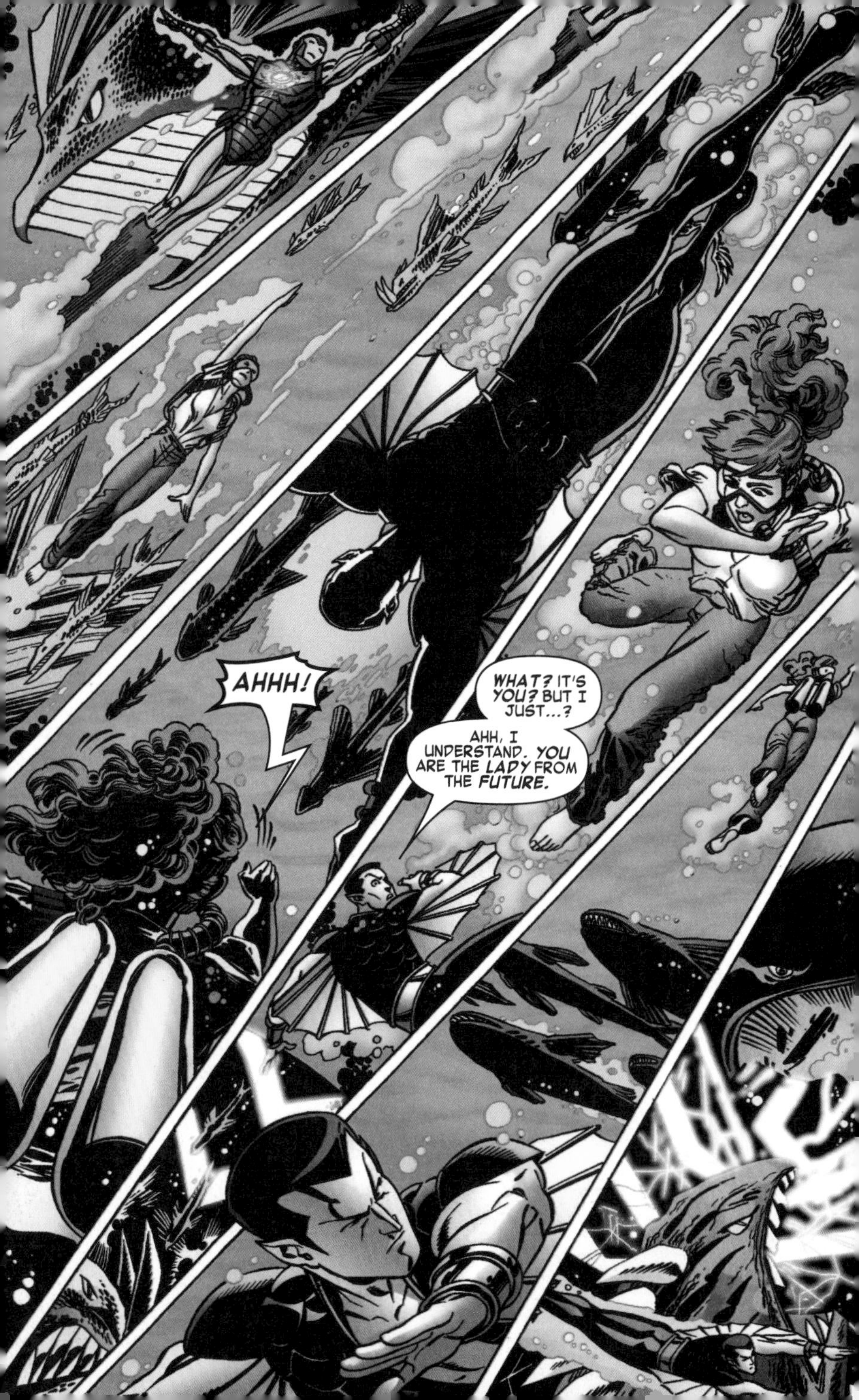
AHHH!
WHAT? IT'S YOU? BUT I JUST...?
AHH, I UNDERSTAND. YOU ARE THE LADY FROM THE FUTURE.

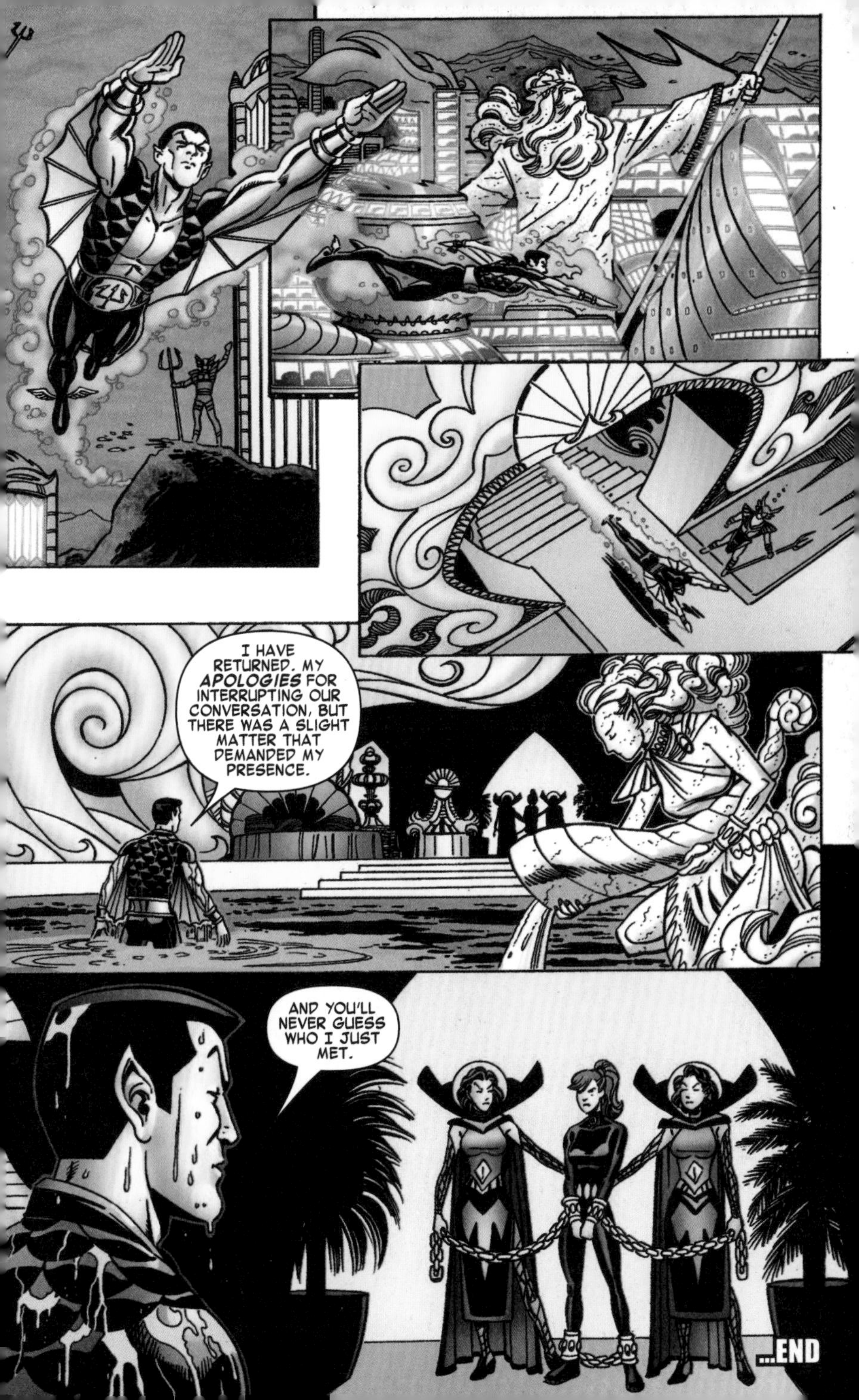
I HAVE RETURNED. MY APOLOGIES FOR INTERRUPTING OUR CONVERSATION, BUT THERE WAS A SLIGHT MATTER THAT DEMANDED MY PRESENCE.
AND YOU'LL NEVER GUESS WHO I JUST MET.
...END

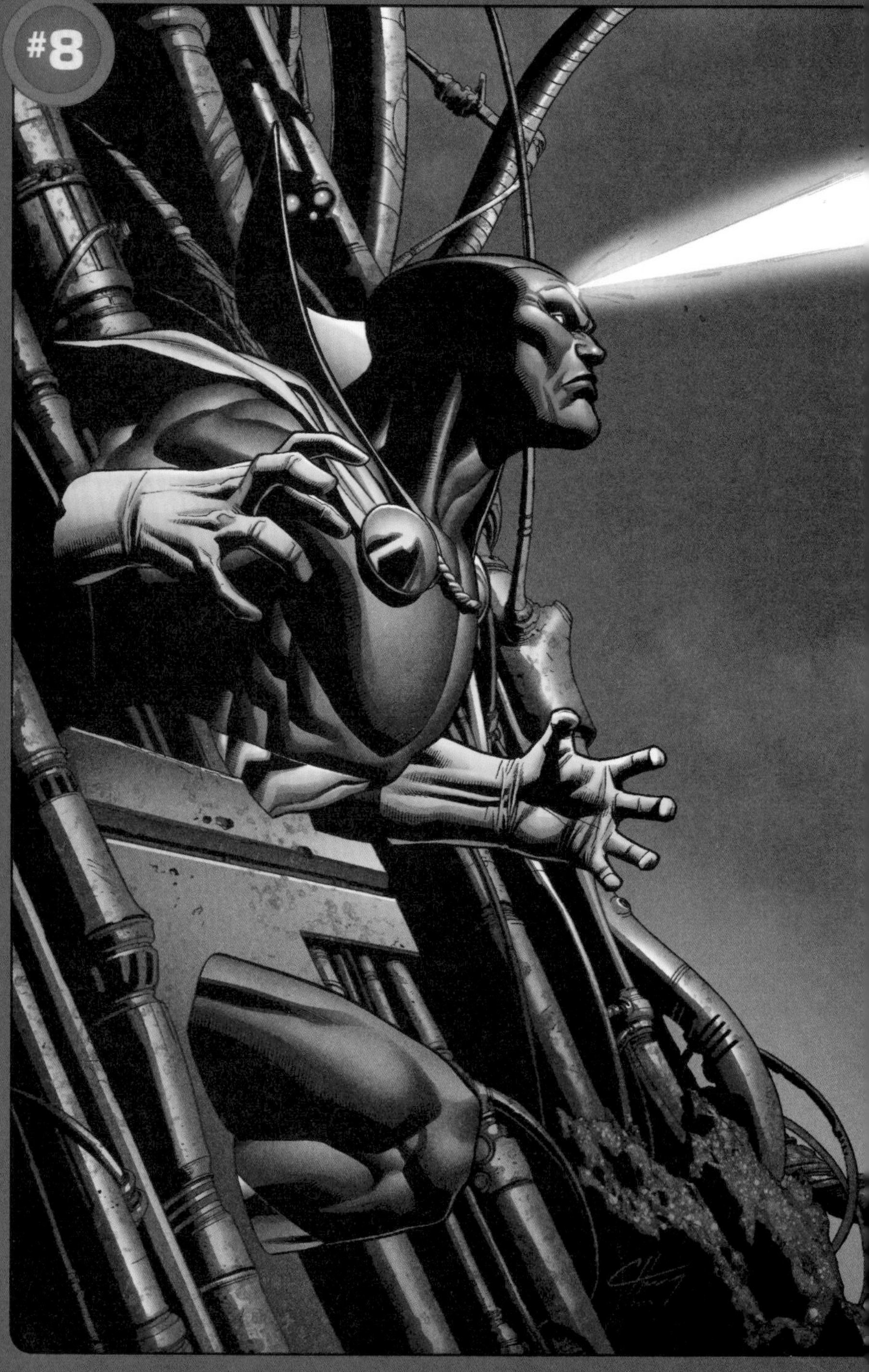
#8

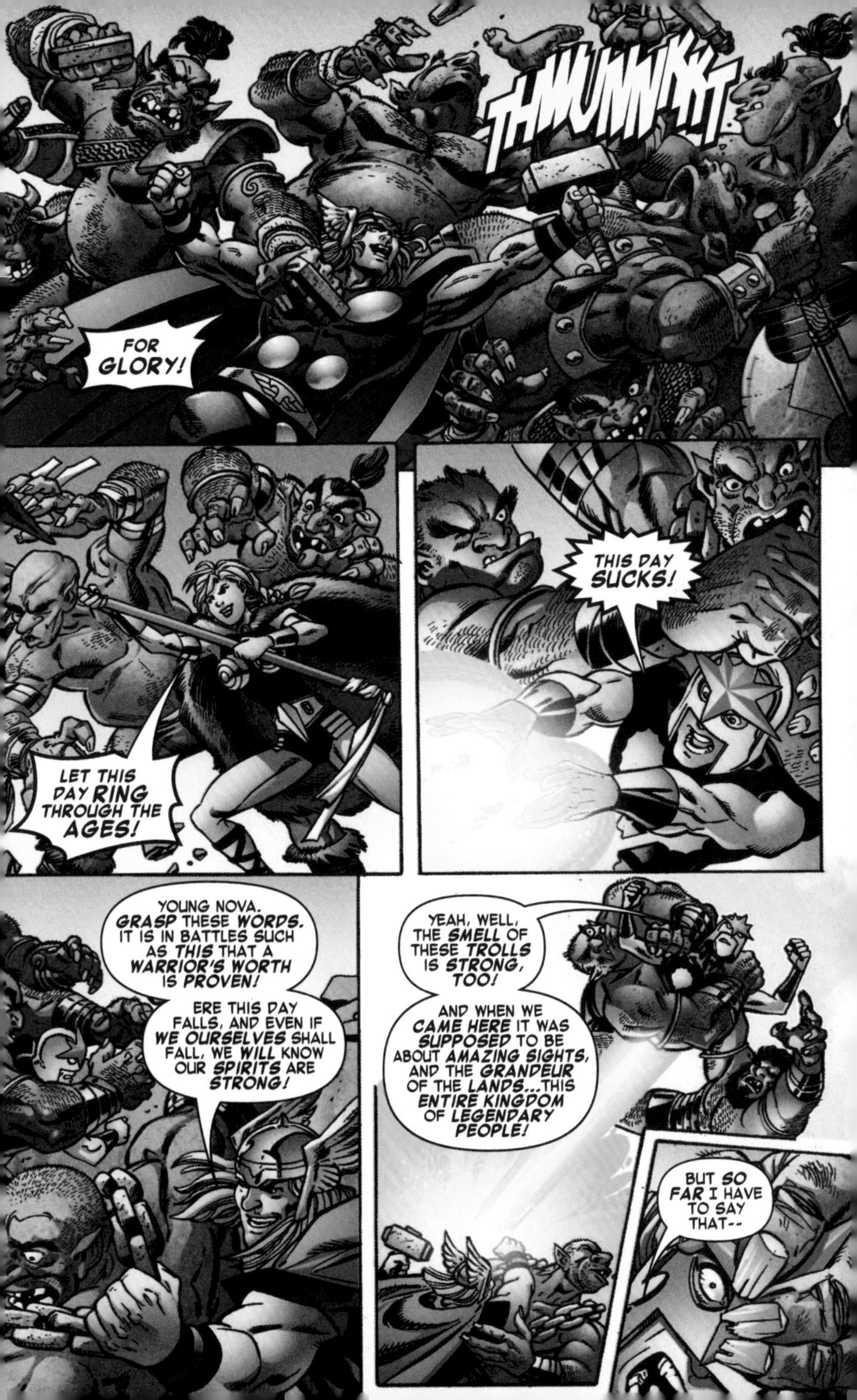
THMUNNKKT
FOR GLORY!
LET THIS DAY RING THROUGH THE AGES!
THIS DAY SUCKS!
YOUNG NOVA. GRASP THESE WORDS. IT IS IN BATTLES SUCH AS THIS THAT A WARRIOR'S WORTH IS PROVEN!
ERE THIS DAY FALLS, AND EVEN IF WE OURSELVES SHALL FALL, WE WILL KNOW OUR SPIRITS ARE STRONG!
YEAH, WELL, THE SMELL OF THESE TROLLS IS STRONG, TOO!
AND WHEN WE CAME HERE IT WAS SUPPOSED TO BE ABOUT AMAZING SIGHTS, AND THE GRANDEUR OF THE LANDS...THIS ENTIRE KINGDOM OF LEGENDARY PEOPLE!
BUT SO FAR I HAVE TO SAY THAT--

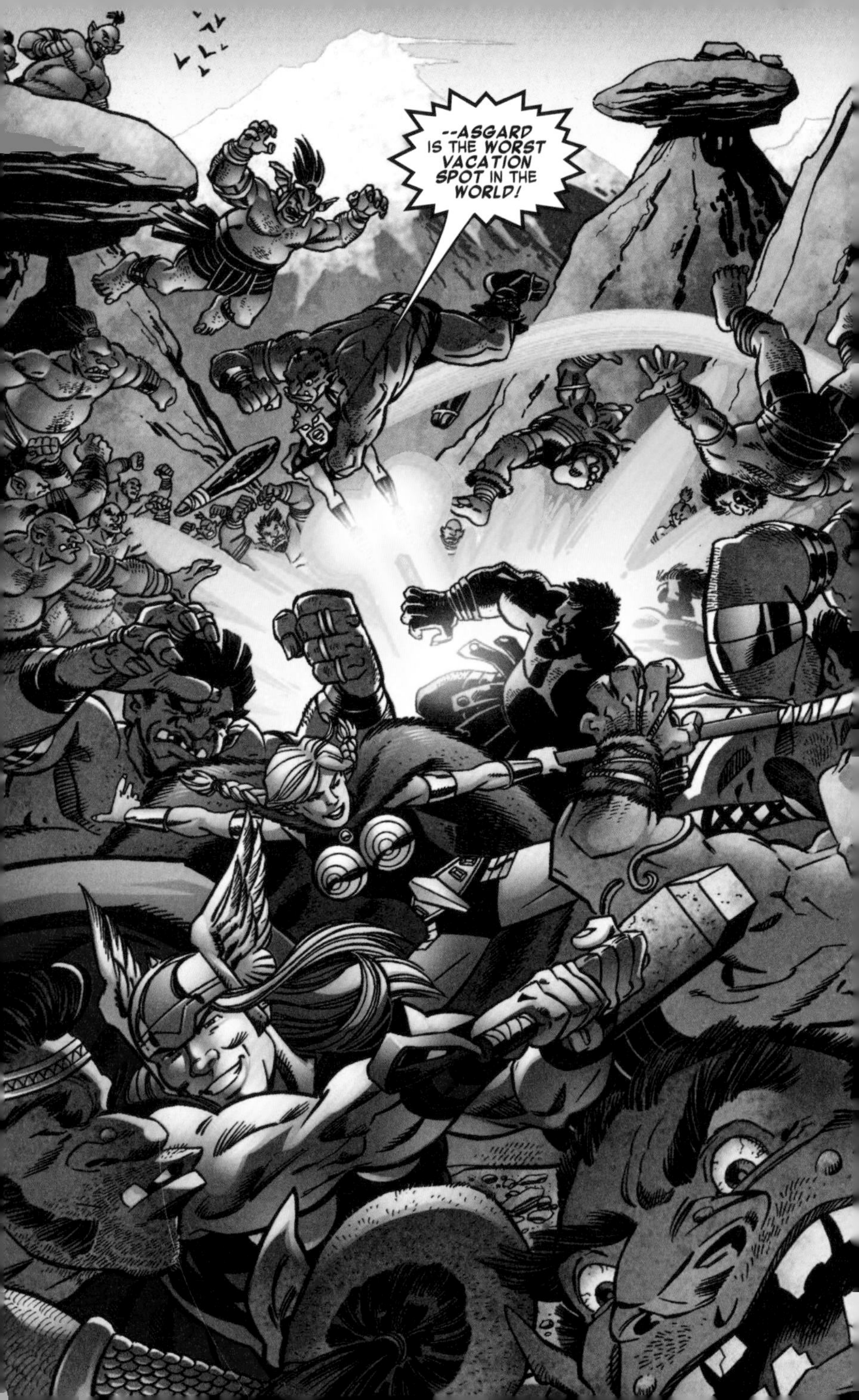
--ASGARD IS THE WORST VACATION SPOT IN THE WORLD!

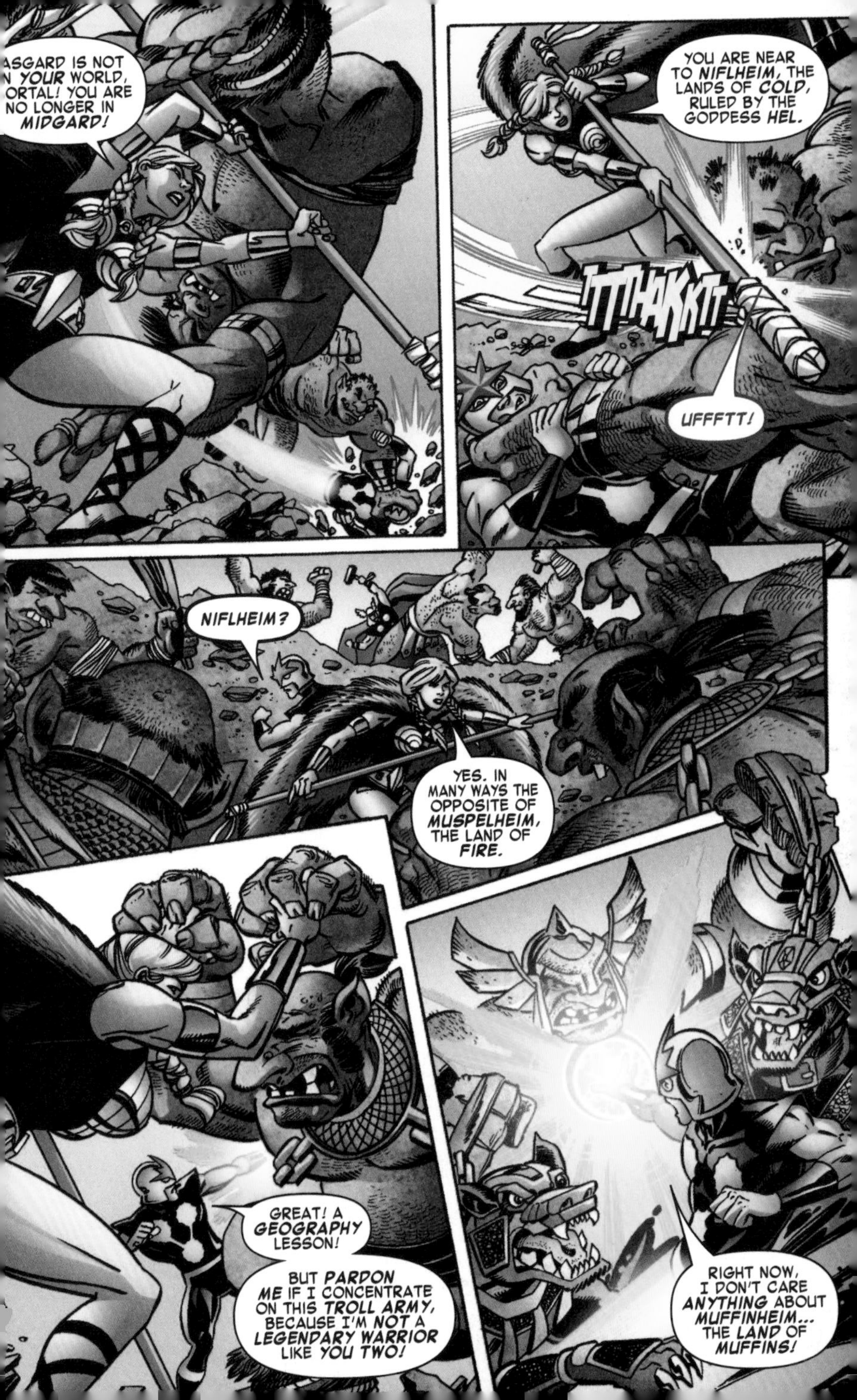
ASGARD IS NOT
N YOUR WORLD,
ORTAL! YOU ARE
NO LONGER IN
MIDGARD!
YOU ARE NEAR TO NIFLHEIM, THE LANDS OF COLD, RULED BY THE GODDESS HEL.
THAKK!
UFFFTT!
NIFLHEIM?
YES. IN MANY WAYS THE OPPOSITE OF MUSPELHEIM, THE LAND OF FIRE.
GREAT! A GEOGRAPHY LESSON!
BUT PARDON ME IF I CONCENTRATE ON THIS TROLL ARMY, BECAUSE I'M NOT A LEGENDARY WARRIOR LIKE YOU TWO!
RIGHT NOW, I DON'T CARE ANYTHING ABOUT MUFFINHEIM... THE LAND OF MUFFINS!

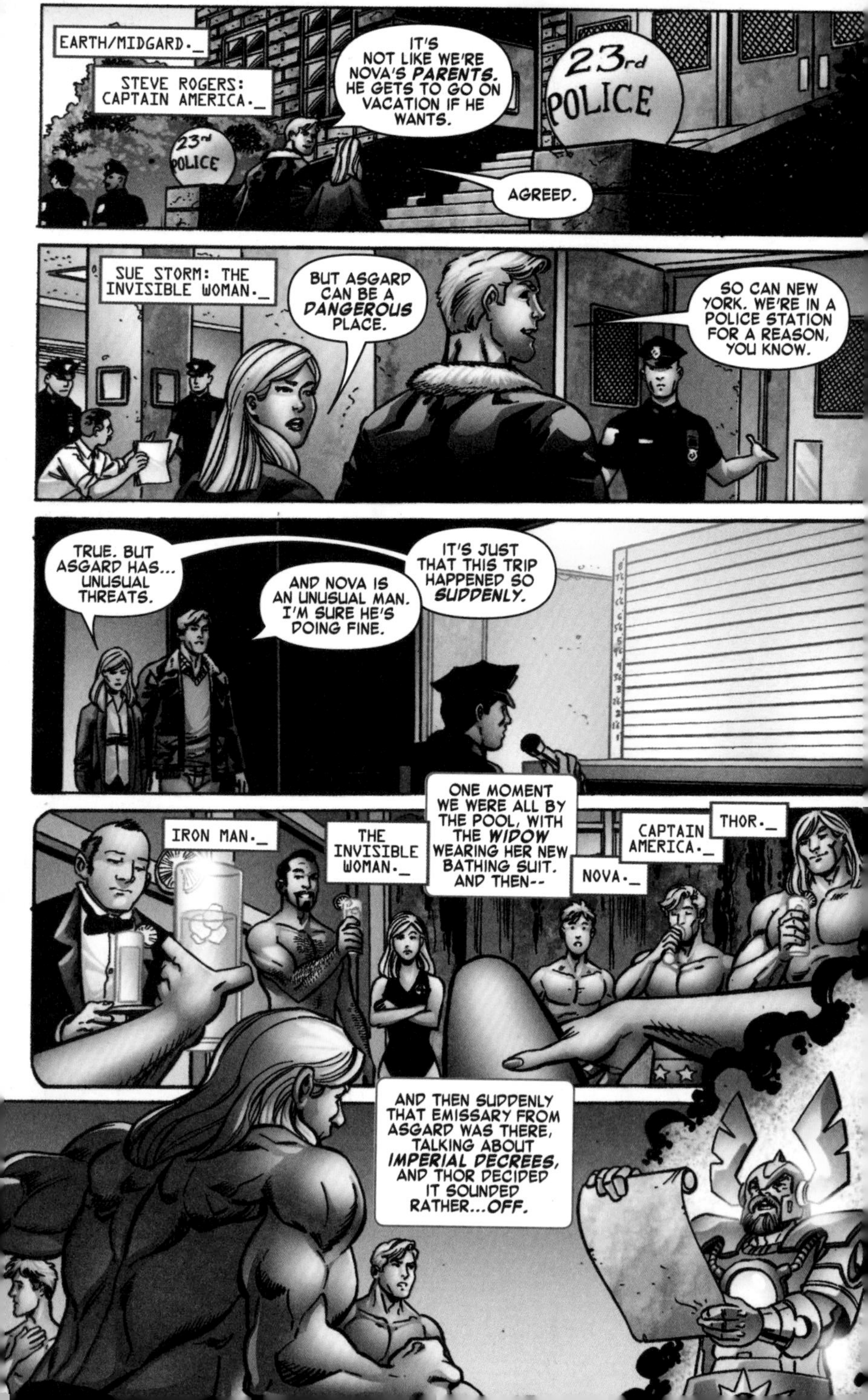
EARTH/MIDGARD._
STEVE ROGERS: CAPTAIN AMERICA._
IT'S NOT LIKE WE'RE NOVA'S PARENTS. HE GETS TO GO ON VACATION IF HE WANTS.
23rd POLICE
23rd POLICE
AGREED.
SUE STORM: THE INVISIBLE WOMAN._
BUT ASGARD CAN BE A DANGEROUS PLACE.
SO CAN NEW YORK. WE'RE IN A POLICE STATION FOR A REASON, YOU KNOW.
TRUE. BUT ASGARD HAS... UNUSUAL THREATS.
AND NOVA IS AN UNUSUAL MAN. I'M SURE HE'S DOING FINE.
IT'S JUST THAT THIS TRIP HAPPENED SO SUDDENLY.
ONE MOMENT WE WERE ALL BY THE POOL, WITH THE WIDOW WEARING HER NEW BATHING SUIT. AND THEN--
IRON MAN._
THE INVISIBLE WOMAN._
CAPTAIN AMERICA._
THOR._
NOVA._
AND THEN SUDDENLY THAT EMISSARY FROM ASGARD WAS THERE, TALKING ABOUT IMPERIAL DECREES, AND THOR DECIDED IT SOUNDED RATHER...OFF.

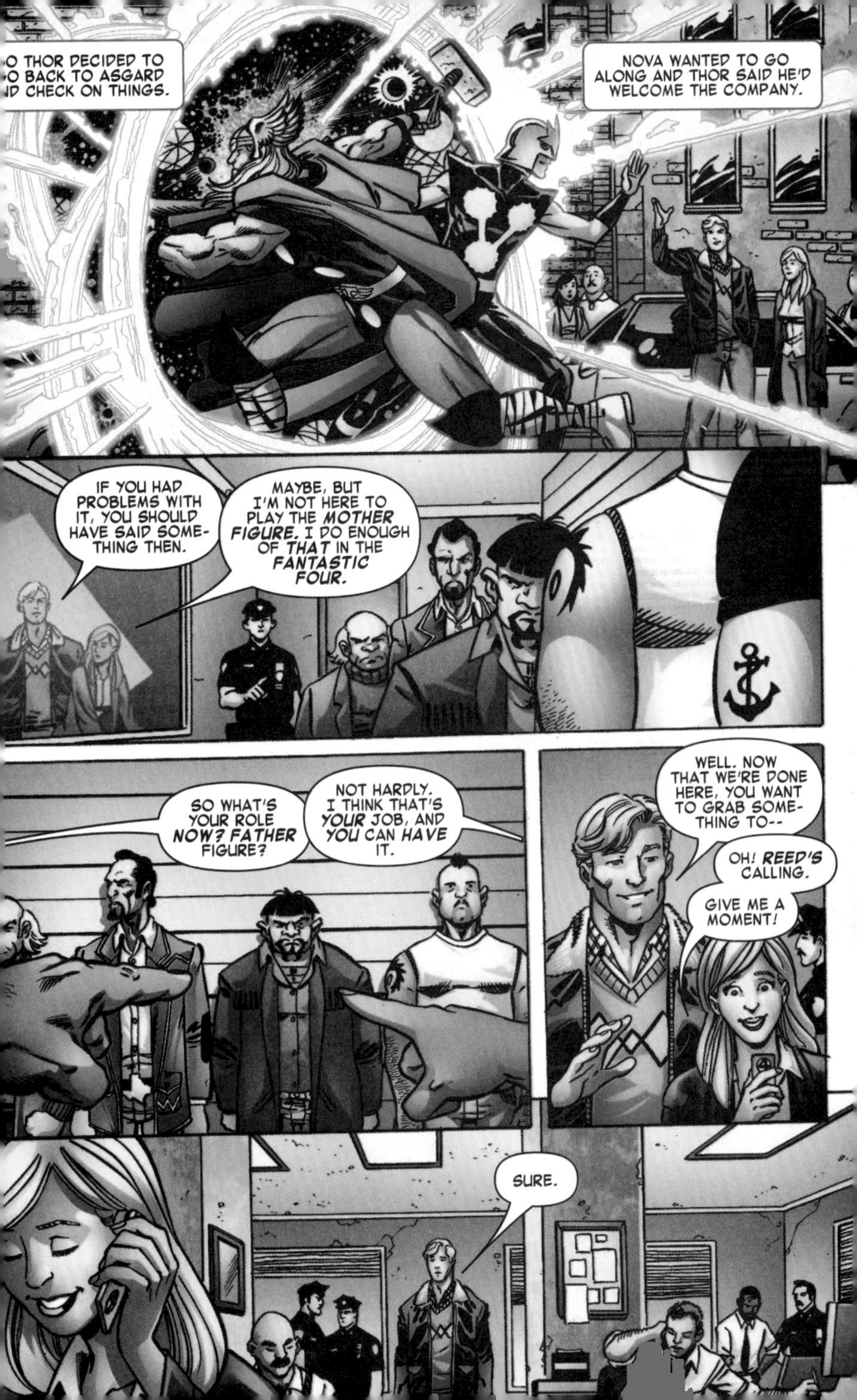
O THOR DECIDED TO O BACK TO ASGARD D CHECK ON THINGS.
NOVA WANTED TO GO ALONG AND THOR SAID HE'D WELCOME THE COMPANY.
IF YOU HAD PROBLEMS WITH IT, YOU SHOULD HAVE SAID SOME-THING THEN.
MAYBE, BUT I'M NOT HERE TO PLAY THE MOTHER FIGURE. I DO ENOUGH OF THAT IN THE FANTASTIC FOUR.
SO WHAT'S YOUR ROLE NOW? FATHER FIGURE?
NOT HARDLY. I THINK THAT'S YOUR JOB, AND YOU CAN HAVE IT.
WELL. NOW THAT WE'RE DONE HERE, YOU WANT TO GRAB SOME-THING TO--
OH! REED'S CALLING.
GIVE ME A MOMENT!
SURE.

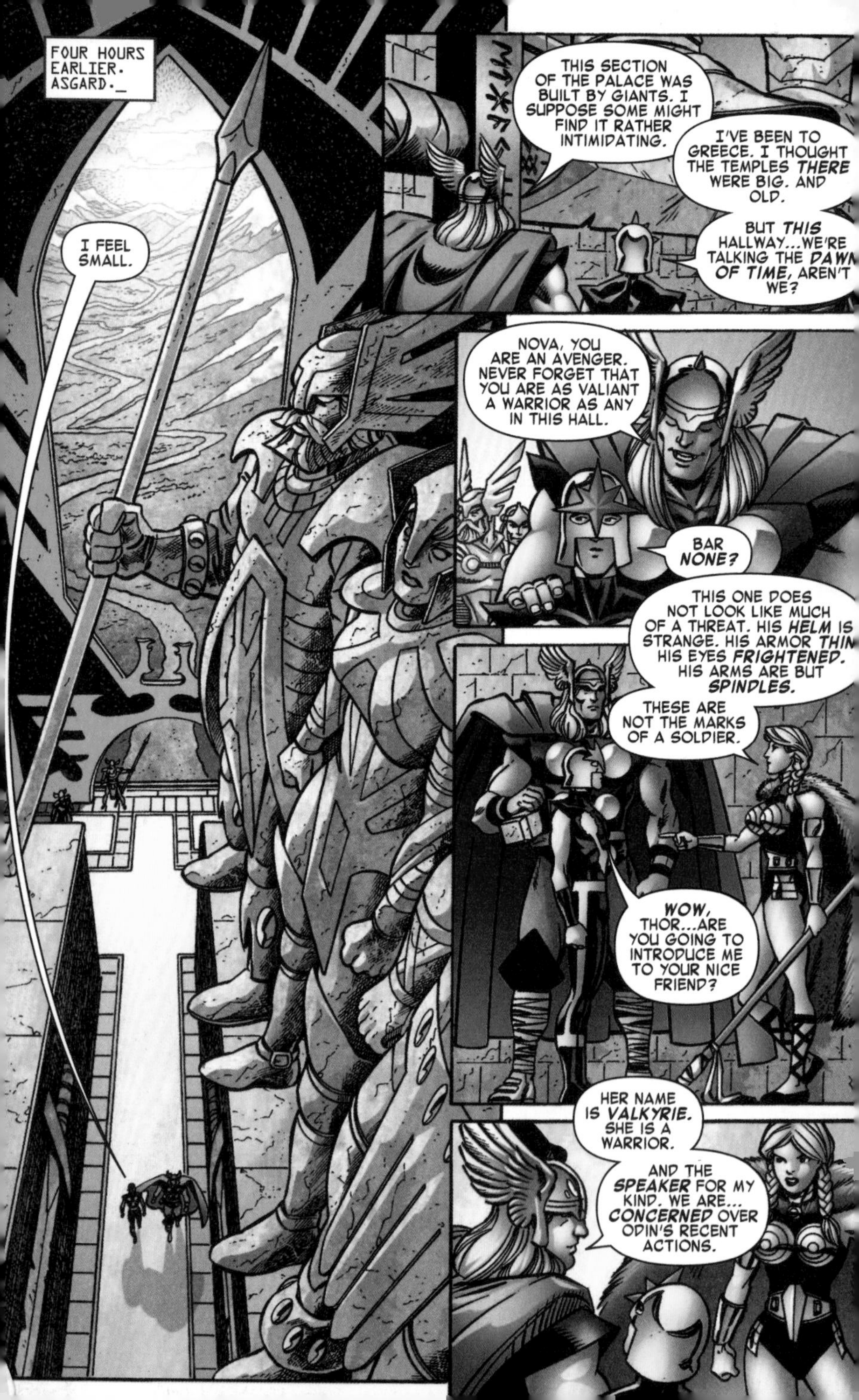
FOUR HOURS EARLIER. ASGARD._
I FEEL SMALL.
THIS SECTION OF THE PALACE WAS BUILT BY GIANTS. I SUPPOSE SOME MIGHT FIND IT RATHER INTIMIDATING.
I'VE BEEN TO GREECE. I THOUGHT THE TEMPLES THERE WERE BIG. AND OLD.
BUT THIS HALLWAY...WE'RE TALKING THE DAWN OF TIME, AREN'T WE?
NOVA, YOU ARE AN AVENGER. NEVER FORGET THAT YOU ARE AS VALIANT A WARRIOR AS ANY IN THIS HALL.
BAR NONE?
THIS ONE DOES NOT LOOK LIKE MUCH OF A THREAT. HIS HELM IS STRANGE. HIS ARMOR THIN. HIS EYES FRIGHTENED. HIS ARMS ARE BUT SPINDLES.
THESE ARE NOT THE MARKS OF A SOLDIER.
WOW, THOR...ARE YOU GOING TO INTRODUCE ME TO YOUR NICE FRIEND?
HER NAME IS VALKYRIE. SHE IS A WARRIOR.
AND THE SPEAKER FOR MY KIND. WE ARE... CONCERNED OVER ODIN'S RECENT ACTIONS.

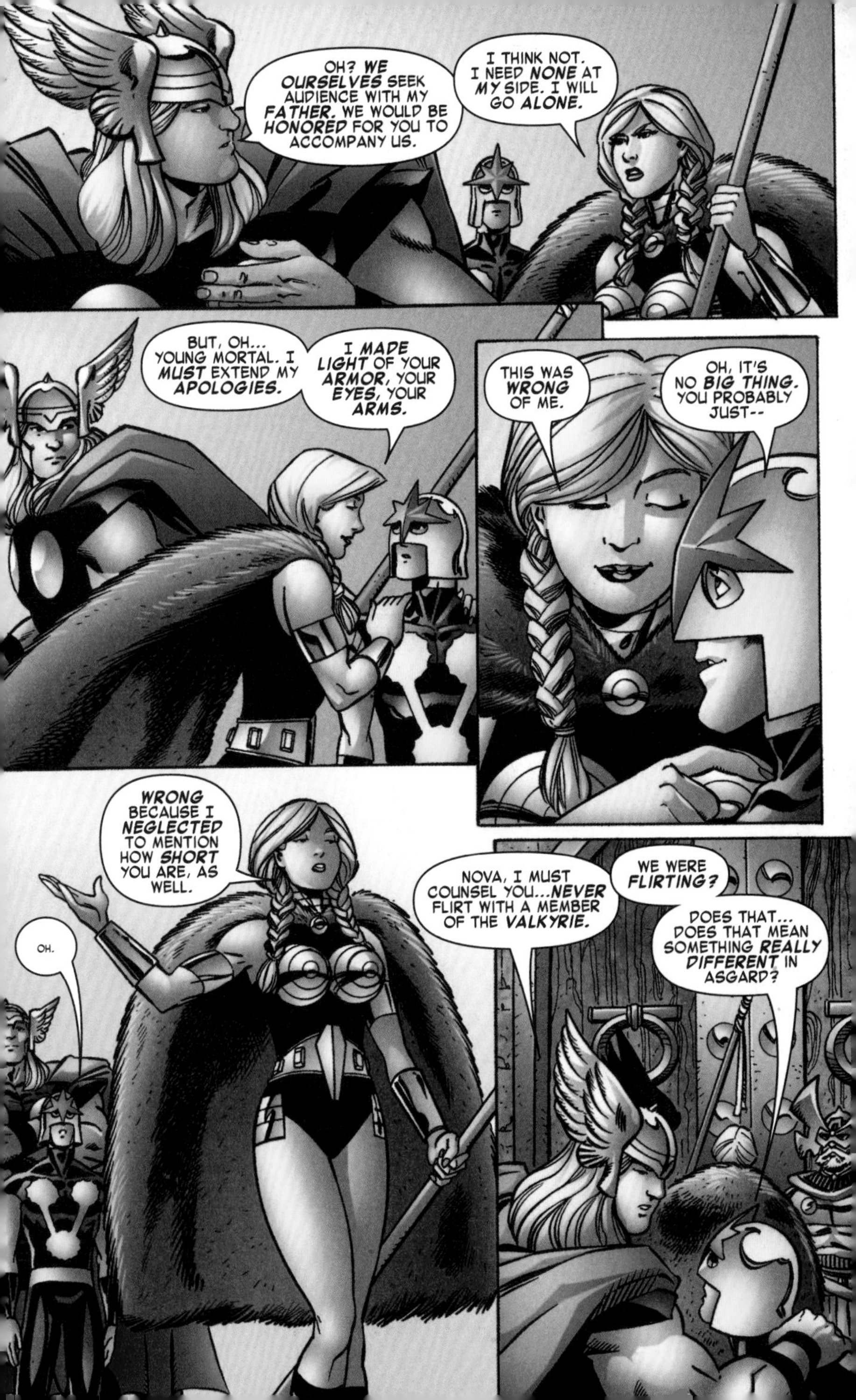
OH? WE OURSELVES SEEK AUDIENCE WITH MY FATHER. WE WOULD BE HONORED FOR YOU TO ACCOMPANY US.
I THINK NOT. I NEED NONE AT MY SIDE. I WILL GO ALONE.
BUT, OH... YOUNG MORTAL. I MUST EXTEND MY APOLOGIES.
I MADE LIGHT OF YOUR ARMOR, YOUR EYES, YOUR ARMS.
THIS WAS WRONG OF ME.
OH, IT'S NO BIG THING. YOU PROBABLY JUST--
WRONG BECAUSE I NEGLECTED TO MENTION HOW SHORT YOU ARE, AS WELL.
OH.
NOVA, I MUST COUNSEL YOU...NEVER FLIRT WITH A MEMBER OF THE VALKYRIE.
WE WERE FLIRTING?
DOES THAT... DOES THAT MEAN SOMETHING REALLY DIFFERENT IN ASGARD?

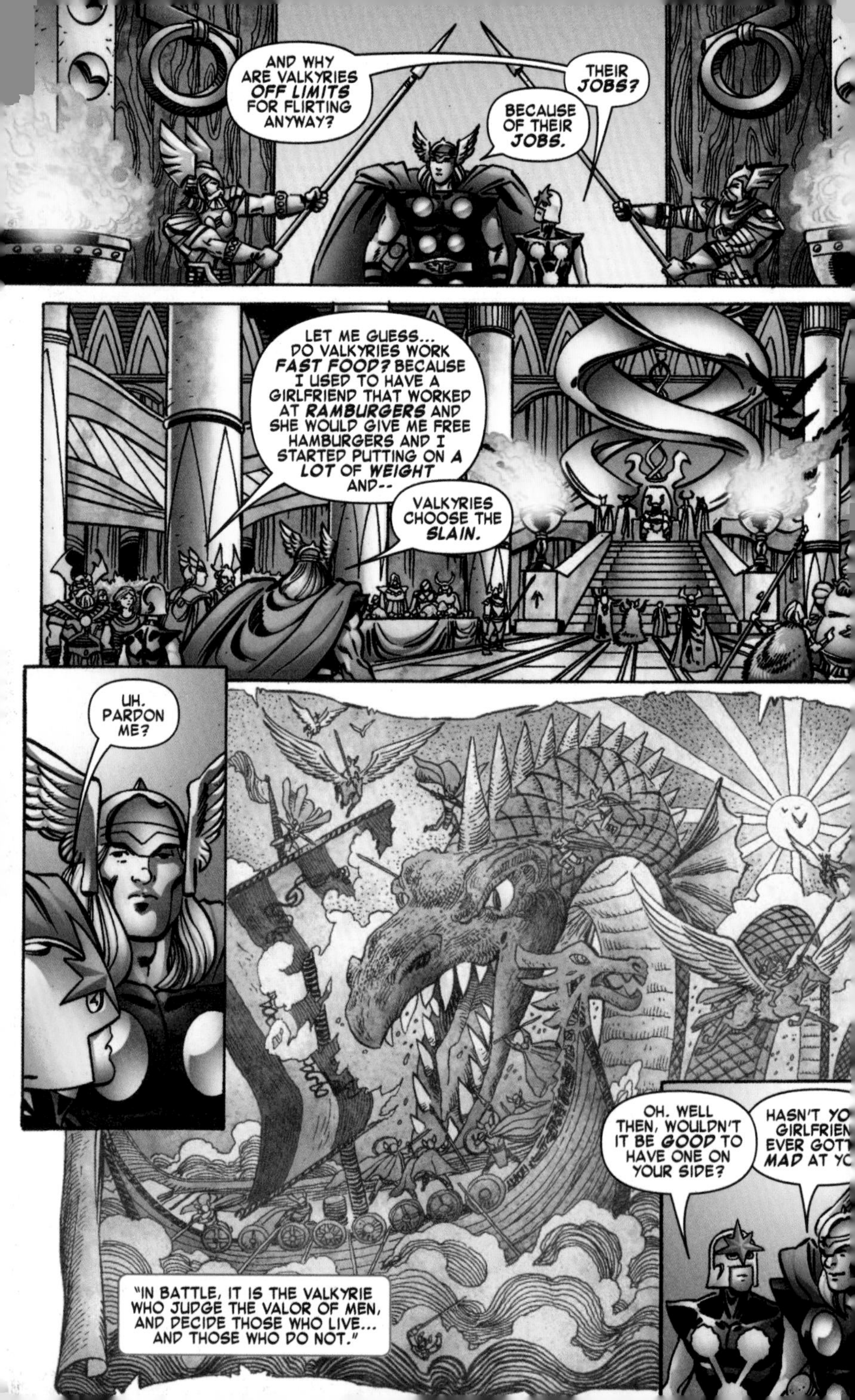
AND WHY ARE VALKYRIES OFF LIMITS FOR FLIRTING ANYWAY?
BECAUSE OF THEIR JOBS.
THEIR JOBS?
LET ME GUESS... DO VALKYRIES WORK FAST FOOD? BECAUSE I USED TO HAVE A GIRLFRIEND THAT WORKED AT RAMBURGERS AND SHE WOULD GIVE ME FREE HAMBURGERS AND I STARTED PUTTING ON A LOT OF WEIGHT AND--
VALKYRIES CHOOSE THE SLAIN.
UH. PARDON ME?
"IN BATTLE, IT IS THE VALKYRIE WHO JUDGE THE VALOR OF MEN, AND DECIDE THOSE WHO LIVE... AND THOSE WHO DO NOT."
OH. WELL THEN, WOULDN'T IT BE GOOD TO HAVE ONE ON YOUR SIDE?

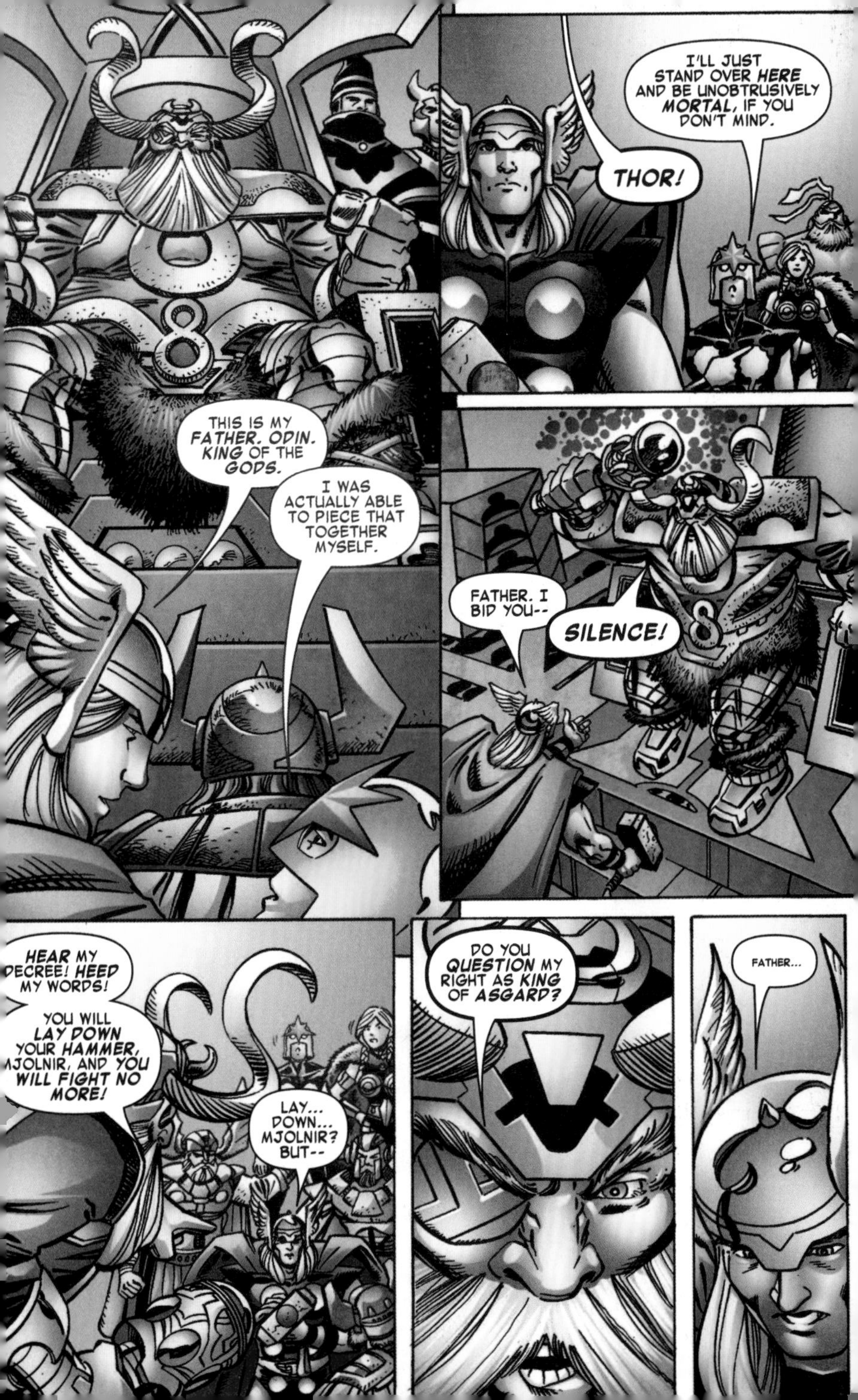

THOR!
I'LL JUST STAND OVER HERE AND BE UNOBTRUSIVELY MORTAL, IF YOU DON'T MIND.
THIS IS MY FATHER. ODIN. KING OF THE GODS.
I WAS ACTUALLY ABLE TO PIECE THAT TOGETHER MYSELF.
FATHER. I BID YOU--
SILENCE!
HEAR MY DECREE! HEED MY WORDS!
YOU WILL LAY DOWN YOUR HAMMER, MJOLNIR, AND YOU WILL FIGHT NO MORE!
LAY... DOWN... MJOLNIR? BUT--
DO YOU QUESTION MY RIGHT AS KING OF ASGARD?
FATHER...

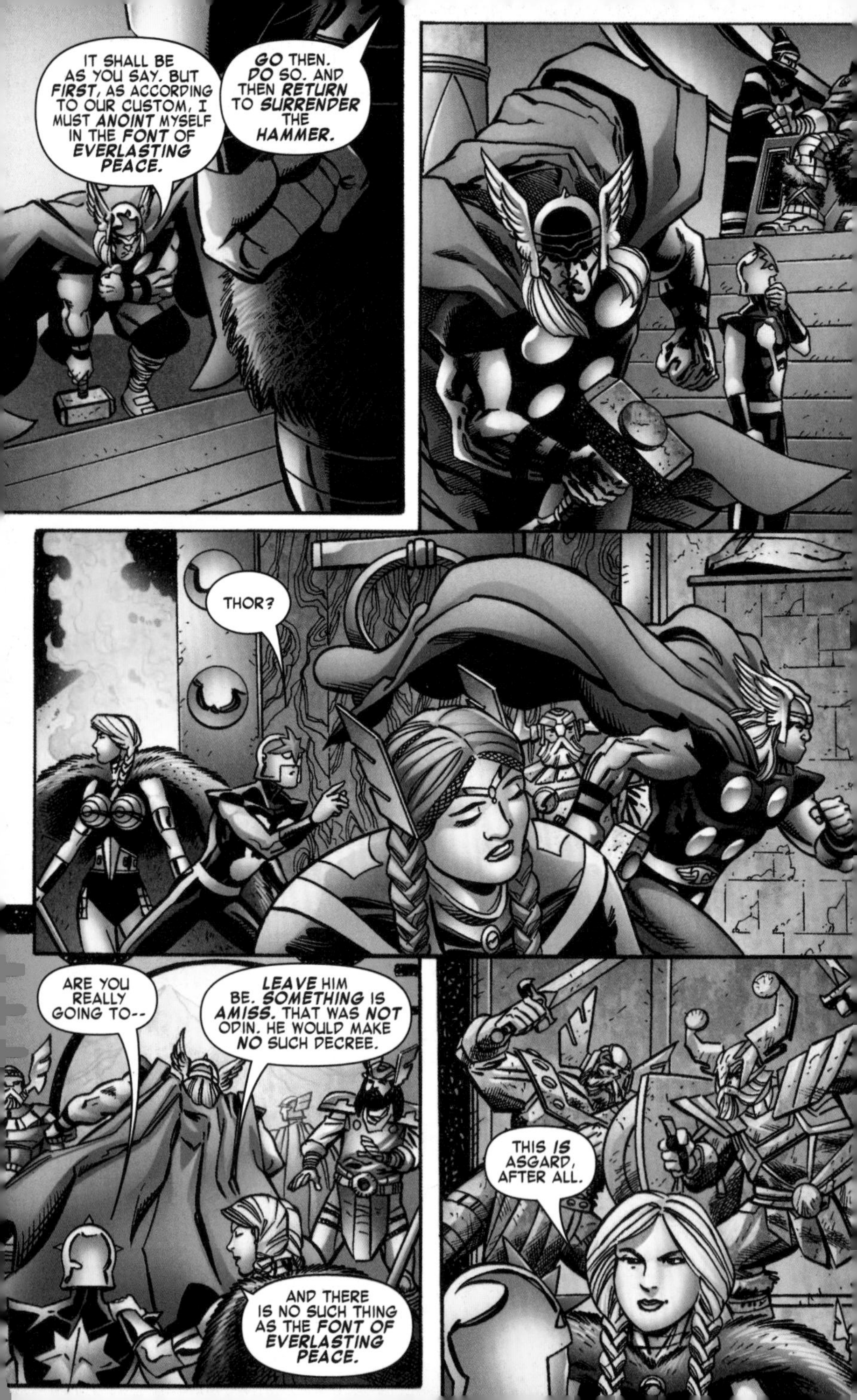
IT SHALL BE AS YOU SAY. BUT FIRST, AS ACCORDING TO OUR CUSTOM, I MUST ANOINT MYSELF IN THE FONT OF EVERLASTING PEACE.
GO THEN. DO SO. AND THEN RETURN TO SURRENDER THE HAMMER.
THOR?
ARE YOU REALLY GOING TO--
LEAVE HIM BE. SOMETHING IS AMISS. THAT WAS NOT ODIN. HE WOULD MAKE NO SUCH DECREE.
AND THERE IS NO SUCH THING AS THE FONT OF EVERLASTING PEACE.
THIS IS ASGARD, AFTER ALL.

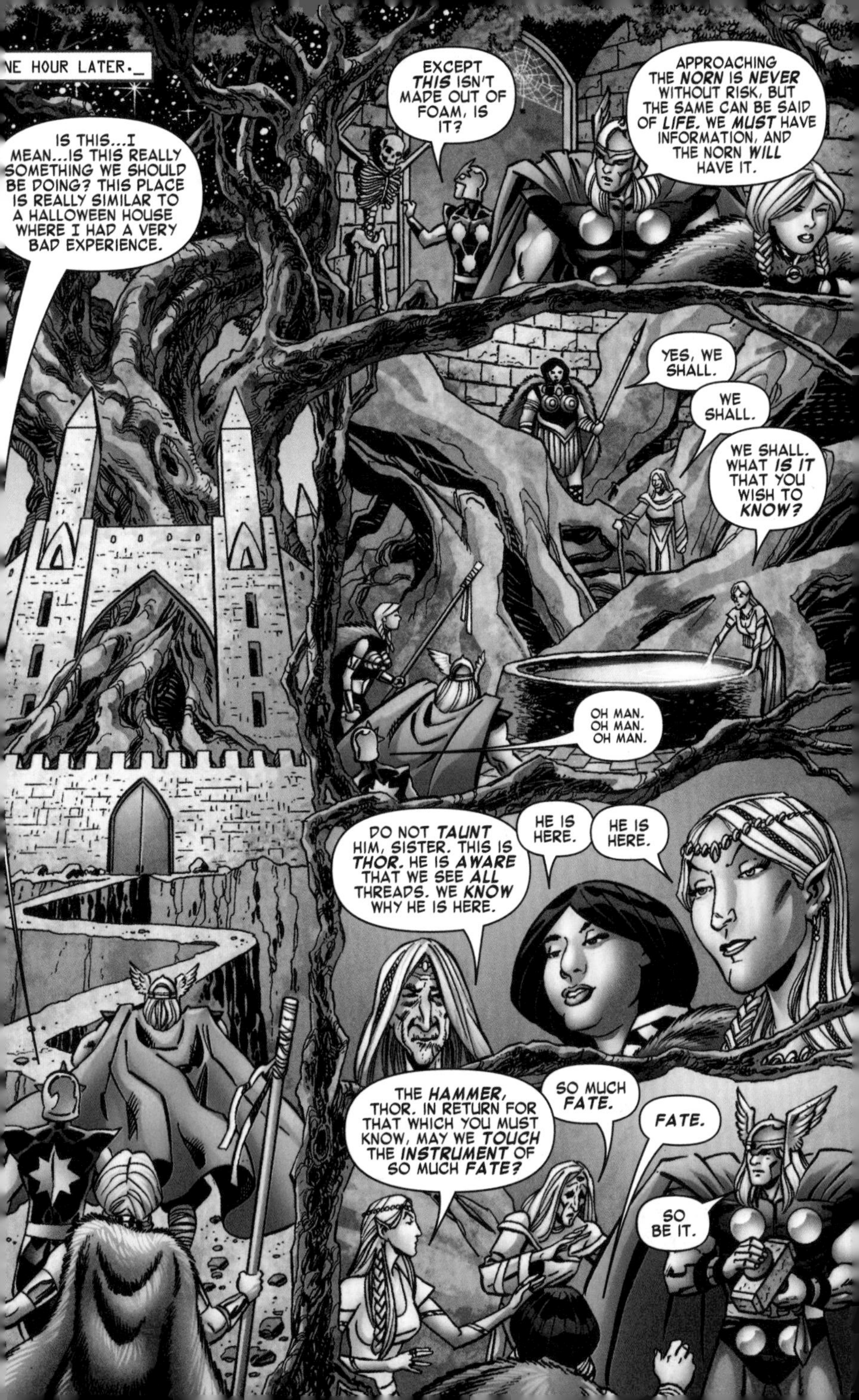
NE HOUR LATER._
IS THIS...I MEAN...IS THIS REALLY SOMETHING WE SHOULD BE DOING? THIS PLACE IS REALLY SIMILAR TO A HALLOWEEN HOUSE WHERE I HAD A VERY BAD EXPERIENCE.
EXCEPT THIS ISN'T MADE OUT OF FOAM, IS IT?
APPROACHING THE NORN IS NEVER WITHOUT RISK, BUT THE SAME CAN BE SAID OF LIFE. WE MUST HAVE INFORMATION, AND THE NORN WILL HAVE IT.
YES, WE SHALL.
WE SHALL.
WE SHALL. WHAT IS IT THAT YOU WISH TO KNOW?
OH MAN. OH MAN. OH MAN.
DO NOT TAUNT HIM, SISTER. THIS IS THOR. HE IS AWARE THAT WE SEE ALL THREADS. WE KNOW WHY HE IS HERE.
HE IS HERE.
HE IS HERE.
THE HAMMER, THOR. IN RETURN FOR THAT WHICH YOU MUST KNOW, MAY WE TOUCH THE INSTRUMENT OF SO MUCH FATE?
SO MUCH FATE.
FATE.
SO BE IT.

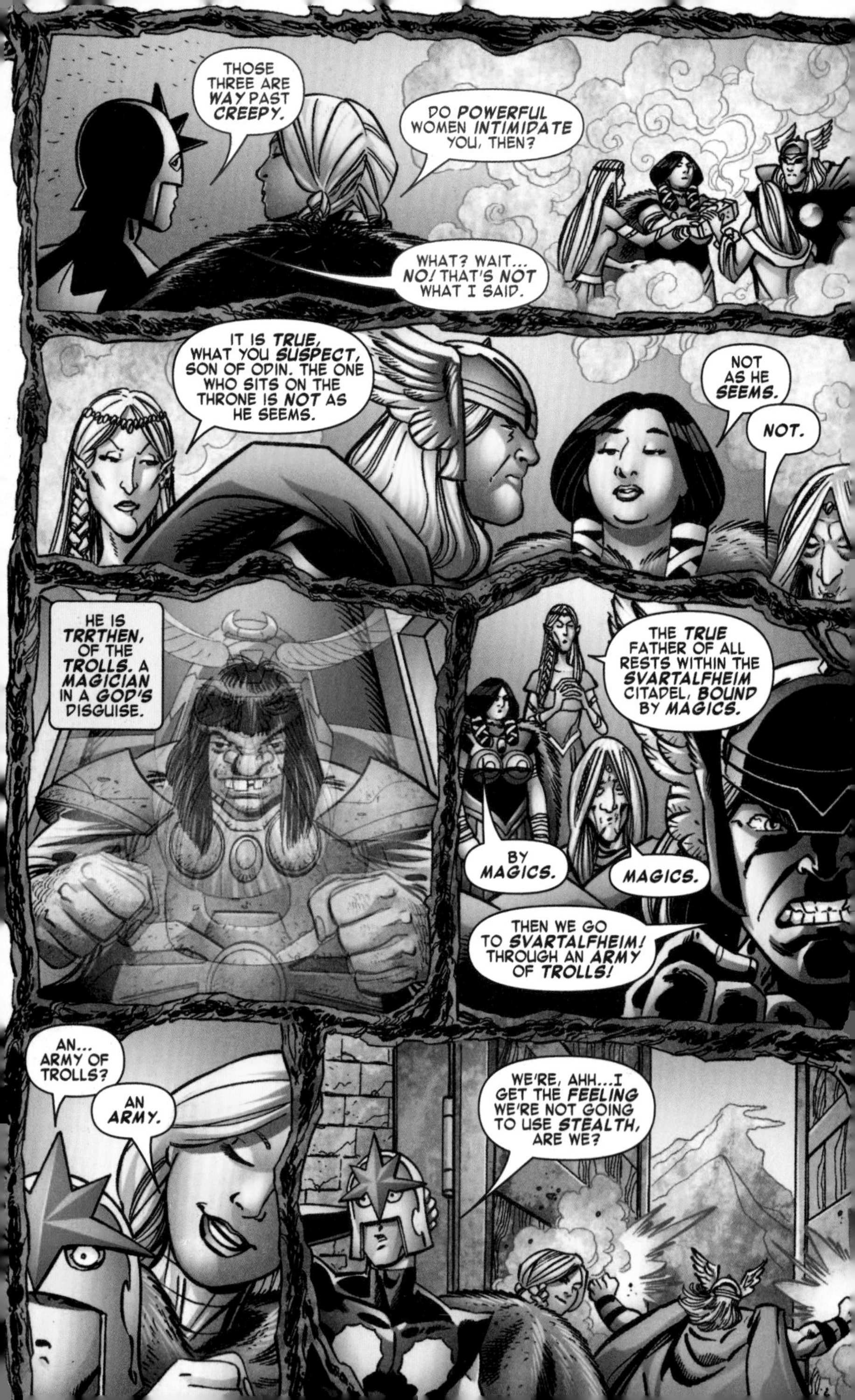
THOSE THREE ARE WAY PAST CREEPY.
DO POWERFUL WOMEN INTIMIDATE YOU, THEN?
WHAT? WAIT... NO! THAT'S NOT WHAT I SAID.
IT IS TRUE, WHAT YOU SUSPECT, SON OF ODIN. THE ONE WHO SITS ON THE THRONE IS NOT AS HE SEEMS.
NOT AS HE SEEMS.
NOT.
HE IS TRRTHEN, OF THE TROLLS. A MAGICIAN IN A GOD'S DISGUISE.
THE TRUE FATHER OF ALL RESTS WITHIN THE SVARTALFHEIM CITADEL, BOUND BY MAGICS.
BY MAGICS.
MAGICS.
THEN WE GO TO SVARTALFHEIM! THROUGH AN ARMY OF TROLLS!
AN... ARMY OF TROLLS?
AN ARMY.
WE'RE, AHH...I GET THE FEELING WE'RE NOT GOING TO USE STEALTH, ARE WE?

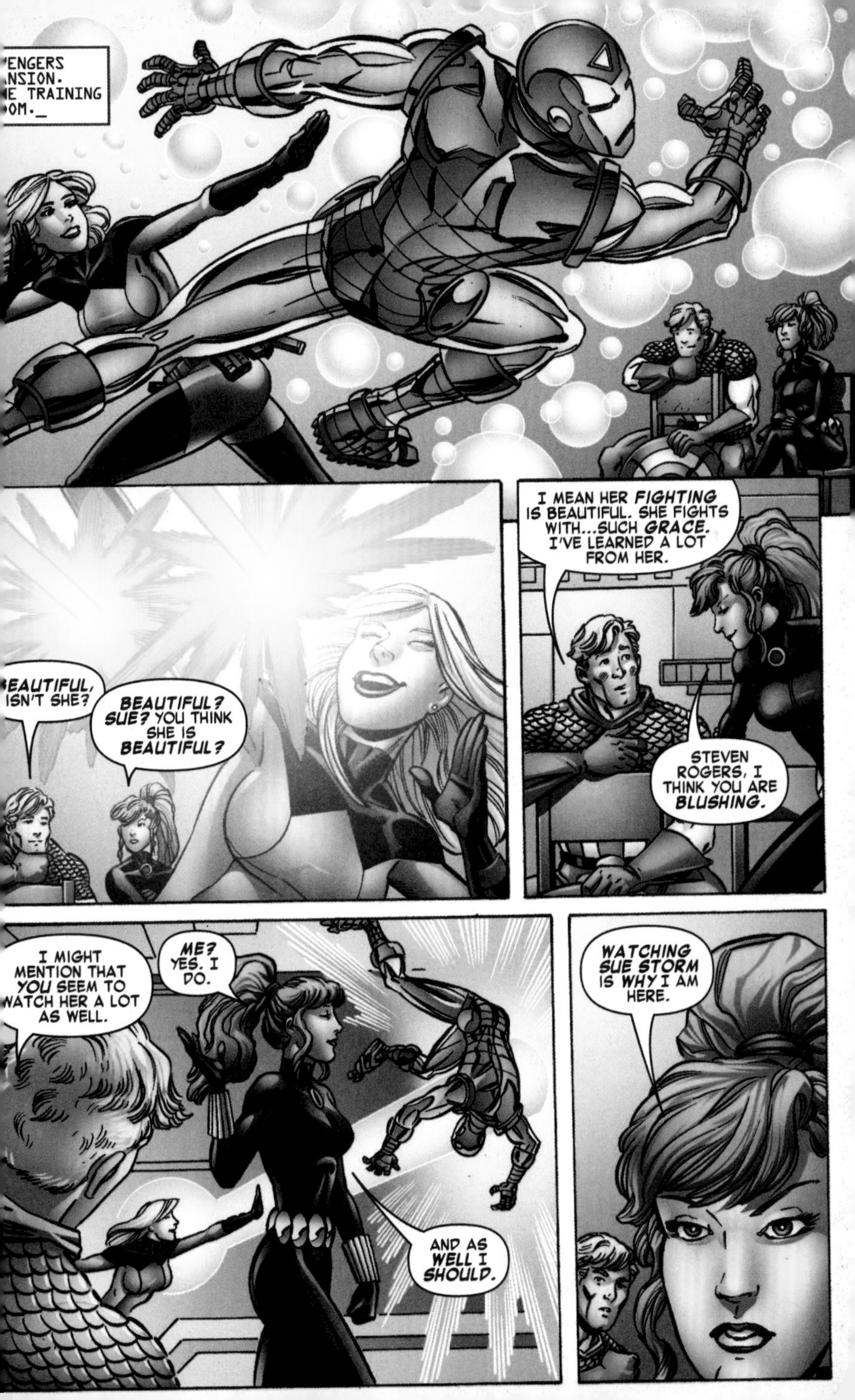

ENGERS
NSION.
E TRAINING
OM._
EAUTIFUL, ISN'T SHE?
BEAUTIFUL? SUE? YOU THINK SHE IS BEAUTIFUL?
I MEAN HER FIGHTING IS BEAUTIFUL. SHE FIGHTS WITH...SUCH GRACE. I'VE LEARNED A LOT FROM HER.
STEVEN ROGERS, I THINK YOU ARE BLUSHING.
I MIGHT MENTION THAT YOU SEEM TO WATCH HER A LOT AS WELL.
ME? YES. I DO.
AND AS WELL I SHOULD.
WATCHING SUE STORM IS WHY I AM HERE.

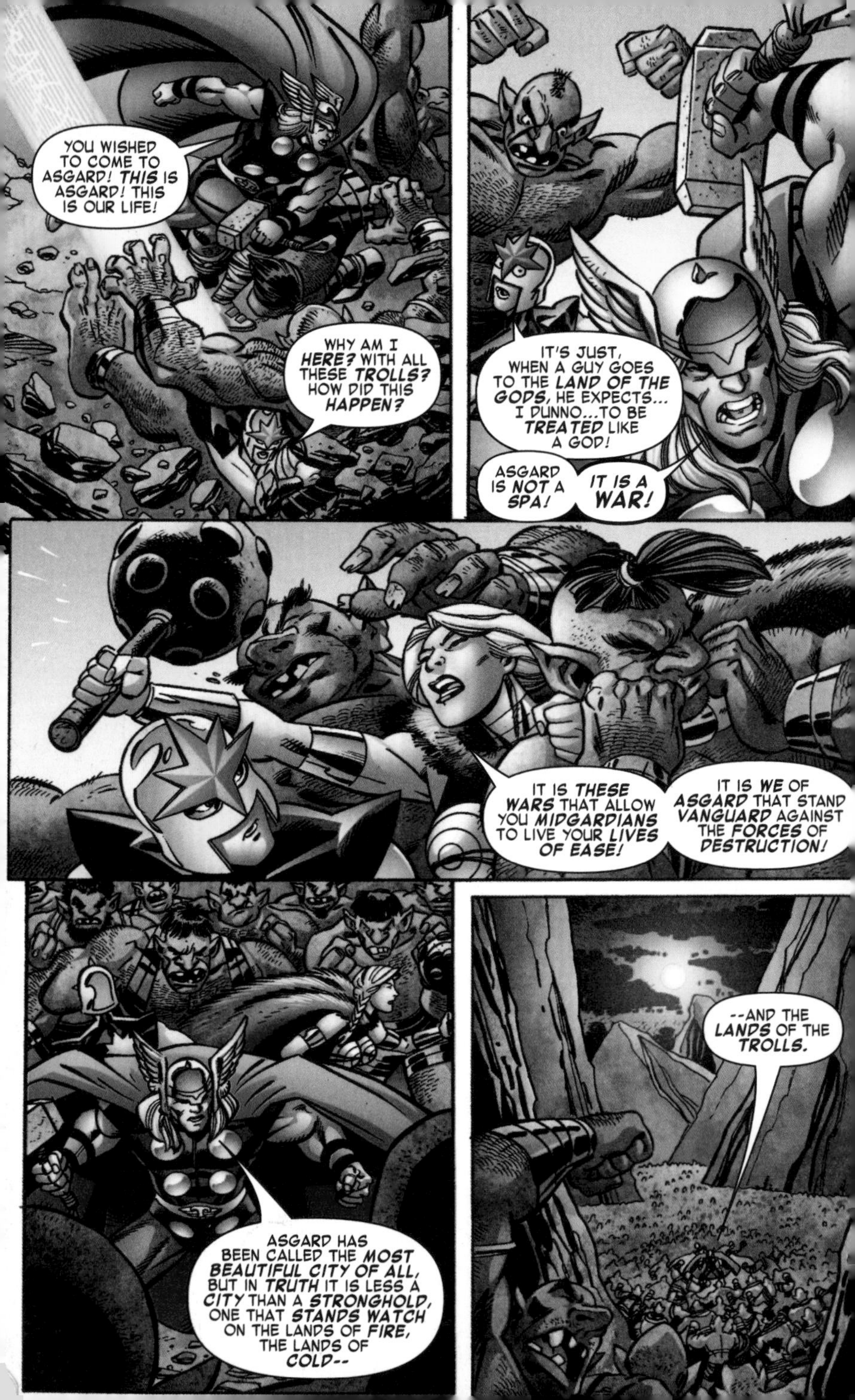
YOU WISHED TO COME TO ASGARD! THIS IS ASGARD! THIS IS OUR LIFE!
WHY AM I HERE? WITH ALL THESE TROLLS? HOW DID THIS HAPPEN?
IT'S JUST, WHEN A GUY GOES TO THE LAND OF THE GODS, HE EXPECTS... I DUNNO...TO BE TREATED LIKE A GOD!
ASGARD IS NOT A SPA!
IT IS A WAR!
IT IS THESE WARS THAT ALLOW YOU MIDGARDIANS TO LIVE YOUR LIVES OF EASE!
IT IS WE OF ASGARD THAT STAND VANGUARD AGAINST THE FORCES OF DESTRUCTION!
ASGARD HAS BEEN CALLED THE MOST BEAUTIFUL CITY OF ALL, BUT IN TRUTH IT IS LESS A CITY THAN A STRONGHOLD, ONE THAT STANDS WATCH ON THE LANDS OF FIRE, THE LANDS OF COLD--
--AND THE LANDS OF THE TROLLS.

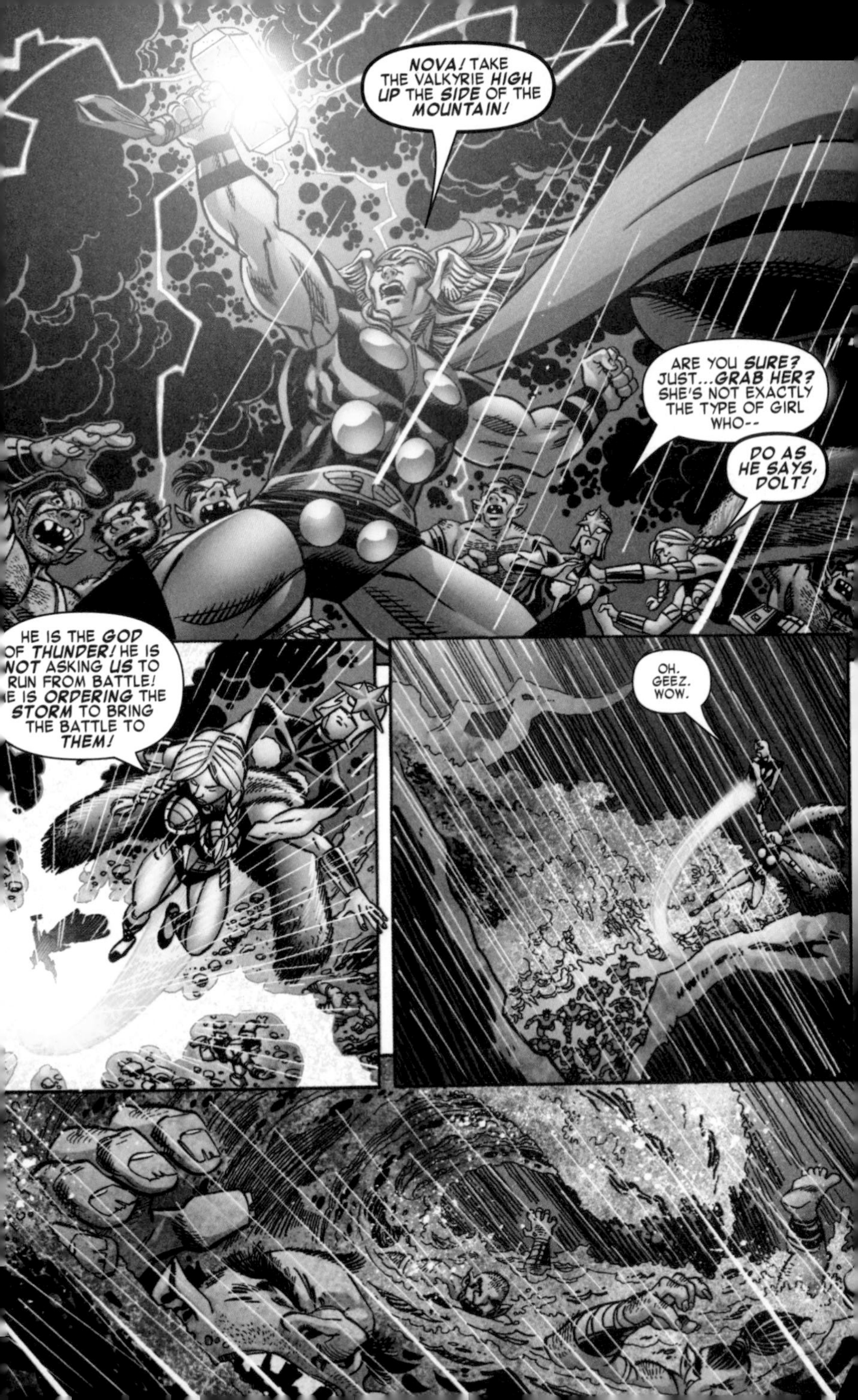
NOVA! TAKE THE VALKYRIE HIGH UP THE SIDE OF THE MOUNTAIN!
ARE YOU SURE? JUST...GRAB HER? SHE'S NOT EXACTLY THE TYPE OF GIRL WHO--
DO AS HE SAYS, DOLT!
HE IS THE GOD OF THUNDER! HE IS NOT ASKING US TO RUN FROM BATTLE! E IS ORDERING THE STORM TO BRING THE BATTLE TO THEM!
OH. GEEZ. WOW.

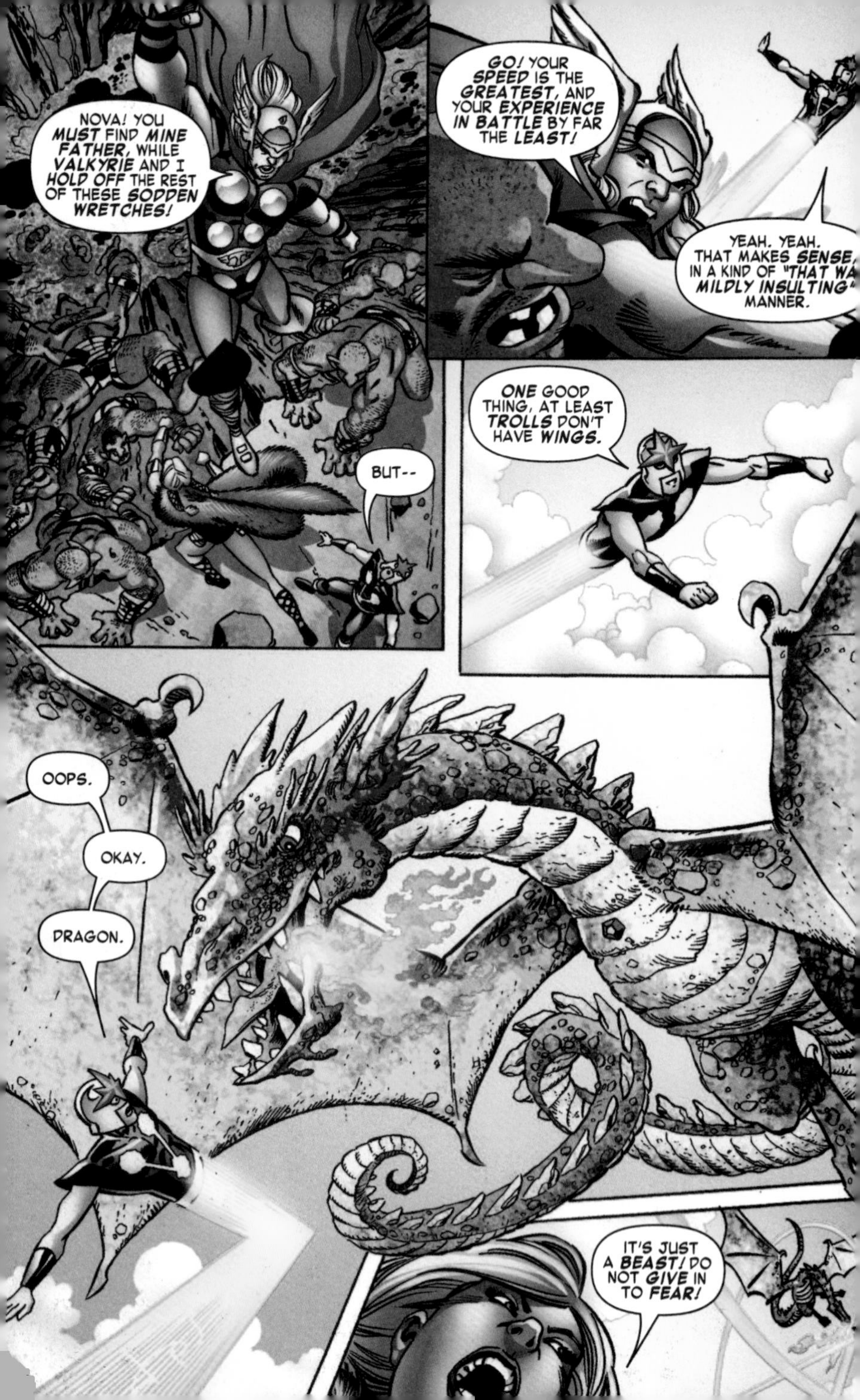

NOVA! YOU MUST FIND MINE FATHER, WHILE VALKYRIE AND I HOLD OFF THE REST OF THESE SODDEN WRETCHES!
BUT--
GO! YOUR SPEED IS THE GREATEST, AND YOUR EXPERIENCE IN BATTLE BY FAR THE LEAST!
YEAH. YEAH. THAT MAKES SENSE, IN A KIND OF "THAT WA MILDLY INSULTING" MANNER.
ONE GOOD THING, AT LEAST TROLLS DON'T HAVE WINGS.
OOPS.
OKAY.
DRAGON.
IT'S JUST A BEAST! DO NOT GIVE IN TO FEAR!

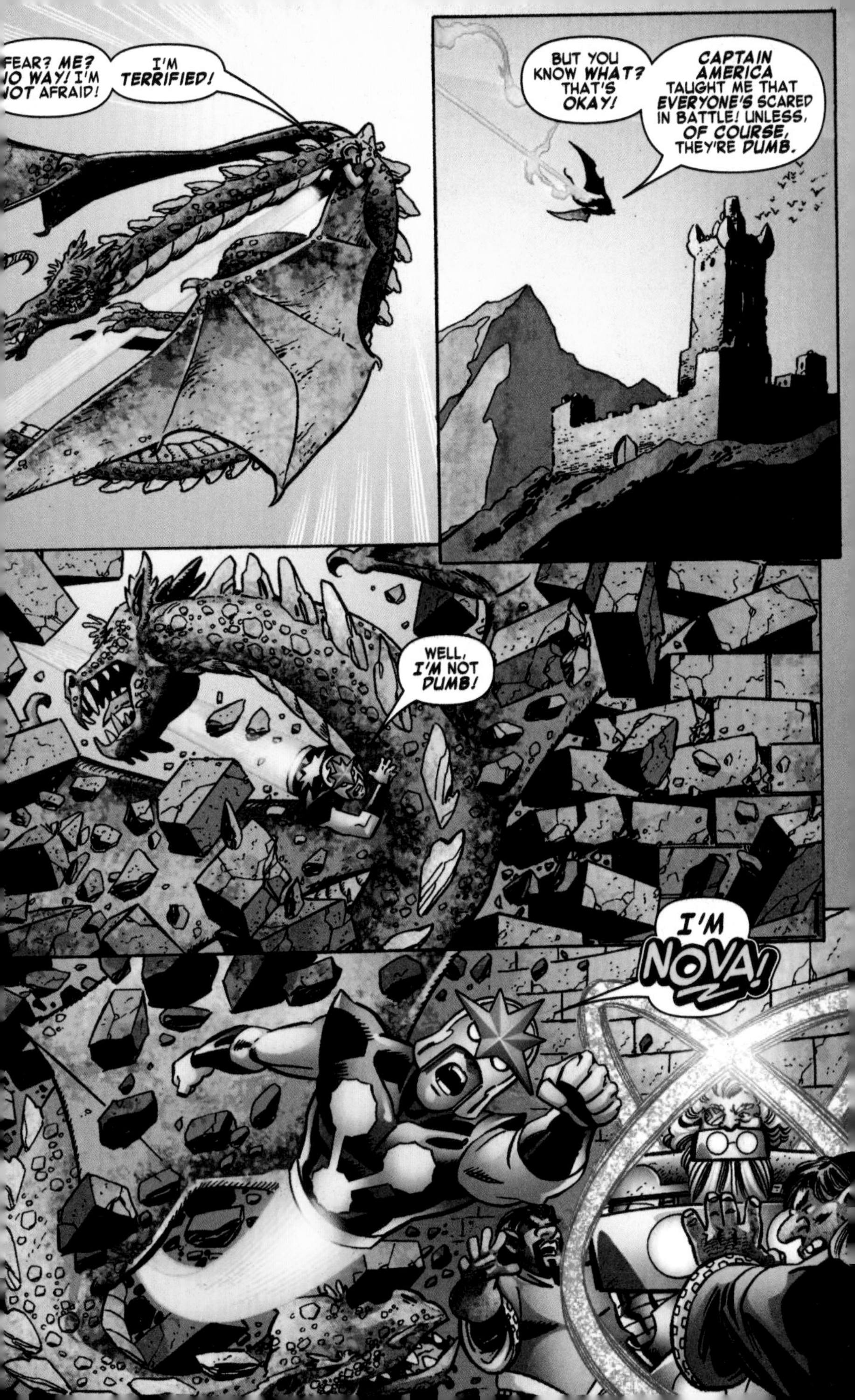
FEAR? ME? NO WAY! I'M NOT AFRAID!
I'M TERRIFIED!
BUT YOU KNOW WHAT? THAT'S OKAY!
CAPTAIN AMERICA TAUGHT ME THAT EVERYONE'S SCARED IN BATTLE! UNLESS, OF COURSE, THEY'RE DUMB.
WELL, I'M NOT DUMB!
I'M NOVA!

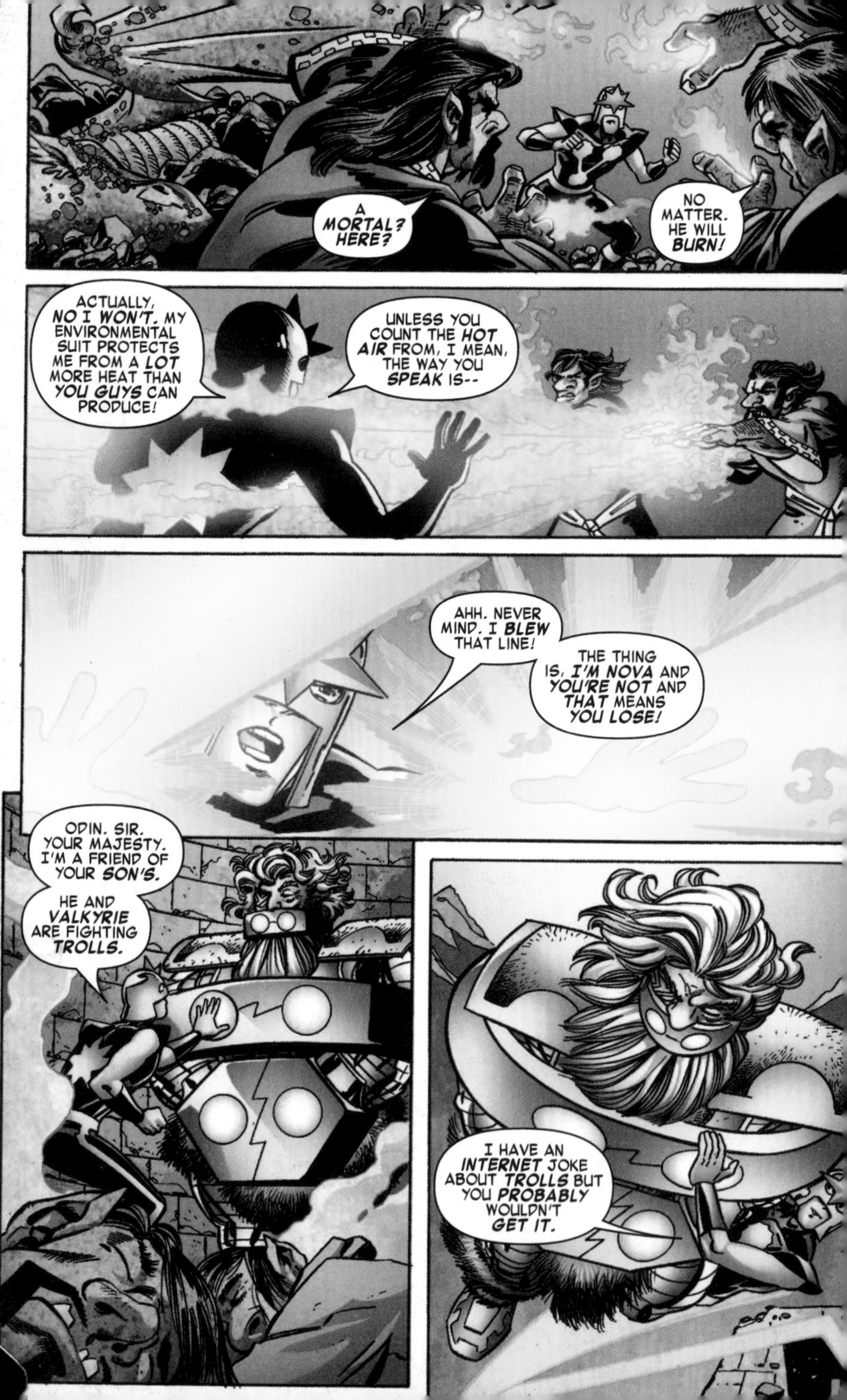
A MORTAL? HERE?
NO MATTER. HE WILL BURN!
ACTUALLY, NO I WON'T. MY ENVIRONMENTAL SUIT PROTECTS ME FROM A LOT MORE HEAT THAN YOU GUYS CAN PRODUCE!
UNLESS YOU COUNT THE HOT AIR FROM, I MEAN, THE WAY YOU SPEAK IS--
AHH. NEVER MIND. I BLEW THAT LINE!
THE THING IS, I'M NOVA AND YOU'RE NOT AND THAT MEANS YOU LOSE!
ODIN. SIR. YOUR MAJESTY. I'M A FRIEND OF YOUR SON'S.
HE AND VALKYRIE ARE FIGHTING TROLLS.
I HAVE AN INTERNET JOKE ABOUT TROLLS BUT YOU PROBABLY WOULDN'T GET IT.

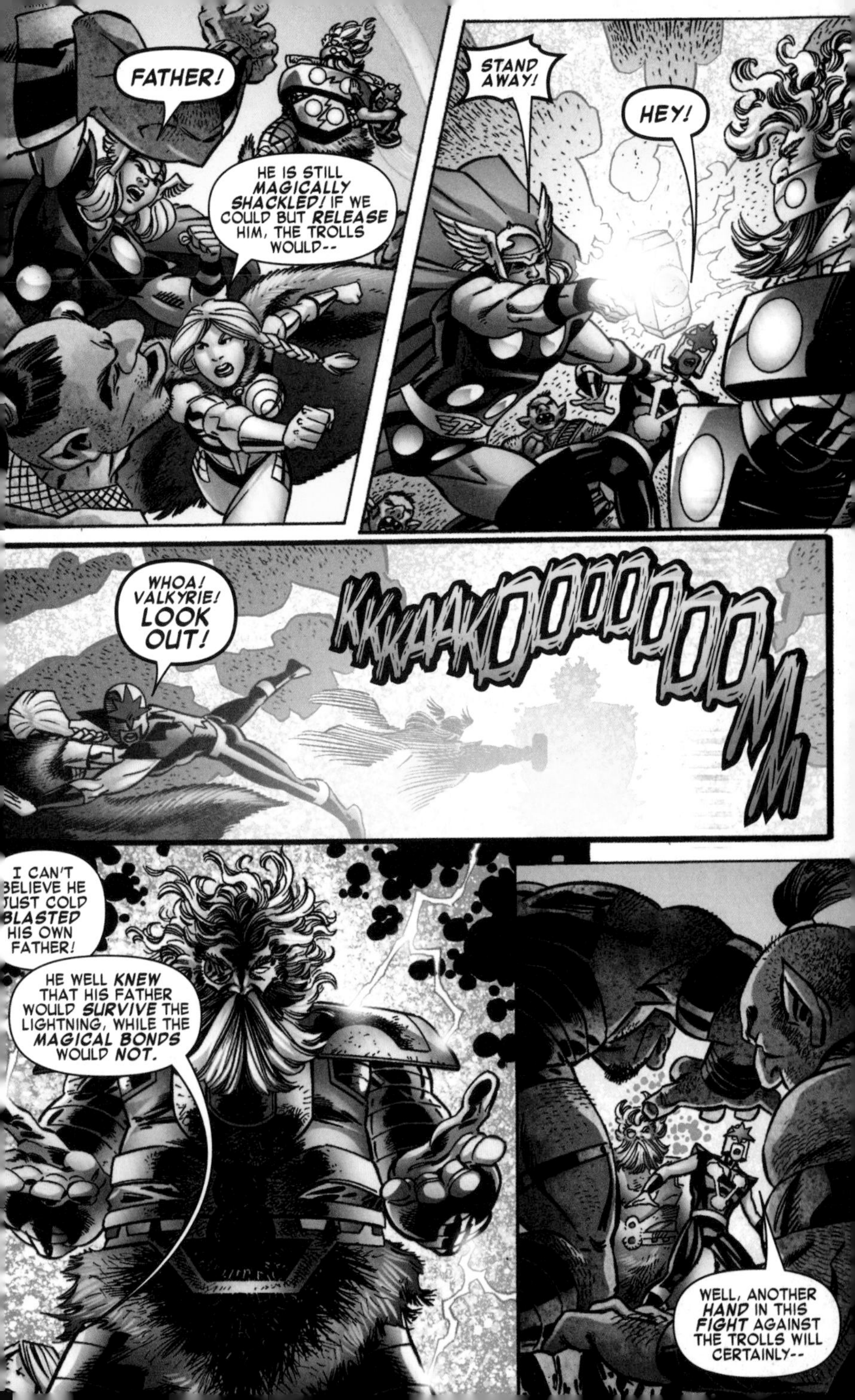
FATHER!
HE IS STILL MAGICALLY SHACKLED! IF WE COULD BUT RELEASE HIM, THE TROLLS WOULD--
STAND AWAY!
HEY!
WHOA! VALKYRIE! LOOK OUT!
KKKAAAKOOOOOOOOOM
I CAN'T BELIEVE HE JUST COLD BLASTED HIS OWN FATHER!
HE WELL KNEW THAT HIS FATHER WOULD SURVIVE THE LIGHTNING, WHILE THE MAGICAL BONDS WOULD NOT.
WELL, ANOTHER HAND IN THIS FIGHT AGAINST THE TROLLS WILL CERTAINLY--

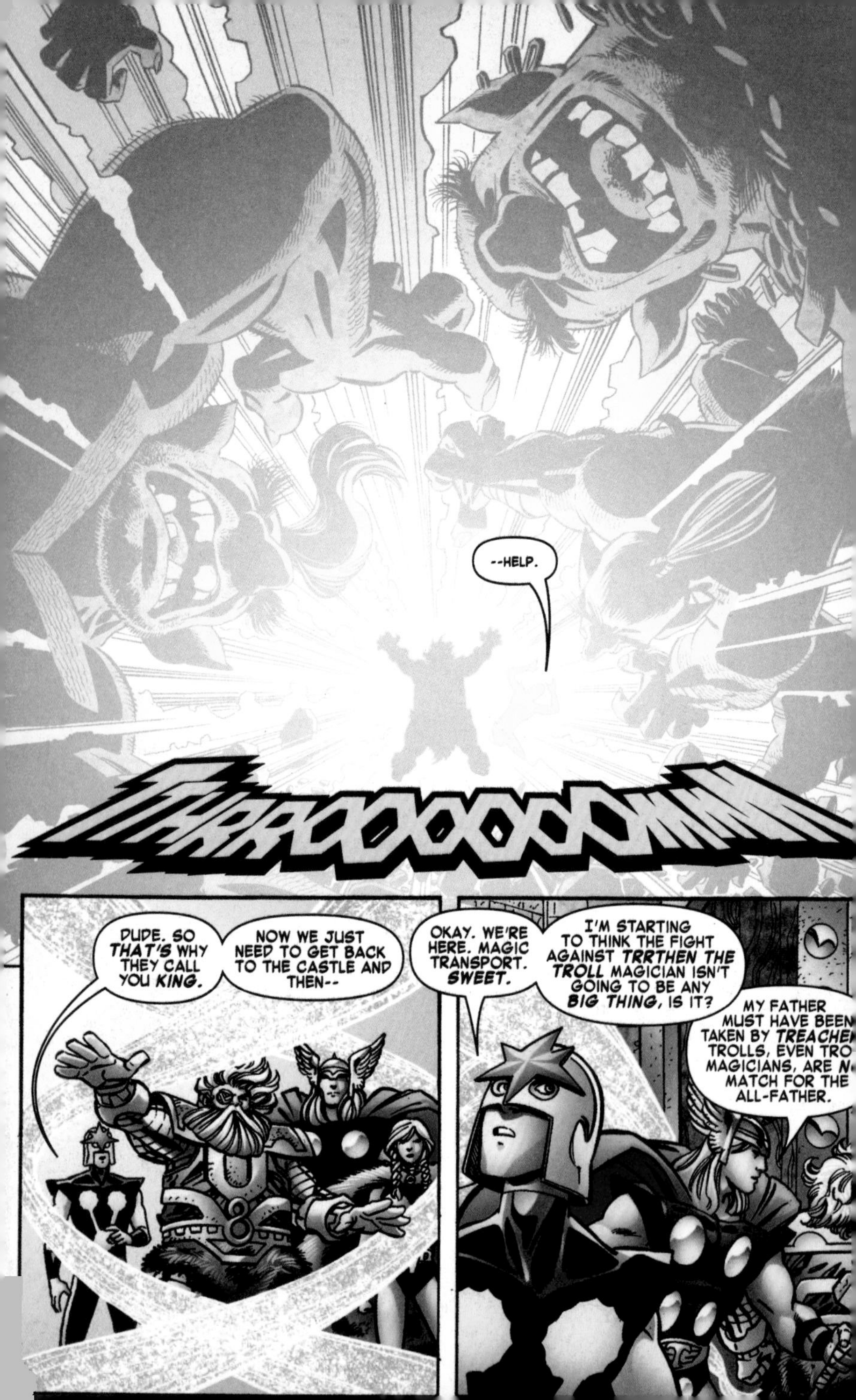
--HELP.
THRROOOOOOMM
DUDE. SO THAT'S WHY THEY CALL YOU KING.
NOW WE JUST NEED TO GET BACK TO THE CASTLE AND THEN--
OKAY. WE'RE HERE. MAGIC TRANSPORT. SWEET.
I'M STARTING TO THINK THE FIGHT AGAINST TRRTHEN THE TROLL MAGICIAN ISN'T GOING TO BE ANY BIG THING, IS IT?
MY FATHER MUST HAVE BEEN TAKEN BY TREACHE TROLLS, EVEN TRO MAGICIANS, ARE N MATCH FOR THE ALL-FATHER.

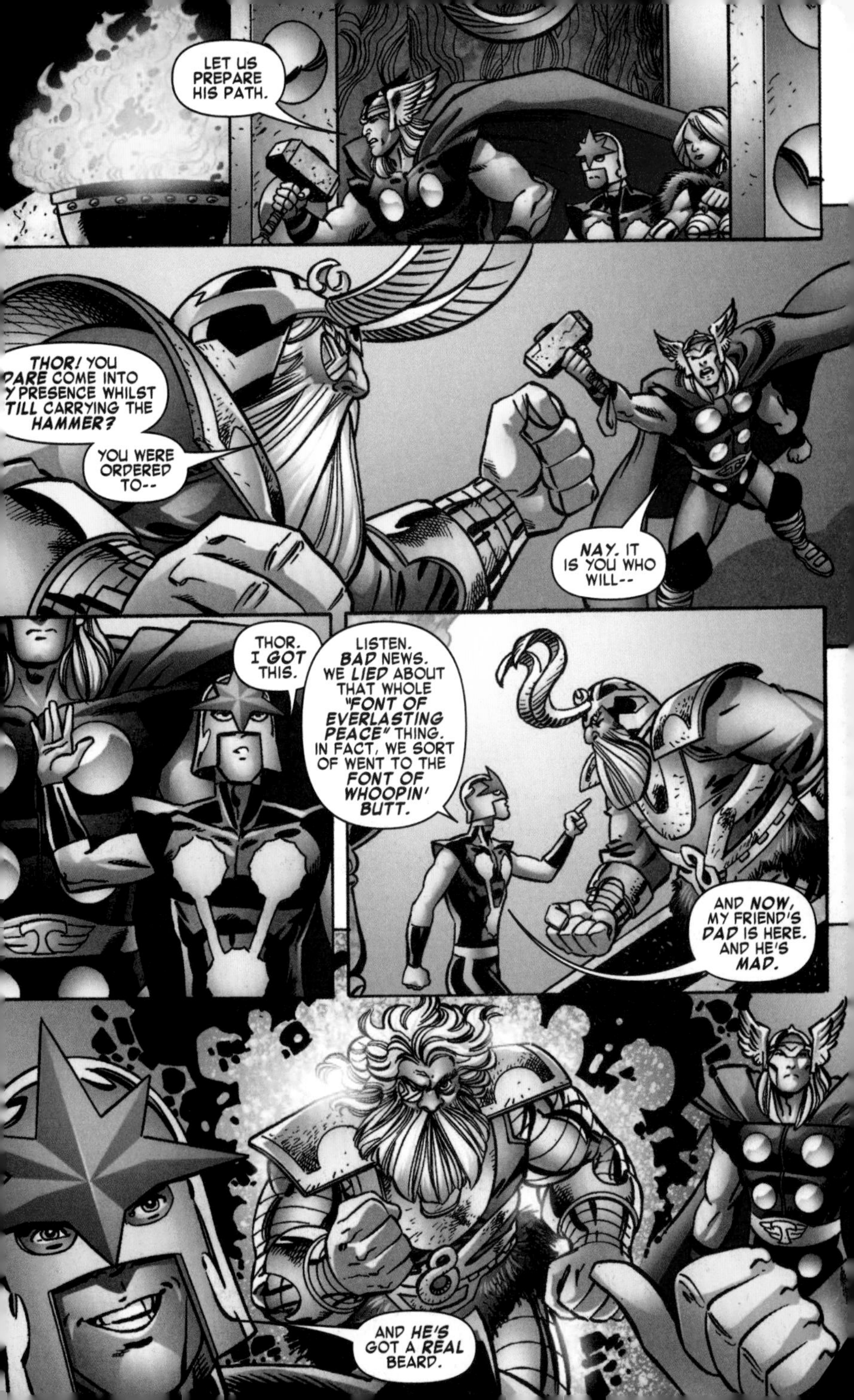
LET US PREPARE HIS PATH.
THOR! YOU DARE COME INTO MY PRESENCE WHILST STILL CARRYING THE HAMMER?
YOU WERE ORDERED TO--
NAY. IT IS YOU WHO WILL--
THOR. I GOT THIS.
LISTEN. BAD NEWS. WE LIED ABOUT THAT WHOLE "FONT OF EVERLASTING PEACE" THING. IN FACT, WE SORT OF WENT TO THE FONT OF WHOOPIN' BUTT.
AND NOW, MY FRIEND'S DAD IS HERE. AND HE'S MAD.
AND HE'S GOT A REAL BEARD.

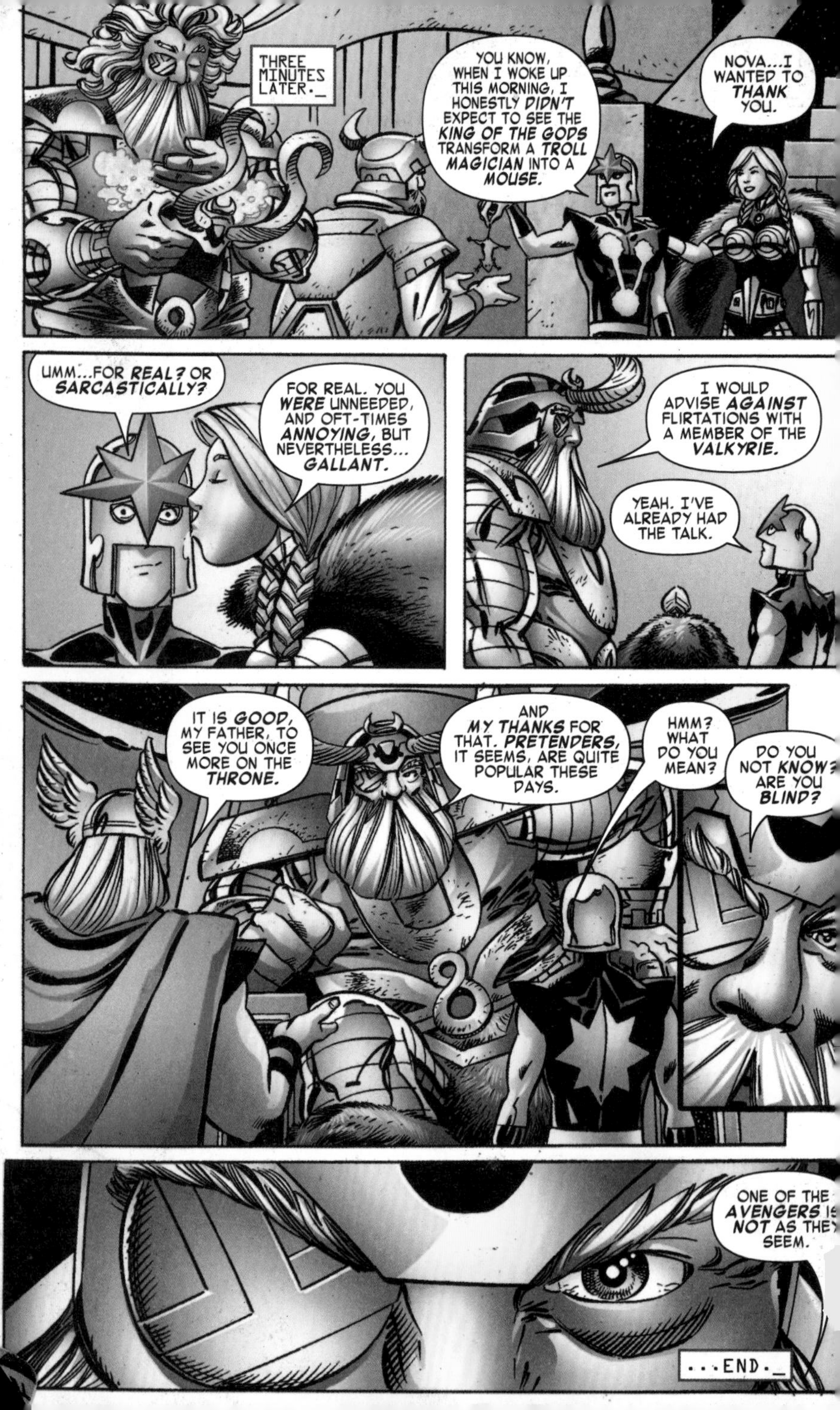
THREE MINUTES LATER._
YOU KNOW, WHEN I WOKE UP THIS MORNING, I HONESTLY DIDN'T EXPECT TO SEE THE KING OF THE GODS TRANSFORM A TROLL MAGICIAN INTO A MOUSE.
NOVA...I WANTED TO THANK YOU.
UMM...FOR REAL? OR SARCASTICALLY?
FOR REAL. YOU WERE UNNEEDED, AND OFT-TIMES ANNOYING, BUT NEVERTHELESS... GALLANT.
I WOULD ADVISE AGAINST FLIRTATIONS WITH A MEMBER OF THE VALKYRIE.
YEAH. I'VE ALREADY HAD THE TALK.
IT IS GOOD, MY FATHER, TO SEE YOU ONCE MORE ON THE THRONE.
AND MY THANKS FOR THAT. PRETENDERS, IT SEEMS, ARE QUITE POPULAR THESE DAYS.
HMM? WHAT DO YOU MEAN?
DO YOU NOT KNOW? ARE YOU BLIND?
ONE OF THE AVENGERS IS NOT AS THEY SEEM.
...END._